Jenny May

JONATHAN LOVEJOY

Armageddon Publishing
All rights reserved.

Cover: *The Young Shepherdess*, 1885
William Adolphe Bouguereau (1825-1905)

ISBN-10: 0692316620
ISBN-13: 978-0692316627

For every Maybelline

Thou art thy mother's daughter—

That lotheth her husband and her children…

Ezekiel 16:45

Book One

Rape

One day, Jennifer Maybelline Breen goes into the woods, to see if there is a baby. There isn't. So she strolls back to her tiny cabin in the twilight. Momma is at the stove. Her expression is sour.

"I been callin' you for an hour, girl. Where you been?"

"I been to the woods, lookin' for a baby for us ta tend."

"Didn't I tell you ta stay outta them woods less'n I tell you to go in?"

"Yes, Momma."

"I'm gon' whip you after supper."

"I know."

"It's fer your own good, Jenny May. Them woods is full of wolves and bears. They'll eat you alive."

3

The twilight vanishes their mountain horizon. The stars are plentiful. After supper, Momma takes hold of the leather strap and whips her nineteen year old daughter until it is done. Jenny May did not cry from the pain.

The next morning came quickly. The mist watered the fertile ground.

"Jenny May! Fetch me some wood for this stove. You gon' have to go to the edge o' them woods to git it. But you better not go in 'em."

Jenny May obeys. While she gathers wood, Jimmy Lee Biggs admires her.

"Hey, Jenny May."

"Hey, Jimmy Lee."

"You still cursed wit' blood?"

"No."

"You gon' let me do it to ya, then?"

"We ain't married, Jimmy Lee. We cain't do that."

"If'n you don't let me do it to you, I'm gon' rape ya."

"What you gon' rape me for, Jimmy Lee?"

"I cain't help it. I need ya."

Jenny May's braided hair is gold in the morning sunlight. Her fair skin glistens with beauty.

He pulls Jenny May to the ground. He lays with her until it is done. Jenny May did not cry from the pain.

She finishes gathering the wood and takes it home. She doesn't tell Momma what Jimmy Lee Biggs had done.

regnant

"Momma, did you find me in the woods when I was a baby?"

"Your daddy found ya, God rest his soul."

"Is that where they find all the babies?"

"Some of 'em are in the gardens and the fields."

"How do they get there?"

"God puts 'em there at just the right time."

"One day, I'm gon' find us a baby ta tend."

"You stay away from them woods. There's wolves and bears in 'em. They'll eat you alive."

Summer turned into Fall. Autumn leaves fell into cool mountain breezes. The north wind came, and the snow covered the woods and the garden.

"Momma, what's happenin' ta me? Momma, I'm gon' die!"

"You ain't gon' die. God is punishin' ya 'cause of what you did wit' Jimmy Lee."

"But how do you know if I did it?"

"There ain't no need a you lyin' ta me, Jezebel. I can *see* the sin on you. And I know Jimmy Lee's been botherin' ya since you was growd. I told you not to go in them woods, didn't I?"

"He came outta the woods to me, Momma. He raped me."

"He raped ya 'cause you was full o' sin."

"Am I gon' die?"

"You just sick is all. It'll be over by the spring."

Spring melted the mountain snow. Jenny May had taken to her bed. She was too sick to gather wood or tend the garden.

Baby

$\mathcal{O}$ne night Jenny May awakens to sharp, stabbing agony in her bloated stomach. A river of water gushes from her.

"Momma. Momma help me! God's gon' kill me 'cause a what I done with Jimmy Lee. God's gon' kill me tonight, Momma!"

"He's chastisin' you. And it's gon' git worse. When it's bout over, its gon' git worse than you ever 'magined."

"How'm I gon' live through it, Momma? Am I gon' live?"

"He probly ain't gon' kill ya this time. But if you ever touch anotha man for the rest o' your life, you gon' die. He's gon' split you in two tonight, so you'll remember."

The late night hours come. Jenny May's suffering is great.

"Now you lay back and take deep breaths. Spread your legs open. The evil is tryin' ta come out of ya, so you push if you have ta."

Jenny May lays back and takes quick breaths.

"You turn your head and don't you look. If you look at the bloody mess that's gon' come out of ya, you'll go crazy. And if I catch you lookin' just one time, I'm gon' whup the skin off ya when you heal. You hear me, girl?"

"Yes, Momma."

She turns her head away. She pushes and breathes until it is done. Jenny May did not cry from the pain.

Momma cuts the chord. She covers the mouth on the thing quickly, to prevent sound. She rushes far away from the cabin, to where the rich woman and her husband wait. She hands them the screaming, bloody newborn and takes their money. No words are spoken.

Through the misty mountain dawn, Momma walks back to her cabin. It is warm inside.

"Look here. Look at the littlest part of what come out ya. I'm gon' bury it with the rest and let the worms eat it. Is you sorry for your sins?"

"Yes, Momma. I ain't never gon' touch a man again for as long as I live."

The spring turns to summer. Jenny May feels so much better that she takes a long walk into the woods, to see if there is a baby. There isn't. So she strolls back to her tiny cabin in the twilight.

Death

ickness looms above their mountain horizon. Souls are taken from both far and near. Momma takes to her bed, sicker than she has ever been.

"I'm gon' die this winter, Jenny May."

"But why, Momma?"

"The sickness." Momma coughs hard. "It's got me."

"But I cain't take care of myself."

"You ain't never been nothin' but a burden, Jenny May. Just tend that garden like I showed ya. And don't you never let nobody see you no more."

"What about church?"

"Just read the Bible and pray. Take good care of them chickens. And you ain't got to never go in ta town 'cause Ms. Simms brings us what we need. She'll keep buyin' them eggs from ya."

"Can I tell 'er that you gon' be dead?"

"No."

Darkness descends. Momma's expression grows somber. Jenny May tends to her dying body.

Soon, the winter winds begin to blow. The earth is covered in a field of winter white. Momma's body is cold and hard as ice. Her eyes are open.

Jenny May wraps Momma in her bed linen. She buries her upon the ridge overlooking Flowers Canyon. She says a prayer over her shallow grave.

She braves the winter wind, trudging through the snow. Her heart is heavy with loneliness. Jenny May did not cry from the pain.

I do not look like my mother. Mother is a lithe, pale woman of breeding, with thin lips and a tiny nose, thin hips and a tiny rose bosom. Her narrow face is pretty. A voice replete with superiority. Colorful dresses adorn her. Her diamonds are plentiful.

The Lady Windsor drifts through her privileged castle, looking for her daughter. The chandelier hangs crystalline from the high ceiling. The staircase spirals high. Mother climbs her pinewood stairs, sliding her hand along the white marble rail.

"Alice! It's time to go. Alice Windsor I'm calling you!"

I stand fit and firm in my thirteenth year. Holding fast to a fleeting moment of freedom, gazing out the huge bedroom window. Overlooking the view of the massive estate, the lawn of green and prosperity. My eyes are fixed beyond my palace prison, to the beautiful mountain peaks rising so near. Hiding so far away from me.

Mrs. Windsor drifts down the upstairs hall. She turns into her daughter's room.

"I've been calling you for an hour, young lady. Where have you been?"

I stand defiant. Arms crossed. Lips pushed out.

"Alice Maybelline Windsor you will answer me or I promise you'll regret it."

"I was playing outside in the woods."

"What?"

"I said I was playing outside in the woods!"

"You hush that tone with me. I don't know what's gotten into you lately but I won't stand for this defiance. And you were told not to leave these grounds to play in those woods, weren't you?"

My long hair is golden in the afternoon light. My young face is tinted with color from the sun.

"Never mind that. I want you dressed and ready to go in ten minutes."

"Do I have to?"

Mother gives a stern look. She leaves me to my privacy. I open the white closet doors, staring disgustedly at the white leotard, and the frilly pink ballet skirt.

Rain

*T*hunder bursts from the clouds. Jenny May hurries to weed the rest of her garden. Soon the rains come, whipping her back coldly, sending her running into her cabin.

Momma's bones lay still on the ridge, three years past their tenth summer season. She wonders why Jimmy Lee Biggs had never come to see her.

Jenny May sits in Momma's comfortable chair, opening her Bible. Under the mountain rain, she reads by the light of her lamp's golden flame. Longing for a baby to tend.

Whipping

One day, Lady Windsor's husband longs for another. Their argument is violent. Soon after, he did not live with his wife and daughter again.

Over time, the Lady's grief begins to show. Her bitterness touches her daughter's heart with cold.

"I'm going to have Sylvia punish you after dinner."

"I know."

"It's for your own good, Alice. There are wolves and bears in those woods. They'll eat you alive."

After dinner, Mother stands by and watches her waiting Lady punish her 13 year old daughter. I did not cry from the pain. When my punishment is done, I hear angry voices from grandmother's upper room.

The ground is covered in winter white. The moonlight shines bright upon the mountain snow. Jenny May looks out her window into the night. Tracks lead from her cabin to the Pine Woods. A wolf howls its lonely voice over the snow covered country.

Winter breezes blow hard against the cabin. Jenny May puts another log in the fireplace and goes to bed.

Brandmere

At the Brandmere school, Lady Windsor's child will not answer to her first name. I disobey every rule. Mice and frogs are common in my teacher's desks. One day, Mrs. Thyme sees a snake appear.

"Ms. Windsor, you were told what would happen if your daughter misbehaved again."

"Do you think I'm going to let you throw her out of here?"

"I don't see what choice you have. Your daughter is so insolent I'm afraid to imagine how profane she is when we're not around. Four letter words flow like water from her mouth. And she is often violent. When Mrs. Thyme escorted her to this office, Maybelline said—"

"Maybelline?"

"Oh yes. Another cog in the wheel that is Alice Maybelline Windsor. She refuses to answer to her first name. Or hadn't you heard? Once, she pushed Mrs. Thyme in her lower back because she walked past her desk and spoke the words *'Alice Windsor you will be silent.'* When Mrs. Thyme escorted her to this office, Maybell... *Alice* said *"get your God-daggon hands off me.* That's cutting it mighty close."

Darkness comes upon Lady Windsor's lovely face. Her aura is powerful.

"Let me have one final word with her. I promise, no... I swear, Ms. Bozen, that she will behave."

Lady Windsor glides into the school hallway. I languish in my grandmother's arms.

"You've been suspended," she says. "You're coming home for three days."

At our palatial home, Grandmother protests the impending discipline.

"Liz, I won't let you do it this time. Why can't you let the past be? How many times do I have to apologize for how I raised you?"

"Mother, Alice will learn to obey me. She's lucky I'm not sending her to Europe. To a convent school."

"I won't let you do this!"

"And you're lucky you're not in a retirement home."

For three days, her daughter is caned. My legs are bloody. My food is rationed. When it is done, my love for my mother dies. I did not cry from the pain.

At the Brandmere school, I do not misbehave again. I spend many quiet days alone. On graduation day, mother is filled with pride. Grandmother's eyes are filled with tears.

London

I have blossomed. My eyes are the color of a mountain sky. My hair is golden yellow. My bosom is full.

At the mansion, mother's plans are laid.

"I can get just as good an education here, Mother. I don't need to spend four years in Europe."

"You'll do as I see fit. It's all been arranged. You'll be leaving for London in a week. From there you'll spend the whole summer traveling. You'll start school there in the fall."

A sudden calm descends. A strength of my will.

"I'm going to school here, Mother."

Without words, Lady Windsor's control over me diminishes. A new war between us has begun.

"Grandmother?"

"Yes, Dear?"

"Why is Mother so angry? She has this mansion. She has you and I to love her. What's the matter with her?"

"Your mother is wounded deep, Maybelline. Some scars can't heal."

Grandmother does not tell what she means. I do not ask again.

In the summer, I travel to London alone. I take residence without joy. I did not cry from the pain.

Many offer a hand of friendship. I politely refuse. Admiration or jealousy is in their eyes.

Freshman

Autumn drifts from the North Region. In the days before Indian Summer, I return to my Carolina mansion home. I attend the first term at the Appalachian University school.

I walk taller than the other girls. To them, I shine like the noon day sun. At registration, every sorority approaches me.

"Hi, my name is Mary. And this is Judith."

Under the September sun, two pretty young women speak to one they believe is more beautiful than they.

"So, where did you transfer from?"

"Excuse me?"

"What school did you go to before you came here?"

"Brandmere."

"Brandmere? That's a high school isn't it?"

"I'll say it is," the other girl says, "and you've got to be rich to go there, too."

"You mean you're a freshman?"

Mary and Judith look at one another. Disbelief colors their expression.

"What's your name?"

Contempt glistens the bluest eye.

"Maybelline."

Angel

Momma is dead eighteen years. Autumn leaves blow over her grave. Jenny May's love for her has turned to loneliness. For company, she walks with the Lord.

"Jenny May?"

Marlene Angel Simms calls her name.

"I thought you might be up here. Come on back to this house, girl, and let's get them eggs."

Jenny May walks arm in arm with her. Angel Simms is 20 years over Allie Jee Breen's daughter. Jenny May is 37. Her body is thin and curved. Her breasts hang like watermelons.

As she walks with Ms. Simms, she remembers when she was twenty one. Ms. Simms had been coming for a year to gather eggs and bring food. Twenty one year old Jenny May was in the garden that day. When she bent over, her white T-shirt stretched under a heavy burden.

"Where's your Momma?"

"I cain't tell ya."

"I ain't seen 'er near two summers, Jenny May. Now, where's your Momma?"

"I cain't tell ya."

"Is she comin' back?"

Twenty one year old Jenny May kept silent. Her T shirt was tucked tightly inside her prairie skirt. Her low breasts hung round and heavy. Ms. Simms tried not to look at Jenny May's bosom.

"If'n you don't tell me, I'm gon' have to whup ya 'til you do."

"Why you gon' whup me Ms. Angel?"

"Cause I'm a growd woman with children and a husband, that's why. And you ain't respectin' me. Now, take off all your clothes 'cause you bein' stubborn. I'm gon' spank bruises on ya til you tell me."

Jenny May did as she was told. Marlene Angel's body twinged from what she saw.

She sat on a chair in the middle of the cabin. She pulled the naked young woman over her knee. For an hour, Mrs. Simms spanked bruises onto her buttocks and legs. Jenny May did not cry from the pain.

In the present day, Jenny May and Marlene Simms walk from the ridge over Flowers Canyon. At the cabin, they gather eggs laid from two dozen chickens. When the eggs are in the carton, Ms. Simms admires her.

"Lemme see 'em."

Jenny May does as she is told. They hang low and heavy outside her bra. Fifty seven year old Angel Simms takes hold of them, and nurses until she is done. Jenny May did not cry from the pain.

Book Two

$\mathcal{J}$ennifer

$\mathcal{J}$ languish at the Appalachian University school. My acquaintances are many. Relaxed and natural kindness colors my expression. My golden spun braids are tightly woven.

In every class, I sit in the last seat against the wall. Sometimes, the window beckons my attention far away. I imagine myself at a cabin by a mountain woods, breathing the Indian summer air. The lady professor drones about *Madame Bovary*.

"It's such a lovely day," she says. "Let's go outside."

The class lifts sleepy bodies. I drift tall and blonde behind them. I notice I am not alone.

"You too?" the stranger says.

"What?"

"Ready to blow your brains out."

I look kindly at the pretty brunette. Her eyes are Asian.

"I'm sorry. It's just that Miss Madame Bovary there is on my last nerve."

"I thought I was the only one."

"I'm Jennifer."

"I'm Maybelline."

"Jen and May."

Déjà vu grips my soul.

"Since I was a little girl, I've been dreaming that name."

"What?"

A cooling wind pushes the Indian Summer heat from us.

"Jenny May."

Jennifer's amazement is great. Fear and uncertainty come together in her spirit. "I can't do this. I've got to go. You coming?"

"I want to, believe me. But I can't do it to her. It's too pathetic."

"Well, I've got stuff to do."

"No, stay here. Please don't make me sit here alone."

Jennifer smiles as we walk to join the class. My relief is epic. The Indian Summer breeze is cool on our skin. We sit together on the brick décor lining the space where we have gathered. I watch the students press through the boredom.

The morning sun shines hot on our faces. I wipe a bead of sweat from my forehead, wishing for the Autumn breeze again. I make eye contact with Ms. Deat. The professor's gratitude is epic.

Grieg

At the School of Music, I sit enraptured. Jennifer's touch on the keys is delicate as she practices. Grieg's melody in A minor touches her soul.

"Why'd you stop?"

"Sometimes," she says, "when I hear that melody… I just want to die and go to Heaven."

"I've felt like that my whole life."

"I feel so much pain inside. I think a lot of it is because of other people."

"I wish I could just go away somewhere. Maybe live in a small cabin by the woods."

"With those braids, I can picture that. You know, you're not like the rest of 'em. They're all bitches."

"Who?"

"The ones that look like you," she says. "You don't have the same cold heart they have. I've walked past a group of these sorority bitches before. Smiling at 'em. Scared to death. I actually heard one of them say '*f*cking geek.*' It was like somebody unplugged my body and my whole spirit drained out the bottom. It was like my heart was going to stop beating."

"The Omega's want me to pledge."

"I guess you have to do it then, huh? They're the best."

"I don't know if I am or not."

"Pardon me for saying so May, but look in the mirror. You've got no choice."

"You're not so bad yourself. Why don't you pledge?"

Jennifer puts her fingers to her eyes. She pulls them to a slant.

I am appalled.

"I don't think I'm quite '*suthern*' enough," she says.

"They're not like that. Really. I've talked to some of 'em a lot. They're nice girls."

"So, you're saying we should pledge them together?"

"Sure. Why not? It'll give us something to do, anyway."

"I've already got plenty to do. But I guess I'd better. How would you ever make it in without me?"

Jennifer's sarcasm is pleasant. She returns softly to her A minor concerto.

Sorority

At the sorority house, Mary Adonna and Judith Spencer admire us.

"A music major," Mary says. "That's great. I think Kerry can play the oboe or something."

"The French horn," Judith says.

"Whatever." Her response bears an enigmatic smile. "Horn, oboe…cock. What's the difference, Kerry's always blowing something."

Jennifer's hand goes to her mouth. Her shock is genuine. I smile and lower my head.

"Girls, I'm sorry about that," Judith says. "From the mouths of virgins."

"I'm just speaking the truth. You know what we saw—"

"Um… Jen, tell us about your parents."

"Typical Asian mother. White father. My Dad's a money tree. Or should I say '*investment broker,*' with a gift for hitting the jackpot for himself. He's home about twice a month. Mom's a former news reporter slash charity queen, my only piano teacher since I was twelve, Julie Chen lookalike, accept with a ghetto ass and juggs halfway to hers…" (She points her thumb at my chest). And yes, my Mom thinks I'm going to graduate and tour the world as a concert pianist. Sorry. But she's got it real bad."

"Did she used to make you practice a lot?"

"Just like the Joy Luck Club. Only this was real and I've still got the bruises to prove it."

Mary and Judith smile attentively. Appreciating Jennifer's ease and comfort.

"Well, we've only got two rules here. Be yourself. And be an Omega. Everything else is just cake. Understand though, that everybody who pledges doesn't become a member. And after you've pledged once, we never ask again."

A sudden protectiveness arises in my soul.

"With your help, I'm sure we'll be fine."

A pause…

"I'm sure," Mary says.

Mary

At the Appalachian Mall food court, the young crowd is busy. They walk and rush to and fro in talk and hunger. In their tight jeans and T-shirts, Mary and Judith comfortably take a center table, taco salad lettuce packaged in both their trays. Mary sips her cup of water through a straw.

"Why so quiet?" Judith asks. Her salad shell begins to die a noisy death.

"Who the Hell does she think she is?"

"Who?"

"Maybelline Windsor, that's who."

"She didn't do anything."

"*I'm sure with your help, me'll be vine.*" Mary's face is twisted to mocking. Her long, blonde hair is golden. "And then she has the nerve to drag her dog up here—that piano geek I see walking by herself all the time, bent over under that back pack like a mule. Who does Windsor think she is anyway? She acts like she's already in."

"She is."

"So *you* say. I don't care what she looks like or what her name is— she's going to have to suffer just like everybody else before she's a member of this sorority. Neither one of their mothers is even a member. They're lucky we didn't ask them to forget about it already."

"Maybelline's got something. I don't know what it is, but…"

"Oh yes you do. You like her 'cause she's got watermelons in her bra."

"I do not. Why would you say something like that? God, you *are* sick."

"Yeah? Well, don't try to act like you didn't notice. She looks ridiculous. Can you imagine her in a bikini?"

The two girls share a quick, mocking giggle.

"Pam just kept running her mouth about how pretty she is. *Maybelline this. Maybelline that.* And she wears those braids like the goddamned Beverly Hillbillies. She better hope she's got a 3.0 or we won't even be having this conversation come pledge time. What do you think about Jennifer?"

"Aren't you gonna eat?"

Mary flips her hair in conspicuous flight from her shoulder. She picks up her black plastic fork.

"What do you think about *Jennife*r," she repeats, in irritated fashion. Judith stares into her memory, taco salad fork dug in and waiting.

"I think they're a package deal," Judith sighs. "Maybelline probably won't join without her."

"How come?"

"They're both nerds. They need each other."

"Oh, Jennifer Lin May is a nerd alright. She's a *geek.*"

"And Maybelline's drawn to her *because* she's a geek. They both are."

"If Maybelline Windsor is a geek then what am I?"

"Look, you asked my opinion. I don't mean a geek like *that.* I mean, she's shy. You can tell. I think she's self conscious about her face, her body, her name—everything. We should all be so lucky. With a face like that she could be a model easy."

"Maybe if she lost about 20 pounds first. Most of it from her *tits.* I've been here two years and I've never seen anything like it."

"Me either."

Mary Adonna pauses to take a bite of her taco salad. She swallows quickly.

"Is she prettier than me?"

Truth holds Judith's lips closed. She shrugs her shoulders and tends to her meal.

Mary's appetite leaves her body. A wave of green ice and heat flushes through.

*S*now

*T*he rains of Indian Summer have turned to snow. Jennifer Lin and I languish together as one in the cold; when the day's study is done, when the classrooms have come and gone, under the Appalachian Mountain Moon. We walk together in the snowy breeze, from the sketchiness of our lonely past, into the fullness of our present and future. *The Two Bitches*, we have been called in jest by them, in screaming laughter as the sorority group walks past. The Beginning of Sorrows, I suppose, for denying them control over who we are. Denying access to ourselves. Refusing to become one of them. As their laughter echoes away, I feel the approach of another inside, so familiar, yet so strangely foreign to me. As the echo of a presence I have felt since I was a little girl, which refuses to reveal itself fully to me, passing by Mary and Judith's cruelty, prompting the feeling of 'Maybelline,' as we begin our brief ascent to the Appalachian Music Hall.

"Somebody call your name again?" she says.

"How did you know?"

"You get that look every time. You're going insane, you know."

The snowflakes brush brightly against her silken black hair. Her Asian eyes are beautiful.

Inside the Appalachian Music Hall, our practice room is a refuge. The baby grand is the hearth by which we gather. Mozart heats the coals of winter fire. Grieg burns our blue flames of torment. Outside the window, the snow falls to earth in A minor misery.

"What are you doing?"

"I think I'll start this sociology paper," I say, settling into the old sofa across the little room. "I'm not doing any research though, I'm gonna write the whole thing from the book."

"Don't you want to watch me practice?"

The question washes over me like a warm fountain in the cold. Of its kind, of its potential, it is the first. Without a word, I stand up, vulnerable all of a sudden, lips tucked in, walking slowly over to her at the piano. "Sit beside me," she says. The skin of her hands is as smooth as cream on the piano keys. Grieg's adagio melody tickles the air like flakes of snow.

"Did it bother you?"

"What?"

"Those girls. What they said."

A sigh. "Why'd you have to remember that?"

"So it did bother you. I mean, it hurt your feelings. Them calling us bitches."

"Truth is, I was more angry than hurt. What about you?"

"Well… if you weren't here, guess what I'd be doing."

I can only gaze through the fog of tension at the keys. Do I really know you, Jenny Lin? Does this flower rise from the east—burning blue and black fire? Our silence is a golden flame.

"Put your hand here," she says. "This finger here… these two here… this is a 'C' chord. You got it… good. Now, press down."

Timidly, my fingers call forth the Heart of Melody. Unnaturally. With ineffectiveness. Un-affective. Ineffective.

"You have to press harder," she says, smiling. "Like this…"

Jenny Lin! From where comes this apprehension! What breath of wind touches every nerve in my body! With her left hand, she presses upon mine, to give proper power to the voice of clarity. These vibrations flow from the touch of her hand, and that of the piano key, to the heart of who I am. I am the lady cello to her piano, made alive by our hands upon the keys, and her stare upon my face and my hair.

"I tried not to do this," she says. "I would have rather died than done something this pathetic and clichéd but you're an impossible person. Look at me. Please?"

When I turn left to look, I watch, I feel her breath quicken, her hand still atop mine at the piano. Asian beauty leans forward to my lips, and I feel the rise and fall of myself at my groin, to my breasts, to my heart, to the stroke of her hand on mine, then back to my lips again.

"Are you a virgin?" she says.

"Yes."

"It's like I said before, May. You're an impossible person. You're prettier than all of those girls put together. And yet, you're still humble. I'm as pathetic and clingy as it gets but did you ever once make me feel bad about myself? You're the only person I've ever known who…"

Her voice chokes, to signal the arrival of the tear from inside. From this pain, I suppose, Jenny Lin did cry.

"When I tell you this, I'll probably never see you again."

My body aches in two fold. Partly, from such compassion as I have never felt. As too from a desire that burns down to the center of my spirit.

"When I was sixteen, my mother raped me. Under her dress, she was wearing a small red strap-on. She tore my clothes from my body, and she raped me like a man. She started to repeat '*so you will learn, so you will learn, so you will learn*'. Then she had an orgasm with her dildo inside me. It was like she sucked the air out of my lungs. I couldn't breathe."

I suppose that my expression is a masterpiece of non-verbal communications. Shock and disbelief being primarily among them.

"I know…" she says. "I know you can't believe me. And when you meet my mother, you'll find it impossible to believe. She's very beautiful. Tell me, is that why I kissed you? Because of what happened to me? Am I a geek dyke like they said?"

"Hey, look at me. Whatever you are, I am. I understand about mothers. When my father left my mother, she took it out on me. She used to have the maid strip my clothes off and beat my skin to blood. My mother didn't rape me but I felt the same pain, the same fear and humiliation you did."

Close beside me, she looks away, towards the black and white keys of discontent.

"Can you promise me," she says, "that you won't be like everybody else I've ever met? To smile and laugh *with* me, then without explanation, start smiling and laughing *at* me instead? Can you promise me?"

"I swear I won't, Jennifer. I swear to God and Jesus."

"Will you do me a favor then?"

"Anything."

She goes to the two windows in the room, to close out the late afternoon snow and gray. Daytime dark permeates the winter warmth. She returns to sit beside me.

"Take off your top," she says. "And your bra."

I am unable to hesitate. My fingers make such quick work of my sky blue shirt. When I take the collar shirt off, unashamedly, she raises her hand to her mouth in un-pretend shock, at the size of what my white tank t-shirt holds.

"I've never seen anyth—"

"I know. They're too big. It's embarrassing."

"How can a goddess be embarrassed?" she says, her voice filled with awe. Truly, I do understand. There are times when I am held by my own reflection, at what freakish appearance my body obtains. A tallish white girl with thick golden braids on either side, with two big, heavy breasts above a small, curved waist and wide, rounded hips. Beauty, I suppose, is in the eye of the beholder.

"Those are million dollar breasts," she says. "I know, because I…"

It's as though she can no longer speak. Only stare.

"Turn to the side," she says.

As she directs, I turn to the side, straddling the piano chair, with her behind me doing the same. I don't know from where this is, the feeling in my breasts, when my friend's hands reach from behind me—lifting them. Mashing, squashing, pressing them together. When the front of them is pulled, I hear the involuntary grunt from me, and I feel her slide closer behind me—establishing a dominance I never knew existed, squishing a sensation through me I never imagined before. For every desire she has had, she takes it out upon my breasts; the fervent cushion for her fall, I suppose. O Teachers, O Mothers, O Daughters, O Sisters of the Halls of Learning! What possibilities lie exposed, behind the closed doors of your security! O Mother—what churns beneath cultured civility! When I think of the beautiful Asian woman, and what it is that she must do! The Red Dragon of Fire, which hath breathed into the womb of her daughter! Ah, but this Red Dragon's flame is as those from the ancestry, as all of this dragon's breath, the breath of azure flame, and cerulean fire tinted by fire the color of night.

Yes… the heat of this burns my breasts through her daughter's hands, whose fingers tirelessly shake and wobble and pull my breasts as has not been done to them before, until my head is pushed back to her as far as it can go, and every new breast pressing pushes my body closer towards a trembling I will not survive. In the daytime dark, hidden from the icy mist of snow, I gather my strength against the tingling, crashing fire in my breasts, which has joined the burning in my groin, to cause me to lose my ability to focus my eyesight, nor can I hold back the quick and violent yelping voice from within.

Ice

At the White Tower dormitory, Mary and Judith recover from their snowy walk. Their blood is as cold as ice.

"I wonder."

"About what?"

"How long sushi stays fresh in the snow."

Judith's mouth opens wide. Her shock is genuine.

"Mary, you didn't…"

"No, I didn't. But *she* did."

In the private dorm, their screaming, cruel laughter is hidden.

"Did you see the look on their faces?" says Mary. "They're so full of guilt and shame they couldn't even look at us. They've been playing 'crouching tiger' for weeks baby. Believe it."

"You really think so?"

"How can they not? They probably cum before they get their clothes off."

"Wow. That's just… wow, Mary."

"Look, don't act like you don't know what I'm talking about."

Judith allows knowledge to disperse denial. Their brief look is filled with knowing.

"Well, even if it were true," says Judith, "Is there really anything wrong with that? I mean, they're both beautiful aren't they?"

"*Damn* it," Mary says, closing the Cosmopolitan magazine, slamming it on the bed. "What do you bitches *see* in those two?"

"Nothing, I'm just saying…"

"You, Colleen, Melissa, all of your mouths are watering, aren't they?"

"No."

"It's because she's got those braids and those big tits isn't it?"

Without a word, Judith picks up the magazine. Pretending to be mesmerized by the cover.

"Oh, my God. You want to fuck her."

"I do *not*."

"My God… Judith you have a boyfriend. You're not even gay and you want to suck her tits."

"Shut *up*, Bitch," Judith says roughly. Throwing the magazine hard at her friends face. Mary blocks it violently.

"I'm just joking, okay. Put you're knife back in your purse, why don't you?"

"Stop joking about me sucking Maybelline Windsor's tits, okay? It wasn't funny the first ten times and it's still not funny."

"Okay, I'm sorry. Come sit back down."

Brunette, dark eyed Judith reluctantly walks back over to the bed. She sits beside her friend. Un-amicably.

"Those two weirdos have got me upset too, Judith. Besides, I know who's tits you want in your mouth again."

The delighted, appalled spirit settles again over Judith. "Now?"

"No, not now you crazy dyke. Look, I'll admit it. I want to see Maybelline Windsor in her bra myself, okay. I can't help it. She's got the two biggest tits I've ever seen. It's ridiculous. I'm sure she'll be deep-throating half the football team soon enough anyway. But that's not what bothers me. What is the number one sorority on this campus?"

"We are."

"Why?"

"Because when they look at us they see what they want and can never have."

"That's right. That's *exactly* right. But you guys just might be right about the two of them. Together, they do look pretty damned good. Almost impressive. They turn heads when they walk by. And I know they've been approached by every good sorority on campus. Hell, the cheerleaders have been sniffing around her like dogs."

"She's too tall to be one of them," Judith says.

"But with those stupid braids and that face and those balloons on her chest, who cares? She'll be head cheerleader before she's a junior."

"So, what are you saying?"

"I'm saying we need her."

"But she already turned us down."

"I know," Mary says. " And I know that country bitch is too strong to change her mind. Unless she had a reason."

Judith stares boldly. Dark eyes of bewilderment glisten.

"I want you to go to Jennifer. Be as pathetic as you need to be. I want you to make her think the only reason we wanted Windsor was so *she* could join. Convince Jennifer that we only really want her. Make her believe that we need her. That we can't go on without her. That no matter what Maybelline says, Jennifer should accept her Fate, and take the opportunity that Fate has given her. Convince her that it's her Destiny."

"And if she says no."

"She won't. I have her address. I'm going to her house if I have to. I'm going to talk to her mother. Just in case."

"And… if Jennifer says yes?"

"Then, it begins."

"What begins?"

"For her? The end of the world."

Twilight

I am at one with this planet. Lying on my back, on this sofa of dreams, I am transported by the smooth and incessant pulling at both my breasts, the warm suckling by the lips and tongue of this lovely Asian girl, this lovely young Asian woman on top of me. Each pulling, each call by her mouth for the phantom milk raises me up higher towards another plane, where I think it might be the Evening Day in my mind, and there is but one star which rules the twilight sky. This has more power than even the squeezing did, to set my body aflame, to make me breathe and writhe underneath her with a small fury, pressing. Grinding my lower self against her through the underwear cloth, the outside voices and footsteps whirling and fading into a haze of distant noise. This noise dominated by the loud nostril breathing of the woman above me, who presses so heavily down upon me, from whose spirit flows the A minor melody in such desperation and sorrow. When I hear this melody strike, it aligns itself to a new chord in me, as the Asian woman attaches herself to one breast of mine, bobbing her head up and down deeply upon the nipple in the Virgin's Intercourse, where my mind carries me to this other plane of waiting; where the ghost of my second orgasm waits for me.

In the Theatre of My Mind, I am suddenly inside a mountain cabin in full braid, with nary a stitch of clothing on my body, seeming so much the mature version of myself, while this girl is as unclothed as me, bent down to one of my breasts in a desperate sucking for the milk that flows forth so pure and white. I am at a loss for control at this, as I tremble inside this mountain cabin, a voice uncontained in the Evening Day, to suckle my Asian Doll to satisfaction. And I find myself transported from the cabin, falling, falling backward until I am on the Sofa of Dreams again, my body convulsing hard from the waves of pleasure passing through.

ledges

"*F**uck* Maybelline Windsor."

A refrain in bitterness gazes the winter window. The snowfall is plentiful.

"You said that, remember?"

"If the truth be told," Mary Adonna says, turning her head in facetious delight, "fuck you too."

Judith Spencer can hardly maintain the flow. The flow of energy to her school work pen in motion. Judith Spencer is a girl interrupted. A girl corrupted by one of the seven billion secrets to know. This secret turns her head to look at her captor.

Her mistress.

"Get your ass over here."

Fear touches the brunette soul. It lifts her up, and drifts her to the blonde at the window.

"I've got the strap-on hidden in my drawer," the blonde says. The pause in her effect is epic. "I'm gonna strap it on… and I'm gonna watch you deep throat it."

With nonchalance, she returns her gaze to the Appalachian snow.

"That Asian bitch," she says. "If it's the *last* thing I ever do."

From whence doth this tear fall, as a drop of rain from a sunny sky? Fascination guides the brunette stare. Watching a tear fall from the maiden's eye. An eye without sorrow.

Without pity.

other

From the Penthouse window of the White Tower Dorm. To the frosted window of Whitaker Hall. Across the snowy landscape—these promises fly, until they are frozen in motion along the timeline. Promises cold with purpose. Promises unfettered. Unhindered by the glass window at the Whitaker Music Hall.

"My mother cried when she raped me," Jennifer says. I feel the penetration of her voice at my bosom as I lay, with her resting on top. The beating of her heart still plays a rhythm at my chest. "But her crying wasn't sadness or regret. It was a release. An explosion of something that had racked her body with lust for God knows how many years."

"Is your mother a housewife?"

"A housewife whose never home. Dad's never home either so it doesn't matter. She was a local news woman when I was little. I don't really remember it but I've seen the pictures. The tapes. It all looks so ridiculous. Like she was pushing against something that wasn't meant to be."

"A TV news woman. Why'd she quit such an important job?"

A pause. To eternity.

"ABC. CBS. NBC. CNN. They all rejected her. One of them said she was... too distracting, whatever the Hell that means. At least that's what Mom told me. And she could be telling the truth about that. She's as pretty as Ann Curry and Julie Chen both, and that's no lie. But with a big, shapely bottom. Like J-Lo in *Ass*aconda. Small, curved waist. And her breasts are huge. Big and long when she's naked. No where's near as big as yours though. But they're so sensitive that she..."

"That she what?"

"If I..."

I feel her breath quicken again, and too, the beating of her heart.

"If I nurse her long enough... she can get off. Even with all her clothes on. Or if I get behind her and massage her right... same thing."

"Wow. Just like me, huh?"

"I'll bet you didn't know you could do that, did you?"

"No. I never even wanted to before."

"Sorry I corrupted you," she says. Coldly. "My mother was born Anna Lin Chow. Chow spelled 'C-A-O.' Her parents only spoke Chinese. She said that her mother hit her or beat her every single day. Is that why Anna Chow is a sex addict? Is that why she's a closet dyke like nobody's business? But she would never cheat on my father...*oh no*. I think she respects him too much because he's rich. I think he's worth about 5 million dollars. At least he was at my high school graduation."

Old memories of my own father coalesce. A mustache. A kind, smiling face. A fortune five times five million.

"Am I just a bored, rich bitch?" she asks. "Like my mother? Did I attack you because my mother attacked me?"

"You didn't attack me. You needed me."

"I needed you alright. With both hands."

A giggle tenses her body. Her hands squeeze my overdeveloped bosom once again.

"There's something else Anna's good at. One of her many… 'private talents.'

In the heart of her memory, I see the beautiful Asian woman form as a mist of white tinted blue, with a center spot of red at the pit of her soul and spirit. These do come together, until the mist is solid in human form; and from Jennifer's voice I see Anna May come to life and purpose, standing at the piano in the nude, as her daughter sits nude upon the keys of Grieg, sliding and bouncing up and down the scales of Melancholy Bay, imprisoned by the chords of pain and grieving. The red welts on her back tell of her mother's discipline, I see, and the unyielding frustration of her own requited life. *You will be perfect,* she says, *through every distraction, until the feeling and power flow through your hands like magic. In these last days, in the dying light of classical music, you will be one of the last great performers on this instrument; they will sit in the audience with their legs together tight, enraptured by what they see, and what they hear...* and now, the beautiful Asian woman places her birch wood cane on the black piano wood, harmlessly, dangerously in front of her pupil, whose learned and mechanical playing she hears undergo a sudden metamorphosis, brilliantly flowing, but still as red as the rivers of Armageddon. What is the end of the mechanicus, with no feeling beyond wrote and practice? It is the beginning of an unheralded young master, channeling what energy that must have tormented Mendelsohn, Schubert and Bach.

In the Heart of Memory, in the projection of Jennifer May's voice, I see the teenager at the piano, already past corruption, and the gore of Chastity's Demise. I see her gaze from the keys to the periphery, to where her mother stands with her long breasts pulled down and twisted by both nipples, her face anguished with a pain so wide and deep, and so unique to her own private grieving. This pain, in a formation anew, to a pleasure come together and sent to far and down below, as her daughter sails the waters of this adagio, with this pain having grown and come to life at her groin, where hangs the violently red member, to project the burning of blue and black fire. In the Heart of Memory, I am a prisoner, to see and hear the sound of perversion which has no end, except to be uncovered in the droves of overnight one by one, as we spin along our blue path among the stars, headed for infinity.

Yes, end of the world mother, I see your heart projected at your nipples hung low and out, to complete the Triangle of Life and Death; the left breast, the right, and the opening to thy womb. But this opening is electrified by you, dear woman, to the strains of Grieg in the air of your home around you, as you are able to abandon your breasts in part, and begin to stroke the red protrusion down below, as your daughter plays so robotically, so robustly along, I see you test her resolve, her concentration at the keys, as you begin to feel the red phallus as a protrusion of your own body, as your arm begins to hammer on its own, while the perverted dominance, the sadistic control you must take becomes a part of your breasts, up into your backside in phantom grieving unrealized, and to the member you push and pull like the wheel rod of a moving diesel, your face already twisted towards the ugliness of agony, the unbearable beauty of orgasm by deviance, which has you now shaking uncontrollably while your hand still moves the member, as you scream a scream only your daughter can hear, your free hand slammed so noisily in such atonal clamour upon the keys, the red member spewing the depravity of yourself that only you can see, which rains white upon your daughter's hopeless hands, and the white and black piano keys she hath long since ceased to play.

As to this perversion, Anna May, how many mothers hath ceased to know? At the end of this age, Anna May, how many daughters hath ceased to know?

Church

In the mountain church, Angel Simms listens to the pastor. His words are dripped with eschatology.

> "...and it won't be water, but fire this time,
> just as it was in the days of Noah—the Almighty
> God, who sits on high, and looks down low—this
> Almighty God, shall rain fire down from Heaven,
> to consume every particle of sin from his
> Creation—to burn the rainbow of Promise from

the clouds in the sky, to burn these clouds with fire, to boil the skies aflame, to send a wave of eschatology from one end of the world to the other—until there is nothing left but cinders, ashes, and the smoldering remains of every sinful man, woman and child—to melt the elements with a fervent heat—from the North, the South, the East and the West—every valley shall be exalted, every mountain and hill laid low, the rough places will be made plain, the crooked places shall be made straight, and then the glory of the Lord shall come upon the clouds of glory, and every wicked eye that is alive and remains, shall see him return—as it was in the Days of Noah, so shall it be again, in the coming of the Son of Man, in the Second Coming of Jesus Christ our Lord—this same Lord, who came the first time, wrapped in swaddling clothes, lying in a manger—whose arrival was foretold by the arrival of a Star in the East—the brightest star in the Heavens— the brightest star that this sinful world has ever known—this selfsame Jesus, would grow up in righteousness, and in the power of the Almighty God, this selfsame Jesus, who was without spot or blemish, who knew no sin, who lived blameless, who was despised and rejected of men..."

From the stained glass window, a winter breeze touches the face of Angel Simms, distracting her from the burning of blue and black fire. The winter draft caresses her soul. Lifting her in spirit. Drifting her across the miles, to a cabin nearby the deep Appalachian Woods.

The preacher's voice fades to a drone without words, in the mind of Angel Simms. She opens herself to the breath of snowy winter. Rescued from the heat of judgment, and the fires of Armageddon. This, to seek refuge, in the heart of her own fervent memory. The refuge of what must be. Of what bust, what lust there is to see. These last eighteen years. The daughter of Allie Jee Breen.

The swallow in Miss Angel's throat is the swallow of hunger. Of thirst. As Calbert Simms takes Angel's hand, in the rain of fire and brimstone, the preacher's voice is morphed to that of a woman. A woman who screams the Second Death of Chastity, after 37 mountain winters. A young woman some twenty years her junior. A score of years younger than Angel Simms. In the heart of Memory, Angel listens to Jennifer Maybelline Breen exclaim to this self same Lord and Savior, upon the second death of her chastity. When the years of lengthy nursings and kissings and grindings could no longer suffice. When the device that burns bright blue, is brought from the far city. Brought by Angel Simms, without shame or remorse. When this phallus is raised about the hips this past Sunday, one week preceding this fiery sermon. The sermon which is now a woman's voice—whose body created a scream a week ago. A sound unlike any heard by man. A sound Jennifer Breen did not know she had contained. When she stood unclothed in the mountain cabin of no unnatural light, heated barely warm by fire.

In the orange fireplace glow, in the crust of newly fallen snow, they had stood on bare feet and nudity, the two of them. In Angel Simm's heart, they stand together, the two of them. Jenny May is bent over in front of Miss Simms. Miss Angel. Marveling the new and unfamiliar pain of a curse bestowed. Jumped from the Angel family tree—over to the Maybelline Breen. Bent over standing, gigantic breasts hung down and free in the winter dark. Receiving the Snow Goddess' Intercourse. The mimicking of that which pertaineth to a man. Feeling the rise of a voice that cannot be contained within. A series of many long thrustings, for the greater part of a half hour. Until Angel hears the sound. The sound she had craved, but could not find before. Holding Jennifer Breen's arm tight up behind her back, Jennifer bent over on her feet. A prisoner of what she has never known. Not the clumsy fumbling violence of Jimmy Lee, done when she was nineteen. But the seasoned, learned motion of a deviant heart. Hidden. Suppressed. Unknown to her husband and her sons. Unknown to the family Simms. Thrusting in determined rhythm, like the chopping of a stubborn tree. But a tree that will soon fall. In the Heart of Memory, Angel Simms thrusts the back of a screaming young woman without mercy. Hearing the pain of trauma in her voice.

Upon the vanishing winter draft, an invisible scream flies into the snow. From the beating heart of Mrs. Angel Simms, she remembers. She remembers that… no. Jenny May did not cry from the pain.

Choke

"Choke on it bitch. I said *choke on it!*"

In the White Tower room, bathed in Sunday morning light, the sorority girls have a passion. One bestowed from the Fall of Man, from the death of the Garden of Eden. Written into the timeline from the Curse of Eve, from the birth of Fate, and her twin sister Destiny. Both the same, yet altogether different. Two forces sent to curse mankind with the desire to go his own way, but to prevent and hinder every step therein. To give so many the pain of knowledge so deep and inherent, but to deny them the fullness of it, so that even the most intellectual become the most foolish concerning human life, and whether or not it is guided by the hand of God. Chaos, Chance, and Free Will, these three, are dispatched into the hearts of the unbelieving—to blind them to the Truth, that Caesar is Caesar by Fate alone, as Christ went to Golgotha by Destiny. Our thoughts, our actions, our consequences in life—those are in the stone tablets of Predestination, written by the finger of God— protected by powers and principalities light and dark, so that those who would be king may be, and those who might be slave as well. It is the Curse of Adam passed down, that some are a magnet for prosperity, even by pure wickedness, that the more sinful they behave, the more prosperous they become—this curse bestowed, to vex those who are condemned from birth to have not, so that their desperation is put upon, and increased by every step along the way, as they watch the less deserving be blessed and rained upon. No, they will not prosper, says sister Fate, and yes, they will die in sorrow, says sister Destiny.

Of this predestined motivation, of what is inescapably meant to be, the brunette chokes upon the eight inch member strapped on—pushed so deep into her throat to coughs and choking, with requisite tears running free, her arms handcuffed behind her back, gazing helplessly upward at her blonde captor. Feeling the thunderous pain of a hard slap across her face, the lightning agony of a hair pull. The brunette Judith pulls back in desperation, having choked upon the phallus, feeling it rising now from her throat in spit and gagging. Spit that flies in lovely crystal strands downward, to fall cold upon her breast and thigh.

"That's it, the Adonna Blonde says, standing on the bed. "That's what I wanna see. That's what I need to see, bitch.. No...spit on it some more," she says, to the tune of another painful slap and hair pull. "You thought I was joking, didn't you? I *told* you you were gonna choke on my cock didn't I? Now, what did I tell you?"

"You told me I was gonna choke—" And the brunette's words are choked now, by the rising, the so-called lump of sorrow in her throat.

"Oh, so you're going to cry now. Listen, shut the *fuck* up or I swear to God I will give you something to cry for. Do you want your nipples bitten?"

"No..."

"I said do you want me to bite your fucking nipples until they bleed—"

"No!"

This 'no', on the wings of sadness and submission.

"Now, bitch. I want you to suck and choke on my cock so I can cum."

The Spencer Brunette must oblige, hands still bound, but now upon the Doll's member with fire and passion—sucking, biting, pulling and shaking, amazed at the blonde girl's loud and fevered bellowing, her hands at her own small breasts in desperate squeezing. "Choke on it. Please choke on it," she says, her entire body tensed up, her pretty face anguished, mouth open now on its own. "Go back and forth," she says, losing her breath. "Yeah, go back..."

It is the sight of a brunette beauty on her knees on the bed, breasts so high and round, waist so soft and curved outward to hips extraordinary, her mouth around the long ivory color, in the fellatio of the Sapphic, working her head back and forth (forward and backward), until the small breasted pretty blonde standing up grabs her by the head, to better anchor herself for the involuntary thrusting, until depravity screams a raspy siren from her young body, as she stands bent over the head of her brunette slave, shaking like a flower on the Eve of Armageddon.

Viper

The Earth flows the River of Time—from one snowy hour to the next, until another Sunday has come and gone. In the biology classroom, students are cold and heavy laden in the winter spirit. From the bottom row of the theater style seating, to the top and far and distant row, winter souls sit un-enraptured by the serpent lecture, nor does the poison of their misdeeds challenge any frozen winter heart. While the lady professor drones so impatiently onward, so appropriately forward in knowledge to be learned and lost, Judith Spencer sits with a lesser maiden from the Psi Alpha Omega sorority. Through the lady professor's impressive string of brute force facts, Judith gazes unawares through the veil of poisonous snakes and their venom, to pinpoint the face of the freshman Asian beauty, who is smart enough to take this class now, and end all further speculation on Biology 101. From her seat high up and toward the back of the room, Judith gazes down at the beautiful Asian, whose hair is such that Judith briefly considers that it has to be a wig, then reconsiders quickly.

So few, such a blessed few among them can hear the last warning; as their interest wanes and dies at the head of the Gaboon Viper on the giant screen below. Judith is one of the disinterested. The masses too consumed with themselves to care.

She rises with the Sea of Youth, bidding a quick and dismissive goodbye to her lesser sorority companion. Watching the Asian student leave in a hurry to go nowhere fast. Feeling the instinct of a black leopard eaten alive by hunger, when the feral pig grunts over the forest leaves below.

What to do? Push through the cold, lazy crowd to the doorway down at the bottom of the room? Or do a lesser, but more crowded pushing to this door up high, and meet her outside in the snow? But these instincts do override free will, and she is helpless but to push downward through the exiting crowd of students below, unafraid to be the bitch she is known to be, pushing and shoving without mercy to get through the door and into the hallway, where there is hardly much more lonely room to breathe.

"Jennifer—hey Jennifer!"

The lovely Asian turns in bewilderment, in time to see the beautiful brunette push through the remaining winter crowd of students in the hall, pale blue eyes glistening from a fair skinned face, underneath hair almost as black as her own.

"Hi, I'm Judith, Judith Spencer. I've seen you around campus. You're Jennifer May, right?"

"You're Mary Adonna's friend. From the Omega's."

"That's us. The Alpha *and* the Omega."

A sudden pressure brushes Jennifer's lonely spirit. Demure, humble. Lips tucked in. Her smile is genuine.

"You wanna go somewhere and talk?"

"We'll, I sort of have to practice. And I've got somebody waiting for me."

"I tell you what, let me walk you over there. It won't take that long."

"Well, okay."

Fungalooga

*H*eavy veils of snow form high in the clouds of weeping; those tears frozen in the nick of time, where the veils of ice crystals formed break into billions of pieces, all unique in six part formation, but identical in origination and regret. This new veil hath broken up in the clouds, each part shattered gently again and again, until the crystals are pulled downward in lost hope, adrift on winter winds of tragedy, which send them into the current of wickedness flowing, where they must bear fearful witness to the fallen angels they see—all of the powers, principalities, and rulers of the darkness of this world. In terror, and the sorrow of the ages—

lamentation falls further and further downward, to the invisible cesspool of air closest to the earth, and the corruption that hides in a tapestry of pain, and the abiding icy façade of beauty in winter white.

"The reason we didn't approach you before is that we were afraid. You're a gifted student. You have a full scholarship. You're beautiful, and not that it matters, but you're a minority and that makes you special. And no, it's not tokenism. We're not trying to collect minorities to make ourselves look good. We need somebody like you, and you need an organization of lifelong friends like us. Our mothers and fathers are connected and networked like you could never imagine. You'd only have to play for them once and they could set you on the road to becoming a concert piano player. If that's your heart's desire. Is that what you want most?"

"It's what my mother wants most."

"It's what you want too, isn't it?"

"I guess so."

'Our sorority is only about 25 years old. We're still trying to make a name. To carve out an identity. We're on the edge of starting chapters at some of the best schools in North Carolina. Schools way better than this place. Mary says Appalachian is a dump but I think it's beautiful here."

"But I thought you were only interested in May Windsor. And I thought you were all mad because she turned you down."

"We wanted *both* of you. But I told you we were scared to ask you because we knew you had a piano scholarship. And you're right, Maybelline turned us down already. You might even get her to change her mind, who knows? But it's not really her we want anymore Jennifer. It's you."

A force unseen, unmeasured, stops the bewildered girl in her tracks. On this part of their long walk, the trees are few. The veil of snow drifts down quiet and plentiful around them.

"What?"

"I said we want *you*, Jennifer May. That's so weird, Jennifer May... May Windsor. It's like you guys were meant to be together. But whether she joins or not, we want you to become an Omega Girl."

"Wait," says Jennifer, turning to walk again, "will I have to pledge or haze or something dumb like that because if so, I don't—"

"Only those losers in those drunken slut sororities still do that. We don't do that... for everybody."

"What does that mean?"

"Look, if you mean do we have a big blue paddle with 'Omega' printed in black across it then yes, we do. "We gotta have some fun, right?"

"I don't think beating somebody in the name of sisterhood is fun, alright?"

"I said we don't do it for everybody. The paddling is a choice, and some girls would rather be paddled than look like a coward, that's all."

"So if I don't take the paddling then I 'm a coward."

"The girls that don't get paddled have it worse, okay?"

"Like how?"

"They have to... *dee throw a fay ca.*"

Judith's voice is low. Almost whispery.

"What did you say?"

"The girls that don't get paddled have to... deep throat a fake cock."

This train is forced to another stop along their snowy path. In every life, there is the ride upon this train—a train to Tucumcari. Through unanswered prayers, hope found and lost again, the horn whistle blows, and the train wheels screech a siren to every mountainside, and one learns that through all resistance and futility, yes. This train will stop at Tucumcari.

"What did you do?" Jennifer asks. Seeing Whitaker Hall afar off, and a lonely figure in the snow. Judith takes a fervent step in front of the Asian girl. Her pale eyes glisten in guilty delight.

"Oh, I think you know."

The two brunettes stand face to face in the field of white. Teaching and learning. Giving and taking without a word.

"Yes," Judith says. "I don't like paddles either."

Jennifer glances downward, at the canvas of snow, where she can see the image of herself at the piano nude, her mouth around what red is strapped to her mother, jaws drawn inward by the fervent sucking motion.

"A boyfriend's cock is fun. A girlfriend's cock is fungalooga."

"Funga… what?"

"Fungalooga. To the mind. To the body."

A pause…

"To the spirit."

Library

"girlfriend's what is *what?*"

"I know. It's crazy, right?"

"Well... remember Whitaker Hall the other day?"

"Forever."

The all encompassing library quiet is a refuge. A welcome respite from the cold.

"I can't believe she told you that about herself. I would die before I'd tell anybody what we did."

"Maybe that means it's for real," Jennifer says. "That they really do want me to join."

"How can you talk to them? Don't you remember the way they were laughing at us? They called us '*The Two Bitches*' for God's sake."

"May... I don't have your strength. I can't survive on my own. I need people."

"But I thought... I mean... after the other day."

"I know. I'm being pathetic. Disloyal. Maybe even sort of treacherous. But I can just hear my mother's voice *"you did what? You turned down Psi Alpha Omega? Because you're scared of a plastic cock?"* And then, the requisite slap, the ear twist, the hair pull, until there's just enough tears to satisfy her. Besides, she already told me to find a good sorority to join. I have no choice."

"But those girls," I say. "Can you trust them?"

Deep breath.

"No."

Ashes

In the winter wind and snow, loneliness touches Jenny May's heart. Though the mountain cold is severe, her winter coat is thin.

In the twilight snow, Jenny May gazes above, at the new wire stretched from on high, down to the roof of her mountain cabin. She remembers the new, fan powered space heaters inside. The warmth they bring is oppressive. Sometimes, she opens the window to breathe the ice cold mountain air.

The glow from her mountain cabin is artificial now. The unnatural lights of earthly progression. The embers in the fireplace have turned to ashes for the last time. Ms. Simms told her not to burn wood for heat anymore.

She remembers the death of her new chastity, having known only one sin on one day when she was nineteen. When the curse of her sin split her soul in two with pain. Having not known another such sin, until Ms. Simms put the fire inside her shaped like a man's private thing. To cause the death of new virginity. To cause the second death of chastity.

"We cain't do our business in this cold cabin no more," Ms. Simms had said. Then the men came and put the telephone pole by the trees down the path. Then they strung a black wire down to Jenny May's cabin. After this, the kerosene began to smell like poison. The smoke from the wood and ashes, like death. The fire looked like foolishness and pain.

A box at the top of the pole hums in the dying mountain light. The high pole tops off in the shape of a cross. As Jenny May stares at the cross, Angel Simms' vulgarity burns the theater of her mind. Tonight, in the modern heat and light, with no covering on either window in the cabin, 57 year old Angel Simms had stood 37 year old Jenny May up nude again bent over. The pounding had not ended until an hour was done.

"Why you got ta stick this thing in me Ms. Angel?"

"Cause my momma did it ta me, and her momma did it ta her."

"But you ain't my real Momma, Ms. Angel."

"That don't matter. Ain't I been carin' for you since your momma died?"

"Yeah."

"Then whose your momma near 'bout twenty years now, girl?"

"I guess you, Ms. Angel."

"Then you like my real daughter ain't ya?"

"Yeah."

"Then I gotta do it to ya, girl."

"Why you wait near 'bout 20 years to stick that thing in me?"

"Cause God called me ta tame the sin growin' in you girl. I dreamed that I grow'd one a these and stuck in ya. Then you was white as snow. Like a angel from Heaven."

In the Heart of Memory, Angel Simms grabs Jenny May's bosom from behind. They are big and heavy in her hands. Angel shakes and falls over onto Jenny May's back.

"It's been burning in me since I was little. I got behind my momma and did it to her when I was 12. My momma's titties was watermelons like your'n. I used ta get behind her and hold on to 'em when my daddy died. If I pulled on the front of 'em for a few minutes she shook and screamed like it was killin' 'er. You shook a lotta times girl, but you ain't never hollered 'til I bought this thing and put it in ya. You want me ta keep makin' you holler don't ya?"

"I don't know."

"Why not?"

"It feels too good, I guess."

"Is that why you have ta holler? 'Cause it feels too good?"

"Yeah."

"Better then when I suck on your bosom?"

"Yeah."

"That's a sign then. That we found what we was called ta do together. I'm gon' take good care of ya Jenny May. And we gon' make each other holler sometimes. Now stand up and turn around. Put the front of your titty on mine."

In the mountain twilight, Jenny May sees the first and brightest star appear. The mountain pines fade to a black forest in the evening day. She remembers the years of gathering wood for the stove. Momma's voice warns of the wolves and the bears. There is no baby to tend.

Loneliness touches her heart again. Jenny May did not cry from the pain.

Book Three

*P*rivilege

*T*he houses in Jennifer May's neighborhood are pristine; each brick mansion drifting by as we drive these snowy streets, on our winter break from the Appalachian school. These are the houses of upper class strivings, where through a rocket powered leap upward, have managed to escape middle class poverty; the treadmill of want and greed, where the middle class run tirelessly to their graves—buying and spending, borrowing and lending themselves into a stupor of self denial, that their lifestyles are not as fragile as a soap bubble, kept from popping by desperation, drive and Destiny itself. But these are the houses of privilege. Them who have escaped the bubble of high hundred thousand dollar burden and million dollar façade—these brick houses are of Million Dollar Truth instead, where Talent and Perseverance are joined by Luck itself, to provide the low seven figure salaries—saved and spent with such skill, until the brick mansions are paid for outright in less than 10 years with no drain on the lifestyle. I can see, and feel the echoes of what I know in these beautiful brick palaces, that if this is where we are going, then the girl I love is *rich*, and free from Poverty's accursed sting.

In our little blue chariot, we roll the black streets of privilege. Past the snow covered golf course lawns and landscaped forest trees white with winter ice, until we approach a lonely house of gray brick, which seems to sit alone on the neighborhood open plain.

And as we turn into the driveway, rolling up to where a silver gray Lexus rests in winter reserve, I know that even the comfort of what they feel is only the smallest part of what the Lady Windsor has grown accustomed to.

"Anna May's home" she says, unlatching her seat belt. Unable to mention, even with her eyes, the things she has told me in secret.

In Jenny-braids and white winter coat, I step from our little blue ride into luxurious winter air, untouched by the stench of hopelessness, or the loneliness of Middle Class Poverty and Despair.

Anna

The air inside the mansion is blessedly warm, as the spirits are so inclined, to remind us that so many are protected from the icy cold. In the fungalooga warmth, the shelter and winter refuge, the Queen of Harvest Lake Drive appears; bewildered at the top of the stairs, face more deeply Mongoloid, the purest Asian echo of her half-white daughter she sees below. I bear witness to the Truth—in the tightest gray business skirt and like high heels, looking all of Julie Chen's long lost sister as she drifts toward us, her red blouse buttoned so tight over breasts at least half as big as mine. The woman is an Armageddon Flower, whose power is apparent in just her face and figure alone, whatever intelligence or personality or talent may be withstanding or no.

Anna May's beauty is the saving grace of our lonely visit, her long black hair fluffed and styled in perfect contrast to the fearless red lipstick and bosomy red blouse below. She waves at me the cutest smile and flutter of the hand, then exchanges a look of such relaxed, joyful understanding with her daughter—"*Jenny Baby, come 'ere,*" flowing out on its own. They hug so tight and without a spark of the slightest tension, so that I cannot imagine a single word of what Jennifer told me about her is true. Their hug is hearty indeed; like sisters or best friends who have shattered all barriers of separation long ago. The smiles, the hugging, the look exchanges are profoundly genuine, lacking any undercurrent of discord or strife.

"Mom, this is my best friend. Maybelline Windsor."

"Hi," she says. Her air kiss at my cheek smells of lilac and mint.

"Maybelline. Now that's a name."

"I know. Everybody just calls me May."

"Jennifer May. May Windsor. Jenny May is here to stay, huh?"

"Mom, stop. Please."

Alright, you little grump slides so effortlessly from exotic lips, while she takes her daughter's face by the hand and rubs their noses together.

"We're going up to get settled," Jennifer says. "We'll be here about a week. Is that alright?"

"The longer you stay, the better. You know that. You go on up and let me steal May for a few minutes. We'll go to the kitchen. For some coffee or cocoa or something."

"Well…"

"Go on," Anna says, "she'll be up in a minute. I want her to get used to me before you take her and hide her from me."

As if in slow motion, I am touched by the Anna May hand. Caressed at the small of my back, and carried by the current of time—from where I glance over to the staircase, seeing my friend take each step in this self-same slow motion. Not needing to make eye contact, her expression relaxed in complete, good-natured knowing and acceptance. As if I am suddenly unimportant, and her mother's will must surely be done.

*K*itchen

*T*he kitchen is every bit as palatial as would be expected, with the light oak wood cabinets so smartly chosen, to deliver the overall impression of substance and beauty.

"Open the fridge honey, look in there and get what you want." A pause… "Or would you rather have something hot?"

In the last days, thus saith the Lord, *I will pour out my spirit upon all flesh… and your sons and daughters shall prophecy. And your young men shall see visions, and your old men shall dream dreams.* When I look at the beautiful, mature Asian woman, to answer concerning the apple juice I hope she has in her refrigerator, I am captured by a look I've never seen before from a woman. Her face flashes the most somber, determined gaze—from my face to my breasts and back again.

"Do you have apple juice?"

A forty year old face lingers a serpentine look, a full second more. Then I see the fungalooga smile again; lips closed this time. A knowing grin, intentionally forced and laced with an invisible wink.

"Honey, we've got every kind of juice you could ever want. I love juice. Don't you?"

"Yes, Maam."

"I'll get you a glass."

Lips tucked in, I'm at the open refrigerator, pulling at my loose white blouse, reaching for an unopened bottle of the drink I've always loved. When I close the door and turn, I'm nearly shocked, nearly, by Jennifer's mother close by, staring at me with a glass in her hand.

"It's remarkable," she says. Taking the heavy plastic bottle from my hand, opening and pouring a glass for me.

I suppose that shyness is a small part of who I am. But what about naiveté? What does she see, when I take the glass into my smooth, white hand, and touch the glass to my lips as pink as a summer rose?

"Maybelline," she says. "There's no wonder."

I smile, lips tightened already by demurity. False wonder raises my eyebrow, opening my blue eyes wider. The energy of her stare is palpable, to light my braids on blue and black fire.

"And the amazing thing is, you seem to genuinely have no idea…"

"Of what?"

"That with nothing more than lip balm on your lips… did my daughter tell you I was a reporter when she was a little girl?"

"Yes, she did. That's really interesting."

"The only thing interesting about it was why I did it."

"Oh yeah?"

"I did it to rebel against my mother. I don't know what it is about Asian mothers and the piano but, yes. She wanted me to go professional. But after high school, I quit because I knew I wasn't good enough. I knew it was never going to happen. So I did the other thing an Asian girl is supposed to do in college. Journalism."

"But you enjoyed being a reporter, right?"

No answer.

"I've seen beautiful women of every age, every race. When I was running around shoving microphones in people's faces like a desperate moron. What the Hell was I looking for? Oh yes… Beauty. And you want some truth? So far, you're the most beautiful woman I've ever seen in person, young or old. And I spent a lot of time traveling and talking to people…"

She glances at my bosom.

"And I've never seen anything like it."

The quiet, deep tone her voice takes unnerves me to confusion. A flash of her sparks through me like a plug in the wall, where I see her ripping at my blouse to break the buttons.

"How does God… *why* does God bless a girl your size to have breasts that large? Is your Momma big-chested?"

"Actually, no. And neither is my grandmother."

"Well, maybe your father's mother or… may I ask you for a favor?"

"Sure, anything."

"May I see your breasts?"

I feel the plug in this secret wall spark through me again—this time with her holding both my breasts, and sucking one of them as by aggressive, brute force instinct.

"I…"

No sooner than my mouth opens to stammer, we hear the quiet commotion of a young Asian girl in the living room, grabbing my bags like a maid on a family vacation, smiling at me and her mother, unknowingly, dragging my clothes and books up the stairs in lonesomeness unhidden.

"I should go help Jennifer unpack, huh?"

"No," she says. "I should help *you* unpack."

"Oh, you don't have to do that, Jennifer's going to help me. Thank you for the juice, Mrs. May."

As I place the glass on the counter and turn to walk away, her hand reaches out on its own to block my path, with her still looking away from me, toward the glass of apple juice on the counter.

"I… I think Jennifer wants me to help her unpack."

"I'd like to help you unpack too," she says, stepping lightly against me, so that her red blouse is a pressed cushion against my white one. "I'd like to help you unpack what you're hiding in that bra."

All pretense drains from her expression, to correspond with the fearful departure of it from my spirit.

"You want me to take your bra off, don't you?"

"No, Maam."

"Does this feel good? Your best friend's mother? Her breasts pushed against yours?"

"I… I don't feel anything."

"Well, I do. I most assuredly do."

I feel like I can't breathe. I want to take a deep breath. But how? How could it be anything other than an invitation to her to take a deep breath of her own, many of which she has already taken here, still pressed up against me.

"Please, Mrs. May."

"Please?" she says. "You have the nerve to come in my house with this face, this hair, this macromastian bosom, and say please? Please *what*, may I ask?"

"Please don't."

"Why? Are you a virgin? Do you feel *violated*? Abused? Have I crossed a *line?* Sweetie, let me ask you a question..."

The woman adjusts herself, to make her bosom a better fit against mine.

"... has my daughter yet had the privilege?"

I open my mouth, where the words '*I don't think that's any of your business*' sit self-righteously, but trapped in the back of my throat.

"Oh... my ... God. She's seen you naked..."

"Mrs. May, please..."

"*May! I need you! Stop kissing up to my mother and come up here!*"

What energy she has built up begins to dissipate, and I can feel her breath suddenly become less deep, pressing her chest not as firmly against mine. Anna May has mercy on this poor girl, Anna May has mercy on me, and steps back just enough, so that I can breathe free.

"Before you leave this house, I would like for us to talk again. Maybelline."

As if the sound of my name is a horn signal, I'm suddenly able to unbrace myself from her and walk free of her presence. Her power. Her control. She follows me just enough, to watch me take the stairs in humility. In shame. Lips tucked in. Trying not to bounce what she said she wanted to help me unpack from my bra.

By the spirits that govern what I feel, on the eve of the Rapture of the Church—I see the forty year old woman turn upon her own bewilderment, strolling in disbelief back to the kitchen. The small glass of apple juice rests hardly touched. She pinpoints where my lips were upon the glass, lifting it up to her mouth. Drinking the apple juice in deep, sensuous gulps, to put out the fire burning dyke blood. To kill the blonde, blue–eyed breast queen come to life in her body. Tormented now to irresistible impulses of thought—to dreams of rape, and every lewd, like and lascivious manner therein.

Anna May goes to the kitchen table. To the dining place of every dream unbroken. Every dark promise fulfilled. Anna sits at the kitchen table. Hair in beautiful, black contrast to her white skin. Her red blouse and lips. Hair framing her Asian eyes. Eyes as black as the soft hair above them.

Anna rests her elbows on the table, and clasps her hands together in prayer form. Pressing her red lips to them.

Devil

As it was in the Days of Noah, so shall it be in the coming of the Son of Man. In these last days, the sins of men and women will be uncovered.

But the signs have run through men for centuries, shining brighter, screaming louder than those that torment the fairer sex. But these are the last days. The days before the new judgment of mankind. The judgment of mankind in fire and smoke, in preordained contrast to the first judgment in water and mist.

And these are the signs of the times, that the secret and private and quiet sins of womankind must be revealed—the whispers of perversion that run so wide and deep as the hurricane, and those unseemly things they do, with every sensual wickedness and unspeakable thing therein. This spirit of latter day desire, this end of the world lust and craving has haunted me in my dreams, intensified by our time in the million dollar May Estate, as her good-natured smiles and winking innuendo hath not ceased for a time. Every trip to the car, every rolling river ride to the malls and the restaurants and the charity places have been so heavy laden with tension, to where this is no longer a vacation from school for me, but a seven day prison sentence, where the hours drag along like days, and each day is as a fortnight in captivity. The evil that men do is no respecter of persons, and I am as uncomfortable around her as Anne Hathaway was in her training days, when a Devil embodied by Meryl Streep wore Prada.

I ride with the Devil from sunup to sundown, since I learned of her intentions toward me, that coupled with what I now know to be true that happened between her and her daughter. The devil I sense, the devil I feel—pricks me with the precision of a needle-beaked blackbird, raising me up from the paper I type at the laptop, pulling me in mysterious fashion from the room and to the top of the stairs, where I see Anna looking through the fancy front window at the sound of a car door closing. Then, like the screaming of a buzzard hawk over a field of rabbits, I hear the engine of a luxury car start, whereas my journey down the stairs is an epic struggle to keep from running.

"Is that Jennifer," I say, walking so boldly up beside her. "She didn't tell me she was leaving."

"She remembered something she had to pick up at the mall," she says, stepping up behind me, black heels, dress on fire with blue. "She didn't want to disturb you."

"Oh," is the defeated half whisper, while my protection rolls back in silver Lexus luxury, then rolls forward down the long, snow dusted driveway to the street beyond.

Then, upon the turning of silver, upon the departure of a winter chariot, a shock startles me to a yelp, when hands clamp my heavy breasts hard from behind.

reasts

"Don't move," she says. "I want you to stand still. No one can see us."

And perhaps she is right, because though I search with wide and fearful eyes, there are no passing cars to shake her courage, and no houses close enough to shatter her resolve. Of what prying eyes there are, she performs for gladly, her white hands buried in the fabric of my navy collar shirt, which apparently had not been loose enough to hide the great cushioned power within.

"Mrs. May… what are you doing? You don't have to do this."

"Oh, but I can assure you," she says, "that this is *exactly* what I have to do."

And upon this she gives my breasts a mighty squeeze, then another, and I hear her say "*Oh, God*" to herself.

"I had no idea," she says. "No idea they would feel so big. How is it possible you can have breasts like this? Magnificent, mountainous breasts. Breasts as big as Momma Oprah. Breasts as big as Mother Winfrey's, hidden under your clothes."

In her voice is the trembling of hunger. The craving that touches judgment and reason.

"How can breasts this gigantic be on such a young and beautiful girl?"

With that, she sniffs my neck and hair deeply enough for me to feel the air rushing in, then I feel her teeth clamped hard over my shirt fabric and in my shoulder. The grunting in my throat is muffled inside. Then suddenly, her hands slide to my shirt buttons, and begin to undo them one by one.

"I have dreamt of you," she says. "Since I was a little girl in my Momma's house, I have dreamt of you. You were sent to me. You are a Divine gift to me."

When enough of the buttons are done, she escorts me to the front closet and opens it, where the full length mirror lies in wait. In the mirror, I see a tall, fair skinned girl with yellow blonde hair in a single braid hidden behind her head, with two of the biggest blue eyes in humanity, both red and wet with tears. The size of the white bra, and the amount of cleavage underneath the open shirt is shocking. Behind her is a beautiful but stern faced Asian woman in a royal blue dress, with a black belt and black heel shoes to match.

I see the Asian woman in the mirror reach inside the open shirt, and inside the bra, and begin to slide the gargantuan left bosom free of its cloth prison. And before long, the girl in the mirror stands with one globe free, white against the navy cloth, three to four times bigger than a C-cup breast would be.

With the non-chalant study of a physician, she kneads it, squeezes, and gently pulls the nipple until the large areolas shrink, and the nipple grows to an epic rising before my eyes.

"When did you turn nineteen?"

Stubbornness strikes my voice. Holding it silent.

"I won't ask again."

I stare at her reflection, unable to break free from my own will, willing to endure humiliation for Jennifer's sake only. I see the sternness in her face relax to a solemn calm, and she steps behind me again.

In the mirror, I see—I *feel* her hands underneath my shirt at my blue jeans. Unbuttoning. Unzipping. Undeterred. Unremorseful. Unafraid.

What pleasure doth this pinch to my private provide? Of this, I do not know. But the pinching grows in strength, and I feel her fingers clamping to full strength inside my jeans. The requisite *'ow'* escapes. Pitifully, at first. But soon it must grow in proportion to the pain.

"Ms. May, *stop it!*" And upon this, the pain grows to what I cannot endure, and I see the giant breasted girl in the mirror bent over, a single breast hanging exposed outside the partially unbuttoned shirt. "It *hurts!*" I scream angrily, unable to see clearly now through the tears. But the strength in the hands that hold me is absolute, and their power is unmistakable. *"May!* I was nineteen in *May!"*

And as quickly as it started, the pain at my groin—the pinching, biting pain stops. Strong hands stand me up straight again, as my voice chokes more than one squeaky sob and cry. *"Maybelline Windsor, born in May. Her best friend's name is Jenny May*. It's alright Baby," she says, pulling my other breast free. "It's alright." Then through tears, I see the forty year old Asian woman reach her head around from behind me, and I feel the warm, lightning pull of my nipple into her mouth.

For only the second time in my life, I feel a nursing at my breast, but not of tenderness and affection, but with a deep and ravishing hunger—a heavy, warm pulling that sends waves of pleasure through my body with every sucking, and tickling of her tongue. Every release is ecstasy, every kissing sound of release when her mouth pulls away does indeed leave me breathless, I have to say.

Still standing by the closet mirror, I look down at this woman, the mother of my best friend, the mother of the girl I have grown to love—I watch her bent over at my breast— holding them, going back and forth between them like a mad woman, nearly bellowing in the effort, as though the lust channeling through her body is an unendurable plateau.

She raises up from the nursing, getting behind me again, this time with both hands at my nipples, twiddling them just enough to increase my own longing for reprieve. Then, she begins to twist. My voice's realization is swift and loud, to echo through the million dollar house, where pain is too great for coherent words to form.

Up, down. Around. Every which way, the pain pulls my breasts upward, downward, outward and upward again.

Pain

*W*hen she is done, she stands beside me. Stepped back just enough. Her own expression spent, while a lifetime of pain and pent up frustration runs down her face in a slow and steady stream. She sniffs, wiping her own eyes.

She steps close to me and hugs me, and I cannot help but fall prey to kindness; hugging her back, sobbing tears of profound relief and regret.

"Life is pain," she says. "We do what we can to cope. I've learned that… the harder you resist pain, the worse it feels. I cannot deny who I am inside. What I am. But am I a hypocrite, because I don't give a damn about the Lesbian lifestyle? Is it ironic, that Lesbian culture doesn't interest me? I don't know if I'm even sure what a Lesbian is. I just know that since I was a little girl, I've been attracted to women. Feminine, beautiful women. Yet, I never intended on ever doing anything about it. Maybe it was because when I was 13, my mother caught me and my eleven year old sister rubbing our nipples together, and she whipped us every day for a week. So I buried it. I became a plaything for a few nice boys. For my rich husband. Always burning in lust for my female colleagues. For breasts. For hips. For young women. For young girls. A lust I kept to myself. Kept it pressed down. Letting it burn."

My breasts still exposed, shirt still only partially unbuttoned, I accept the spirits passed down through the mother line, and what inevitable suffering and secret pain they cause. She raises up from my shoulder, looking at me with something like pity, but teary eyed and solemn.

Without a word, she escorts me from the entranceway to the large cushioned gray sofa in the living room.

"Lie down. On your back," she says. And how am I to say no, or to resist? What can the tiger's victim say, when the mauling is underway? When the claw hath dug deep, and the life's blood hath none left to lay?

While I am on my back, breasts fallen even more massive by gravity's pull, she opens my jeans all the way, and begins to slide them roughly down. And though I would like to cover up, zip up, and go up the stairs to a bath and a change of clothes, I am as a woman pressed down, held immobile by something that may as well have the strength of Wonder Woman.

My tennis shoes are soon gone, and so too are the tight jeans. I feel the cool air on my bare legs, goose bumped on my skin. In the haze of disbelief, I see the beautiful hands below, just beyond the gigantic bosom, fumbling at my pink underwear in nervousness, while the woman's mouth hangs relaxed and open, her eyes fixed on the shame of my humanity.

And then the beautiful woman stands upright, gazing my nakedness from the waist down, finally undoing the buttons on her dress and lowering her bra to expose both her big, low hanging breasts, the dark areolas presenting thick, large nipples for me to see. And then she reaches under her dress and slides her black underwear down and away, leaving them sprawled unkempt nearby where she had stood.

From the space in time where she had stood, I watch the woman in her deep concentration, phase over and climb onto the sofa on her knees between my legs reluctantly open. From this position, Anna May raises up the front of her dress, to expose the red member burning, strapped on but extended from deep inside just the same, forged in the hearth of blue and black fire.

I am so unable to comply, but not with this beautiful Woman of Straw! It is with the spirits of fight or flight, which have cursed me for my stubbornness and left me unprotected in the storm. As I see her looking, holding her member, trying to pry my legs further apart—the words *"I'm a virgin Ms. May,"* come out on their own, along with tears of regret and defeat.

"I know," she says, voice already trembled deep by Testros, "don't fight the pain. Release your pain with me...."

And I feel the tip of who I am push wider apart in stretching, as the doorway discovered, as the portal to a forbidden place is found.

"No, please don't," comes out in a wailing, pathetic voice, which causes her to adjust herself on top of me and move her hips forward, her face every bit as anguished over as my own, as the sword of battle forged

in fire, that must endure the icy waters of contempt. She pushes until we both feel the barrier stretch to the point of breaking, myself tensed up to a resisting that can never be, as though trying to grab hold of an approaching mist and push it fervently away. But this mist is soon and quickly broken, and my soul's resistance is pierced through, to my spirit which strains *Oh, God* and then *Oh God!* again, loud enough to wake the dead.

In this call and answer, I hear her response of *Oh God* and *Holy Jesus*, spoken against my face, as somewhere our mouths meet in a kiss we must have to survive, the woman's tongue pressed so far and deep into my mouth. Then she thrusts again, much greater than before, to bring another cry from me, this time muffled by the fit of her mouth over mine.

From somewhere inside her, I know not where, comes a sudden power and control that raises her up, staring at one of the great breasts lying big underneath her; and she reaches down in mid thrust, giving one of them a great and sucking pull. She releases it in a grunting, a powerful kissing release, watching it wobble back into place, watching me grimace in pain, listening to me sob and weep with every thrust within.

And from the selfsame reservoir of her desire, from the eternal mass of want and dreaming, the energy flow writhes her hips into perfect up, down and forward rhythm into me, until I understand that though this is my first true raping, I understand that some are blessed or cursed—with a gift for this burning of fire within. The look upon her face is pent up agony, the pre-release of an energy build, hazing her eyes glassy and unfocused, her mouth open from passing shock within…

And as her pounding settles into a powerful, steady rhythm on its own, the force of a lifetime coalesces and comes to life inside, and begins to flow out of her mouth in an angry *shriek*, that soon begins to come in waves as her body shakes and lurches forward, knocking her down heavy on top of me, where the shriek is transformed into the wail of a siren so much louder than mine, as her body convulses from a mighty explosion, trembling her on top of me many, many seconds more.

*M*otherlines

*I*t is written, that *we wrestle not against flesh and blood, but against principalities, against powers, against the rulers of the darkness of this world, against spiritual wickedness in high places.* And these are the high places—where so many of us are privileged to live and breathe, where we are protected by the spirits that lord over entire cities, entire regions, and down to the neighborhoods where we live. And there are spirits passed from generation to generation, causing some who even profess to know God to fall. For every such wickedness there is for the world to see, how much does it represent what lies in secret, in the shadows of human existence? Yes, it is the proverbial tip of the iceberg that looms, as such a tiny amount of what darkness there is that pulls us down, and what churns beneath cultured civility.

And I wonder what preordination has kicked in, what dreadful ghosts had lain dormant in the both of us until our bodies came into proximity; until I walked into this house and she saw me. Although the images of her own childhood will not form for me now, I can feel the fervent call of their tragic desire, the weight of years unknown and unseen, passed so efficiently—so irresistibly down from not her father, but through the *motherline* of her birth, which lights her breasts and groin on fire of a lust unbearable, so that what is erogenous alone to most is full blown stimulation to her, so that her magical orgasm can be achieved.

Her body is a conduit for stimulation, I know, so that only the sucking of her nipples long enough will bring the shaking forth, that merely the rubbing of them by hands, fingers, toes, or even the nipples of her partner will bring the shaking forth. This, I am allowed to know of her, that it is a curse passed to her from the old country, from the woman who spoke no English when Anna was born. Whose discipline was swift and brutal and often, done without natural affection or remorse; whether or not maternal love was ever a factor notwithstanding.

The woman who lies dazed, confused and spent on top of me can remember nothing of love and affection from her mother, only the sting of switches and belts and caning rods, and even the occasional extension chord and wooden spoon of legend. And what affection there is to remember, what creeps in as sunlight through cracks in a barn wall, are the memories of her mother's tongue at her nipples when she was only a girl of 12, flicking her tongue around and around, back and forth with hardly a single suck, until the flicking made the girl's breath go loud and shallow, and her young body had to shake its fervent response.

And of these images now and burning in my mind; the young Asian mother's tongue, which hath not ceased from sin—treating the 12 year old and the 10 year old's young breasts like playthings, done in the quiet of night most often, where the father Jim Jung Cao worked two restaurant shifts for their livelihood.

Whenever these two Chinese-American girls, Anna Lin and her younger sister Linda Li were home from school. Not allowed to speak English in the home, both being bilingual already. From the resting heartbeat of Anna May I feel pumped into me, where our hearts are joined by the spirits that flow through us both—I see the girl taught early to nurse and lick at her Chinese mother's nipples until energy was built up and released, while the woman Min Li Cao, did this selfsame return to her daughters Anna and Linda, until they learned to expect that it must happen. Anna and Linda were but 12 and 10, when Min Li's spirit came unto them—Anna and Linda were 12 and 10, when the Spirit of their mother hath come.

And what of myself, and from whence cometh the spirit that lives in me, that has taken this final form? Is it because the Lady Windsor's blood doth not burn the same—that the fire in my breasts must surely be my own? Hath the Lady Windsor placed her mouth to my bosom, to suckle the phantom milk from within? Doth these spirits run through the Lady Windsor to me? Where in the universe, I fear, from deep inside what southern woods, down what mountain path must I stroll, to find where it is that this spirit hath come? Of these high places, where the wickedness of perversion blazes as bright as the noonday—where is the place which is unbeknownst to me, where began this burning of blue and black fire?

Virgin

The minutes mark the revolution of every heavenly sphere, the third planet from the sun—and every inhabitant therein. They mark every moment I feel the weight of Anna Cao May laid so heavy on top of me, as if she is resolved to her fate as a broken spirit, every pretense toward restraint and normalcy like a glass pitcher to a white tile floor. She lays still upon me in half sleep, in full comfort—having accepted that this is the end of her; the sum total of every part of her. And slowly, the life returns to her lifeless body again, and she must raise up just enough, to look closely at the two gigantic bosoms resting underneath her. She shakes her head in profound disbelief, that this fantasy plan of hers is a reality, a big blonde virgin lying underneath her trapped.

To renew this captivity of me, she takes both breasts soundly in her hand, descending upon both nipples, one by one, as though life energy is therein for the taking. My own energy, such as it is, hath not released, and the sight of Jennifer's mother nursing my breasts makes me have to resist a squirm underneath her. Yes. Even as my soul weeps for the part of me she took forever, my body lies here in unwanted response to her tongue flicking across my nipples, and her lips sucking them for the phantom milk inside.

And as she begins to focus, nursing a single breast without ceasing, I can only contemplate the shame of my sluttish libido, which has me grinding against the red extension of herself still inside me. And when she sucks me the hardest, releasing it over and over again in that loud, smacking pull, I am unable to resist the re-ignition, that according to my gift passed down the mountain trail—and before long I have to close my eyes and hold my head back, and let the sound of my motherline curse out into the big house in a loud and single siren scream.

"Yes," she says. Repeating. Nodding her head, still staring at the gigantic bosom. "I knew you were a breast goddess. A woman who can cum through her tits. I knew it from the moment I saw you. The minute I saw you, I knew."

Anna May reaches down, and begins to slide the straps and the red line away. Laid heavy on me, she uses both hands and pushes the harness down and away, letting it fall conspicuous to the floor. Then she positions herself on top of me anew, where her aroused, natural self is pressed against mine. Then she raises up, telling me to hold my breasts up, *"so that our nipples can lock together,"* she says. This, I am obligated to do, as she is the wealthy and dominant mother of my best friend.

I open my sore legs accordingly, watching her raised up, her breasts hanging down, mashed so perfectly, so exquisitely upon mine, so where our nipples and areola are hidden within. And I watch this beautiful Asian woman, wife of the absentee white man, mother of the misfit and unnaturally gifted half-white daughter, lose herself in concentration again, her mouth relaxed open once more, her expression frozen from that inner shock passing through, as the energy builds up so big and smooth this time, and takes a flowing trip to every extremity; and from her mouth in the low pitched bellowing of the animal she has become.

This second passing rolls her eyes back as unto God, in her characteristic *"yes"* repeating, then the requisite begging for mercy, to endure the agony of ecstasy in its purest form...

And as if called forth from another world, phased so casually into our own, we hear the opening and closing of the living room door, and the footsteps of humility move from the hardwood foyer floor, silently over the carpet into our space, where I lie still and trapped, unable to look at her, with her mother laid on top of me in the bluest dress imaginable, the red member harness laid so unceremoniously at her daughter's feet.

Sofa

*P*remonition is a cushion for tragedy. Sometimes, no matter how traumatic and tragic the event, we enjoy the privilege of calm when it happens—as when a wife must endure the next beating, or the girl college student slams into the back of another car rushing to campus, or when the employer hears the gunshots coming down the hall, knowing it is the kook she just fired a week ago. The arrival of devastation is the period at the end of a sentence written into the flow of time, woven into the tapestry of human existence, colored into the symphony of a life. And those that have listened, those that have paid dearest attention to these whispers are prepared at least in part—even for the death ride from the top of the twin tower, and its one thousand foot descent to the burial ground below.

These winds of eschatology have blown here, leaving the three of us gathered up and tossed, churned into the wind and rain, smashed and broken into the wet mud of what offences must come. Jennifer stands there. Pathetically holding the bags of inconspicuous consumption, the nibbling mice of modern retail therapy, hung in the plastic bags, held at her sides, but now dropped to the floor. Through the pain, through the haze of devastation, I see the remains of what I have done—standing in her jeans and winter coat—purse and shopping bags on the floor. Laid on top of me is the force of devastation itself, having been lifted by the twister and slammed down on top of me in the killing. Here I lay. In the rubble of a devastated landscape, dead underneath this thousand pound debris.

This Woman of Beauty lies still on top of me, naked breasts still mashed into mine—her face pressed to mine, both turned to the side and staring into space fully aware of the spirit materialized before us, but being unable to reply. It is as though we have been attacked, compelled, even raped by the unseen, and left for dead underneath skies of gray.

But premonition is a cushion for tragedy. And Jennifer May can only stand there relaxed, and see the culmination of a lifetime of whispers and warnings—to accept what was the drowning inevitable, and to perhaps accept so much of the blame herself, for not going underneath the earth when she saw the winter whirlwind coming; to curse her stupidity for not knowing, that bringing me around her mother would be like bringing a bottle of sweet red wine around an alcoholic.

Is the symptom and consequence of man, that he runs and hides from the truth? That his faith is fleeting, and that he takes refuge in self delusion and denial? But as it is written, the third part of any dark truth is

Cataclysm, and here it is laid on top of me, and standing above me in ghostly devastation and ruin.

Anna raises up only slightly, her heart still pumping a greater rhythm, not looking her daughter in the eye as Jennifer removes her sweater and her top, and slides her black jeans off to the floor.

In the same resignation we feel, burdened by the same tragic, uneasy acceptance of our fate, she kneels down before where we lay on the gray sofa, bra and underwear framing the shapeliness we know, and I watch her kiss her mother full on the mouth. Then she looks at me, defeated, betrayed, but in full understanding of what must be. After the requisite tear falls, she smiles and lowers her head to mine, to bless her mother with this precious gift—to see her daughter press her soft and grieving lips to mine.

$\mathcal{I}$ncest

$\mathcal{A}$s it was in the Days of Noah. So shall it be, in the coming of the Son of Man. Three turns of the world have passed, when the sun has come and gone. Since our time at the living room sofa, and the arrival of Devastation and Ruin.

"I never knew anything like this could happen. I couldn't imagine doing anything like that with my mother."

"You'll notice she's been gone all day, every day since it happened. But that's only because you're here. If I had come home alone... it would've probably happened at the piano... and there would be no shame."

"I saw a movie once on cable… where two sisters did it. But even then, I just couldn't…"

"Grasp it? Process it? Believe it? That's how it started with my mother. With her sister when she was twelve. Her sister was ten."

"Incest?"

"It's a secret that nobody buys, and nobody believes. Except when a father does it to a daughter. But I wonder how many people would believe that my Julie Chen looking mother…"

The look we exchange is laced with doubt and unbelief—the flowering that grows from seeds of denial.

A gust of wind turns my attention toward the winter window. The blue skies of our recovery are vanished again, to blanket the world in a layer of new fallen snow. Part of me is so thankful that we have to return to school on Monday. But the other part of me dreads the sights and sounds of that unholy place, that place of so-called higher learning; every teacher, every student moving, drifting from one place to the next, rolled along with the ease of a roller coaster car on a track, powered by wheels of misery, of secrets hidden and forbidden, and the track of lies they roll so casually upon. All smiles and polite hellos and goodbyes, unaware that these are the Last Days, the days before the new floodwaters of fire, and the rising, drowning flame of judgment.

I know that Jennifer was somehow sent to me like a rabbit in the deep woods, like a deer in the darkest part of this wilderness, as a companion to help guide me in loneliness, and through the pain of this regret I feel. And though the memory of what Anna May did to us has not faded—I have hardly been able to ask her the deepest question, that how can you go on, after having fucked your mother? How can you go on, Jennifer May, after having known the nakedness, and full passion of your mother's kiss?

At the behest of this question inside, as it threatens the tip of my tongue in this newly fallen snow, the two of us hear, we *feel* the winter breeze drift in from outside, by the swing of a closed and open front door.

$\mathcal{A}$ntiques

$\mathcal{I}$n the mountain cabin, the door squeaks in the Evening Day. Jenny May turns from her hour at the stove, to see the trusting, pretty face come in.

"What you got cookin' girl? Smells good in here."

"There's a roast beef in the oven. Carrots and gravy. Rice here on the stove."

"Uh huh. Somethin' told me not to eat 'fore I came here. And I know you cook the same way you is in the mirror girl."

"Thank you."

"They's groceries in the car—we can leave 'em in there 'til later on."

"I'm bout ready ta eat," Jenny May says, taking the roasting pan from the old firewood stove. The new, black electric stove sits cold and dark.

"Jenny May, when you gon' use that new stove I bought you?"

"I'm a git round to it. I aint' used to it yet."

"Well, I want you to *git* used to it. I didn't pay all that money so that thing can sit in here and go to dust. I'm gon' send somebody up here to take that wood stove."

"That's Momma's stove."

"Your Momma don't need no stove in Heaven. And I bet you couldn't sell that old thing even if you wanted to. So I might take it off your hands and give it to a antique store."

"Momma wouldn't like that."

"Look here. Yo momma ain't no ghost in this house, girl. So there ain't no need a you tryin' to scare me with what you hear her sayin' in your crazy head. B'sides, I didn't come here 'bout no stove no way."

Angel Simms studies the face of Jenny May. Her eyes are as blue as the winter sky with no clouds. Her long yellow braids are golden in the lamp light.

"You won't use none a these lights I brought you. And I can smell the fire you built in here today. Didn't I tell you not ta make no more fires in here?"

"Yes, Maam."

Angel Simms steps are slow toward Jenny May. The gaze into her eyes is true.

"I'm gon' have ta whup you."

"I know. I was wonderin' when."

"You ain't gon have ta wonder no more. I'm gon' take a belt I brought with me. And I'm gon' stripe the sass outta your behind."

"What if I don't want you ta whup me, Ms. Simms?"

"'B'fore your Momma died she told me you was full o' sass and sin. The older you git the worse you git. I'm tired o' your sneakin' sass and back talkin' ways ta me. You'd be a skeleton in that chair if I didn't bring you somethin' ta eat cause every chicken you had is dead and you ain't raised no crops worth sellin' in five years. You ain't worth the spit in my mouth girl. And you think you got the right ta smart off at me? Talkin' 'bout *what you know* when I say I'm gon whup your tall, big-tittied behind?"

"I'm sorry."

"If ya ask me, you just a shade over funny lookin' anyway. You slope-backed and owl-eyed, and I'm gon'—"

"I'm sorry, Ms. Angel."

"What was that you said, girl?"

"I'm sorry."

Sorrow touches the bluest eye. Eyes of thirty seven. Jenny May did not cry from the pain.

Harness

"When my mother put her finger in me the first time," Anna May says, "I cried from the pain. It felt like a sharp pointed stick tearing a hole in me. There was blood."

At the bedroom window, Jennifer's mother is enraptured by the snow. Her white hips are full in the winter twilight. Hanging in her right hand, the tangle of leather straps looms, holding the thin red line.

"Maybelline?"

"Yes?"

"When you were with my daughter, did she touch your breasts?"

"Yes."

"Did she massage them from behind?"

"Yes."

"Did it make you cum?"

A pause. From where, I know not. Jennifer stares at me. Fearfully.

"Yes."

"Did you cum in your tits? Or did touching your tits just *make* you cum elsewhere in your body?"

"I…"

"It's an easy question honey. You're a college girl. I know you understand."

"It was both, I think. I felt it in both places."

The response makes her look to the side, away from the window—to better hear what truth I have to tell.

"It started in my breasts. The more she rubbed, the better it felt. Then it went to the rest of my body."

"Your climax… it started in your breasts?"

"Yes."

She turns around. The look on her face is awe and bewilderment.

"You had a true breast orgasm," she says. "Did you scream?"

"I had to strain to hold it in. We were in a piano room at the school."

She lowers her eyes. Smiling a little. Betraying the deepest satisfaction, as her mind tells her: *The piano room. How appropriate.*

"A true Breast Queen. Jennifer, come here."

I watch the lovely Asian girl, fully clothed in her jeans and sweater, walk timidly across to her mother, who stands so casually, so boldly in the nude. Before long, Jennifer removes her own clothing to oblige her mother's order, until the two of them are naked together in the room.

"It's going to be different this time. I want you to put this on."

Jennifer takes the hesitant steps into the harness, while her mother slides it up to her groin and fashions the straps, the red member protruding anew from the daughter's life and blood. Then, the mother and daughter walk over to where I am, and without a word, begin to unbutton my yellow collar shirt, continuing until it lies somewhere far and away, followed by my blue jeans, and then my bra.

Still. In the Quiet of Knowing. The two of them each take one of my breasts into their hands, and I begin to feel the duel agony of this end time revelation, being sucked from the center of who I am, where it flows through both of my breasts in ecstasy.

elt

"*I*t's gon' be different this time, Jenny May. Help me put this on you."

Angel Simms straps the large member onto Jenny May's naked body. Her gigantic breasts hang low. The feeling in Angel's body is epic, as she removes her own clothes quickly.

When Angel's clothes are gone, she takes hold of both Jenny May's heavy bosoms. Angel's mouth on them lights a fire in her own body. When the sucking is done, Angel Simms takes up her husband's old leather belt, and whips the beautiful woman on her shapely hips and thighs. Jenny May did not cry from the pain.

The glow from the cabin is warm in the mountain twilight. The evening stars are aplenty.

Cantonese

Before too long, the feeling in both my breasts is epic. I hear my inner voice gruffling on its own, as the feeling passes to the center of my body. I feel Jennifer's mother take strong hold of me, to anchor me in support, as I begin to tremble so violently, as my voice howls many quick, high pitched screams for mercy.

"Yes, yes, yes…" she repeats, again and again. "A breast queen." Her voice is low. Almost whispery. "That's miraculous," she says, kissing me so full on the face and lips, then leaning over in front of me—to kiss her daughter just the same.

Anna moves us both to her daughter's bed—laying Jennifer down on her back, so that the red member rises straight up and true.

"Get beside her Maybelline, on your knees."

This, I do. On the bed, on my knees, I watch the mature, beautiful woman climb onto the bed to where her daughter lays, climbing herself over the red member, her legs in the shape of a hop frog, raising up just enough—then sliding herself downward onto the fire in which we burn.

I am privy to her great looking away as she begins, her eyes gazing to a horizon only she can see, as she straddles her daughter's *cock* in a hopping position, and begins to grind and bounce herself to a place she may have never been before.

"May… Maybelline…" she breathes. "Come… come close to me…"

I move closer to her, while she hop frogs the red member to oblivion, slowing down only to lick and latch onto my breasts, the sight of which must surely do something to her daughter laid on her back, who suddenly begins to breath and strain in high pitched resistance, beginning to speak her ancestral tongue just a bit. This sound does reach the mother, who responds with a hard bouncing, hopping upon her daughter, herself lost in full Cantonese surrender, her eyes focused so heavily on my breasts while she bounces.

And then, I look down to where the sound of weeping comes from, which is her daughter, my friend, and the girl I will always love, who begins to cry in the beautiful language of her mother's childhood; a weeping without words now, but somehow still in the full tone of her mother's youth, a sound carried to completion as I hold her hand, feeling the strength of her body's climax and calling.

Oh, but what this must do to the mother that hops above! Whose beautiful face has anguished over, and from her open mouth ceases the babble in Cantonese, replaced by a loud and tragic cry for a reprieve from suffering!

Orion

"*I*'m sorry I had to whup ya, girl," says Angel, her eyes focused downward to Jenny May's bosom. "From now on, I'm gon' *have* ta whup ya, 'cause it's in my body."

Angel Simms squats above Jenny May as a hop frog. Bouncing hard on the big member strapped on. As Angel bounces up and down, Jenny May's breasts shake and wobble like soft mountains below. When she sees Jenny May turn her head and close her eyes in pleasure, the sight of Jenny May's breasts makes Angel have to call on the Lord for mercy.

Under the stars of Orion, Angel Simms' voice is loud in the winter mountain night.

Book Four

$\mathcal{S}$*tars*

$\mathcal{T}$he Heat of Summer brings early renewal to this western Carolina countryside, from high in the Appalachian Mountains, down through every forest and field of green. But though the revolution of our heavenly sphere melts the Northern snows for another season, it cannot serve to melt the snows of our fervent memory.

In the quiet of classes gone silent, the two of us have been in and out of one another's room, studying and kissing, kissing and studying, both of us grieving to see the end of this seven day Hell called exam week come and gone. Under the pressure of expectations, by the burden of academic eyes upon her, Jennifer studies as if the world were actually going to go on forever, and that these works of the flesh would matter a century from now. But I find that I am unable to concentrate as I once did, as if my time here is suddenly as empty as a Pharisee's prayer, and every classroom has become to me as a whited sepulcher full of dead men's bones.

But tonight, warm summer winds have dispersed every cloud for us, even in the month of my girlfriend's last name. Out here, on this bench nearby our dorm building, the spirits of privilege are adrift on these late spring and early summer winds, to remind us that we are Daughters of No Want and No Pressing Need, as it was written in these bright spring and summer constellations for us eons ago.

"The North Star. I found it."

"Where?"

"That dim star up from the big dipper," she says. "See? Just follow those two stars in the cup. And there it is."

"Oh yeah. I wonder why it's so dim?"

"I don't know. It's the North Star, you'd think it'd be brighter, huh?"

"I guess so."

We spend the next minute or so enraptured by a dark'ned sky, a sky blessedly with no Moon, so that there is no barrier between the first and the second heaven. And I return again to the North Star—to the star that guides us to the Truth, noticing that it is one of the hardest places to focus and concentrate upon.

"I know why people are afraid to look at the stars," she says. "Because you can see God. And that means we're not as important as we think we are. And if there really is a God, then we're responsible for everything we do."

As I look at the many bright stars above us, I am reminded that the heavens do declare the glory of God.

"I've decided I'm going to do it," she says.

"Do what?"

"I'm gonna join the Omegas."

It is written, that the types of fear are many, and uniquely distinguished. The Fear of Abandonment takes life in my soul, then jumps and slides from my spirit into my body.

"But we swore it, Jennifer. We swore it to each other. You're not really gonna join them, are you?"

"If you really don't want me to, I won't. But… Judith's been talking to me in biology class all semester. As a matter of fact I think we're becoming—"

"Friends?"

"Exactly what do you have against Mary and Judith anyway?"

"Mary? What does she have to do with it?"

"Well… last week they took me over to the sorority house. I met some of the girls. They're all really nice."

Green ice flashes my lungs inside. My deep breath is unseen.

"I didn't know you had gotten that close with them."

"Strange thing is, I know the whole time I'm with them, you're what they're thinking about the most. You know something? You're prettier than every Omega girl. And yes. It matters."

"So what'll happen to me if you join? You'll be hanging around them all the time and you won't have time for me."

"Oh, no," she says, sliding closer in the warm evening. "We're married, Baby. My mother performed the ceremony, remember?"

"Oh, my God," I say. Laughing a little. Trying to pretend it has not burned an icy flame inside me. "I'll admit one thing. You're mother is hot."

"I guess so. Pretty is easy. But sexy is not. And she is both. It's a miracle she never cheated on my father with another woman. Besides with you, I mean. Sorry…"

"Sometimes, I try to convince myself it didn't really happen. Like it was all a cold, winter dream I woke up from."

"Well, I was there remember? It was no dream. It was a nightmare. And I've been in it now for about five years."

She grips my arm tighter, then leans over and kisses me on the cheek.

"Mom was right about one thing though. You are a breast queen. And you can get off just from me workin' on 'em."

Her hands make a determined, but playful assault on my top button. Instinctively, I push her hand away.

"You can't get enough, can you?"

"No," she says.

I smack her hand this time, pushing it away gently.

"Careful," she says. "You'll force me to take one out right here. And I'll have you shaking like Twitch on *So You Think You Can Dance.*"

"Whose Twitch?"

"You, if I get my hands down your shirt."

"I would, but…I feel too much like we're being watched out here. I can't help it."

"As dark as it is out here? How does the prettiest girl in North Carolina get to be so shy?"

"I'm not that shy."

"Oh no? Since you moved into my room, you only leave it to go to class. I have to go everywhere by myself."

"I thought you didn't mind."

"I don't. And I don't mind you walking around the house in those denim shorts and that blue sports bra either. Good *Lord*." The words are followed by a quiet, celebratory *whoo* sound from her. "Some days I look at you, and you look like your name should be Athena or something."

"Why do you say that?"

"Like you don't know. Remember the other week when you wore that pink blouse? The pull over?"

"Oh yeah. Oops. I was embarrassed the whole time. I shouldn't have gone out in that top. Why didn't you tell me?"

"I did. I said you were gonna cause problems in that shirt. But I also said that you should just relax and own your figure for once. I lost count at fifteen."

A pause…

"Fifteen people stared at your breasts like you were in a bikini," she says. "And one poor guy looked like he was afraid and still couldn't look away. His lips were tucked in. He had sad, humble eyes. If you had smiled at him I think he would've fainted."

"You're exaggerating."

"Honey, the only exaggeration around here is your *tits*. Sometimes I think the whole universe stops to watch you when you go out."

"Thanks a lot. And you wonder *why* I'm so shy. I hear the comments. I see the looks. Girls will walk right past me and say "Fake" or "Implants," or "Damn that's *too* much," and they'll laugh out loud. But I get treated differently if I cover up. If I hide 'em. I get treated with more respect. To tell you the truth, people act like they don't really like me anyway. Everybody's either too passive or too aggressive with me."

"They're all afraid of you, May. You represent the Truth. The unbearable. People walk around in total fear every day. Fear of Life. Death. Fear of Hell. And in the Fear of Life, there's this constant, nagging sense that they're going to fail. It's one of their greatest fears. The Fear of Failure. To learn that all their efforts, all their hard work is for nothing. You're like a glimpse into their hopeless future. You remind them that they have no right. No claim to the success they want so bad. They don't even want to get to know you. They'd rather pretend you don't really exist. You're special, May. People like you can change a person's whole outlook on life just by being *nice* to them. Let alone being their friend. Or girlfriend."

I suddenly feel her hands on the outside of my shirt. The gentle squeezing is an alarm signal to my entire body.

"Nobody's watching," she says. Kissing me on the lips.

"What about those guys by the dorm?"

"What, those guys?"

She points at the three college boys that were nearby a minute ago, now too great a distance away to matter.

"What if your sorority friends find out you have a girlfriend?"

"It'd be like they were lookin' into a mirror. I'm gonna let you in on a little secret, May. There's a closet dyke everywhere you look. Whether she knows it or not. I should know what I'm talking about, right? And I know that every girl has a price. The right face, the right body. The right time. Every girl has her price."

The kiss she bestows upon me takes me back. The feel of her tongue inside my mouth, and the pushing of her hand into my shirt are reminiscent of days I have known. I am forced to breathe a deep breath through my nose, and go down deeply on her tongue. Then she begins to kiss my cheek and my chin, and when she kisses my neck, the effect is as a feather upon my nerves, to tingle me down to the ~~soles~~ souls of my feet.

The months of our discovery have not diminished this flame, and though we are outside under the stars, I cannot stop her from reaching inside my bra and sliding one of the white melons out into the night.

"Oh God, somebody's gonna see us… Oh God…"

I am helpless. Helpless to endure my devastation, which is the feel of her mouth to my nipple in a gentle but firm sucking—continuous and unbroken, which seems to send waves to my groin fully clothed in my blue jeans. Even if someone is close by, I'll never know, because I can no longer see clearly in the dark, and the stars above are but jumbled points of light in the night sky.

Heiress

College freshman days have come and gone, in the fervent heat of summer's rising. We languish at the pool of a true million dollar estate, on the anniversary of the day the end of the world began, which was July 4th, 1776. A day remembered by feasts and fireworks, to celebrate the spirit of Liberty, and the birth of the great latter day nation. Even this nation, founded under the power of the sacrifice at Calvary, now courting the spirit of Antichrist, and a move towards the Battle of Armageddon.

"This sun is too hot," she says. "I think I'm getting in."

"Wait. Not yet."

I lay back on the comfortable lounge chair, having bid modesty adieu. At the insistence of my schoolmate, best friend and lover, my gold string bikini covers next to nothing, and I can see the flesh of what it reveals go on for an eternity.

"God, they *are* huge, aren't they?"

"The bigger the better, Baby. Believe me," she says. "I'm just sorry I don't have a camera. Remind me to get one."

"Don't get in the pool yet. Put your umbrella up."

A strong, cooling breeze blows from the green woods in the distance, down the great lawn and over our skin. It makes me take a deep breath in my bikini, and I must admit that I enjoy this temporary reprieve from modesty. Eyes closed, I listen to Jennifer open the old beige umbrella over her chair, blocking out the hot sun rays from her resting place.

"You're right. That is much better. Should have done it already. What a difference."

The breeze from nowhere whispers loudly again, to blow us a gentle breath of renewal.

"I thought *we* were rich," Jennifer says. "We've got a big house and everything, but your mother's the real deal. This is like a 5, 10 million dollar estate isn't it?"

"Seventeen."

"More than seventeen, I bet. What did your father do?"

"He worked at an oil company. Don't know what he did there. Don't care. When he left, he took his 20 million dollars worth of prenup money with him. But my mother... my mother was the one with the real money."

"So, 20 million dollars wasn't real money?"

"My grandfather co-founded a Pharmaceut—a *drug* company about 40 years ago. They went bankrupt a few years after he died. My grandmother lost everything and had to come here. But when my grandfather died, before the company went broke, he had left my mother $100 million dollars."

I hear her chair creak accordingly, causing me to look in time to see her sitting up and staring at me like Carol Ann did when that Poltergeist tree took her big brother.

"You're worth a hundred million dollars?"

"I guess so."

"My God. No wonder you're so lazy... sorry... 'academically challenged.'"

"I'm not."

"Four C's? And a B?"

"I'm just average. Somebody has to be. We can't all have straight A's and a gift for playing the piano."

"I have a *talent* for playing the piano," she says, resting back again. "My mother and I both know I'm not a gifted pianist. Well, at least *I've* accepted it. Juilliard and about four other big schools accepted it with me. But Mother insists that my playing is, 'transcendent.' Whatever. All my mother's hard work. The years I practiced. The '*big sacrifice.*' What was it all for? A scholarship to the Whitaker School of Music."

"What's wrong with that? Whitaker is one of the best music schools, isn't it?"

She turns her head to look at me. To indict my naiveté.

"Mother calls it the *Shitaker* School of Music. How supportive. The whole time she was fucking me doggy style over the piano all she ever talked about was Juilliard, Juilliard, Juilliard."

"*Shhh.* Don't say that out loud." My voice is low. Almost whispery.

"Except for those trees over there, I don't think anybody heard me."

"I know, but still…"

"Just because you don't talk about something doesn't mean it didn't happen. I have earned the right to say anything I want about what that woman did to me."

"Don't get mad. She did it to me too, you know."

No answer.

"What were you saying about Juilliard?"

"There's no talent that a person can have to get into a place like that. Fate decides. I probably wasn't pretty enough. Or Asian enough. Or any dumb, stupid, shallow reason they could never admit to themselves."

"Are you still going to play that concert?"

A pause…

"Is Anna May a dyke?"

Is she?

There is no relationship under the sun as powerful as the mother-daughter dynamic. But most will never come to terms with this—believing that the noise and thunder of their own drama is paramount; husbands and wives, sisters and brothers, lovers of every size, shape, color and gender. Even the great father-son energy fades as we move closer to the end of the age, so that the angels themselves must yawn and turn away.

But oh, what spirit is there that can resist, what ghost is it that hides just outside our view, that can resist following the sensual mother as she goes along, in grieving to know whose life she may endeavor to affect. And woe to that ghost or spirit, if the sensual mother seeks to reach into the heart of the sensual daughter—what end of the world energy there must be! For now, these angels and demons are enraptured both, according to the will of the Most High, held prisoner by the estros wave, what sounds and colors they produce—as it was since Eve marveled her own daughter's manner and appearance, and whether it be love or hatred between them.

Is Anna May a dyke indeed, a question chosen for the affirmative, I know. Is Anna May a dyke indeed? And what of her counterpart—the woman in my own life? Elizabeth Windsor herself. What pleasure did she derive, from watching my nanny strip me nude when I was thirteen, to apply the leather and birchwood to my backside? Oh, what blood runs through Elizabeth Windsor's heart, what spirits were placed upon her when she was a child! I have never had the nerve to ask my grandmother, who always seemed on the edge of telling my why—why my mother has always secretly despised me.

"I wonder how long it would take," she says, as if she can hear what I'm feeling, "before Anna had your mother on her back screaming?"

"The things you say." I can only shake my head in unpretend shock. Staring. Mouth open in something between awe and disbelief.

As the summer breeze continues to blow, I am resigned to what I know of Elizabeth Windsor, that trying to light the fires of her pale, lythe figure, would probably be like trying to get a match to burn laying horizontal on a block of ice.

"Do me a favor," Jennifer says.

"What?"

"Will you take your top off for me?"

I look over at her without responding, held by the longest wait. A grieving to know whether or not this word is true. And why.

Finally, she turns to look at me, but without repeating the question. It is only the look that is necessary, I know, when the unbelievable has already been spoken.

"I just want to make sure I heard you right. You did say... my top?"

"Yes."

I sit up in my lounge chair, turning towards her, my feet touching the white coral tiles, legs together naturally.

"My top."

"Yes."

Lips tucked in, eyes raised in slight bewilderment (or is it embarrassment?), I reach back to undo the string of this hopeless gold fabric, then give a brief and demure glance downward, as the gold cloth is pulled so casually away. And I notice in her expression— even while the breeze touches my sensitivity—the same look of shock and disbelief I have seen a thousand times before.

She opens her mouth to speak, but merely shakes her head, unable to take her eyes off me.

"You want me to take a swim?"

She nods her head, in the aftermath of trauma. Prompting me to stand up and stroll over to the edge of the pool; her Amazon, her Warrior Princess from deep in the hidden forests of Appalachia, her gold and ivory goddess, Olympian breasts wobbling so gigantic, round and heavy on the statuesque and curved body that is mine, so different from the Lady Windsor, whose body is lithe as a wispy waif, flowered by a tiny rose bosom.

In the power of their heavy weight, I dive from the banks of the Azure River, and glide beneath the waters of cerulean tranquility.

Fireworks

The Cloude of Unbreathable Rumor is paramount. It hangs over us like a fog over a lake in early autumn, when summer heat still rises from the waters in a morning mist. But the heat of summer still settles heavy over our resolve, here in the crystal clear Fourth of July evening. This part of the world has turned away from the sun just far enough, so that the evening day is deep twilight, nearby the edge of night.

Mother's fireworks display has been a tradition as long as I can remember. And when combined with the size and beauty of her estate, has the power to draw several hundred people. Some enraptured—to sit captured in the cloud of rumor, that I had quit school and become a waitress, and everybody in this backyard watching these lovely little fireworks pop pitifully over their heads wants to know what restaurant it is where I'm serving. How this rumor got started, I'm sure I don't know, unless it is one of my mother's so-called best friends, who said it over and over again to people this afternoon at the cookout. And the funny thing is that there are secrets about me, truths about me to tell so strong that they would completely dispel the cloud of rumor, and give them something to really talk about.

Jennifer and I are among the lucky few tonight—among the chosen few laid out on the reclining lawn chairs, so that looking up is a fruitful and rewarding proposition. None of the strained muscles in craned, cramped necks for us, as we delight in the first popping of light, sound and color.

Quickly, I notice that my favorites arrive in the sky without any fanfare, as a streak of fiery smoke that stops quietly in the air, then flowers into a gigantic ball of white sparks that become like glitter as they fade. Is it ironic that the fireworks that make the least amount of noise are the ones that are the most spectacular?

"This is really cool," I barely hear Jennifer say, over the sound of John Philip Sousa that began late, blaring from concert speakers hidden somewhere nearby. I'll have to admit that with the Stars and Stripes Forever, it's hard not to be impressed with the Windsor Estate Fireworks Display, which has evolved into something of a local event of late. Money talks and bullshit walks, so it would seem, as I must accept that these fireworks might work at any small venue in the world.

And when the finale begins, all the loud little fireworks popping over the *William Tell Overture* like popcorn everywhere in the sky, my vision is suddenly obscured; by the face of *a beautiful Asian woman* staring at me up close, and I feel the weight of her pressed hard on my body, and the coffee stench on her breath as she licks my face from top to bottom. But I do my best to ignore what I see, what I feel—shifting in my lounge chair while the Light Calvary of the Gods (the *William Tell* finale) rides to victory—uncrossing then crossing my legs again, hoping to knee this wraith in her groin and throw her off me for the last time.

But what powers are there that can be denied, that rule over the desires of men? This, to include womankind as well, as the woman is upon me astraddle, totally nude this time—grinding herself on me as much as it can be meant, grabbing me by the head to anchor herself, her feet steadied on the ground, then grinding me at the crotch of my dress with her naked one, babbling in deep Cantonese, until I am privy to a shriek of such otherworldliness as to be terrifying. I close my eyes to it, hopelessly convinced it will be gone, but there is only a crescendo of inhuman female sound directly in my face, riding the rhythm of this little fireworks spectacular, until the last single firework has exploded in the dark'ned sky.

I open my eyes to a sudden lightness, where I can suddenly feel the warm night breeze on my face where there was none, amidst a heavy scattering of light applause (or is it the other way around?), this clapping risen up from the Unbreathable Cloude of Rumor—of whose husbands are banging whose maids and whose mothers are banging whose sons, etc.

"I'll have to say, that was pretty amazing," Jennifer says. "I see why it's such a big deal around here. It *was* special. And how about that music?"

"That was Mother. She really loves classical—"

"Alice, there you are. I tried to find you before the show started. I didn't know you were this far from the house."

Denise Hayes. Wealthy mother of Elizabeth Hayes. Elizabeth Windsor.

"Aunt Denise, you should have said you wanted to sit with us."

"Well, truth is I didn't really want to bother you. But I knew if I found you I was going to sort of … intrude. Like I'm doing now."

Reassuring her, I kiss my 59 year old grandmother who calls me Alice, whom I call Aunt Denise, because my mother called her Denise my entire life. My mother Elizabeth, the Lady Windsor, who calls her own mother by her first name.

I hug Jennifer and Aunt Denise on either side, escorting her toward the Cloud of Rumor, and the drifting towards where deserts and leftovers beckon in the kitchen and dining room.

"How can Mom stand this? All these people?" My voice is low. Almost whispery.

"Your mother believes it's her calling to "meet people.' To give back. And you have to admit—this little event has raised a lot of money for her charities."

"Well, that still doesn't give her the right to— "

"Jennifer," she sings, changing the subject. "I'm so glad you're here, Honey. I want you to stay all summer."

"I plan to stay as long as I can."

I allow Aunt Denise's successful escape from what negativity there is, concerning Elizabeth Windsor, and whether or not it is a good thing for her to blare her trumpet of alms so loudly, and whether or not the face she wears in public is a false one.

And what face is it that she wears now, I pray? For I am the most unfortunate person here, who hath glimpsed the truth beneath the face of Charity. This I see on the back patio, as we make our way from the Great Lawn to where the water in the lighted pool lies undisturbed.

"Speak of the Devil," Denise says, which I suddenly cannot do, as I glimpse again a look from her into my eyes that is laced with pure evil.

Pulled suddenly on another current. Torn away from her visitors. Knocked free by the wave of me bye and bye, Mother drifts so courteously away from the flood of people moving from the fireworks display into the house and to the desert tables, then to the livingroom where the pledges will be read, then one by one through the huge double front door, then away to the dozens of luxury cars that lie in wait. So casually adrift—this tall, beautiful woman—over to where I stand holding onto my grandmother's arm for dear life.

Without a word to either Aunt Denise or Jennifer, the Lady Windsor grips my arm with fingers stronger than what looks possible, and escorts me on this current of grieving, away from the flow of press and people.

"When my guests leave," she says.

A pause.

"I'm going to whip you."

$\mathscr{L}ady$

$\mathscr{T}$he types of fear are many. And uniquely distinguished. Among these is the Fear of Pain.

They say that activity is the mourners best friend. For the first time as I remember, I embrace this friend in my mother's home. Staying near her for the next hour. Humbly, happily greeting many of the guests. Doing my best to shine like the golden sun for my mother, glad to stand by and help her look good while she thanks them for their so-called charity. One brunette wife in particular, born and raised here in the Tarheel State but living and working in Washington, D.C, always glad to come running when Liz Windsor calls, with her checkbook always unequivocally open. I watch the Washington D. C. lady, brunette hair and white teeth, laugh and joke and pay her way into another year of friendship with the rich North Carolina woman. A friendship she must have as the proper outlet, to help her suffer the agony of living and working among those in Washington and being the wife of a Representative. And what does she do? I don't know. Aide to the assistant to the executive congressional something or another. Does she wish, somewhere beneath consciousness, that she could leave her money grubbing, honey loving husband back in Washington, and beg her friend Elizabeth to let her stay on the Windsor Estate? Who's to say? Did the summer winds that blew today, did they blow a longing of such great desire through her spirit, when she broke away from the crowd for a time to hide under the trees afar off; to gaze at every blade of grass she could focus on, and every window in the front mansion wall, every tall white column of the entrance way, and every tree from where she stood all the way to the horizon? Did the sound of her bitter, back biting friends' voices ring as a clanging noise in her head, and crash like a cold storm wave in her soul?

I watch the genuine, sweet sorrow in the eyes of Constance Brown, the brunette no less pretty than my mother, as she hugs and smiles this after eleven o' clock departure. Their dynamic is truly more relaxed and casual than the rest, and the tone of their last hug and kiss is that of family goodbye. Constance Brown is the closest thing I have seen to a true friend to my mother, and the words "Aunt Connie" very nearly come to life in my soul. Aunt Connie, Mrs. Brown, was the first guest to arrive at one o' clock this afternoon, to help my mother produce this farce.

And now, Connie Brown is the last one to leave. I am privy to the hug. The hug of desperation and denial. Denying the truth that no, you cannot live here. You cannot love my mother as a *Sister, My Sister*. No, you cannot play with me, and pretend that I am your real niece, while you pull my ponytail back like a horse bridle while you're behind me doggy style with a strap on dick up my... or rather, a false member strapped on, pushed deep inside my bottom.

A hug from Aunt Connie. *Oh God*, she says. *Those eyes. That face. Liz, where did you find her?*

Mother takes my hand into both of hers. Smiling a fungalooga smile. One laced with false pride and contempt. And now, Fate locks our hands together. Brief and fleeting, Fate inhabits the hands of Constance Brown. To lock them around my mother's hands and mine. So much longer than we have touched hands in many a year. Perhaps not since I was twelve, when I was left at the boarding school. And we are forced to lock eyes, one with another, both Wrath and Fear hidden away by the fungalooga hypocrisy. A triad of it are we, as the municipal and corporate woman smiles her false promise of false hope. False hope to return again soon. To spend time with what she calls *the prettiest mother-daughter she's ever seen*. The prettiest she's ever felt.

And now, Fate has mercy on the two of us, as Connie pulls away so reluctantly. Turning so smartly in JC Penney flowered casual, a white dress halfway below the knee. Turning so smartly, with a touch of elegance and grace. Her hands, sliding away from mine, as she moves toward the door of this millionaire's home. Blown North, on winds of obligation and duty. Winds of Prosperity, the storehouse of gold for their labour. Representative Lofton Brown, and Constance Brown. Larry and Connie Brown.

Return together, the two of you, to where the glass ceiling looms. To where you are called, and locked into your places of business. To where you will weep and howl for your lost riches, when the hour of judgment is come. Larry and Connie Brown. Go thy way, and leave us be! Leave us to whatever fear and wrath there must be!

Upon the closing of the door, I see Civility fade as the light of a dying day. The Lady Windsor touches her hand to the door, and leans her forehead—her small white and pretty forehead, against the door closed shut. As though to feel where her friend is gone. Where it is that Connie Brown has gone.

I'm sorry, I say. *I tried as hard as I could this year. You know I did. But Mom no matter how hard I study I just can't seem to—*

Mother holds her hand up. Without a word, she turns to me—long navy dress bearing greater elegance than her friend. With not a look to my eye, she walks coldly past me, with only a brief and somber '*lets go*' to remind me. And I know that on this River of Fate I ride, towards where there awaits The Eternal Sea. And it is to this place I ride fully aware, imprisoned to follow her, where there is no setting the captive free. Where there is no relief from suffering. Wrath and Pain take these steps. As seen by the spirits who watch and torment us; each slow and deliberate step. We walk toward the staircase one by one, one followed by one, both resigned to what must be. A mother and daughter in bewilderment, for what whirling chaos hath brought them together again, after the years of allusions and waiting. To what is supposedly done in the name of correction. In the name of discipline.

Spirits watch a wealthy mother walk. Followed by the daughter. Slow motion steps taken in sorrow.

Taken in defeat.

.

Discipline

"Mom, I'm twenty years old. You don't have to do this."

In the upper room, the sanctuary of our most fervent dream, I see the somber, depressive spirit color her expression to ruin, as she reaches back to her zipper and undoes the back of her dress. And then this self same spirit comes to me when she slides the bottom drawer of her dresser open, and so calmly moves the heavy wooden paddle into view.

"Mom? Mom you're kidding right? This isn't funny. If you're trying to scare me it worked okay? I'll study harder next semester, I promise."

The Lady Windsor slips her dress from thin white shoulders and slides it down. Exposing her slip underneath.

"Mom, what are you doing? Mom?"

"I need you to take off your clothes, Alice... *Maybelline.* Every stitch."

"Please..."

"Your clothes, Alice."

Alice! Thy name is a stranger to me! A name I have hardly heard since before I was sent away to private school!

"Take that dress off. Now."

"Mom—"

"I said... *take it off!*"

Thus, the revelation. The remembrance of the temper I once knew. Much of the reason, truth be told, that my father left so long ago. The rise and appearance of the Witch Hazel—the other side of a woman's personality.

My yellow dress is soon down and kicked to the side, away from my bare feet.

"Your bra," she says, now holding the paddle.

I oblige quickly, to rush this humiliation along. Soon, the sensitivity of them is exposed, with me unable to look away from my mother's face, to gauge what lewdness or laughter might color her expression. But her look is as cold and indifferent as a lady doctor on the call of duty.

"Take your underwear off and walk over here to me."

My breasts hang heavy upon my humiliation as I bend over, sliding my white underwear off. My face is suddenly hot while I step over to where she is, still hardly able to fathom that this is not a dream.

"You know the routine."

"Actually, I don't."

"Oh, so you're going to smart-mouth. That's good. That's *very* good. Hands on the dresser."

"I wasn't smart-mouthing. I swear I wasn't—"

"Hands on the dresser."

I'm not sure whether my trembling is genuine, or enhanced for dramatic effect. Either way, I tremble, placing my hand onto the dresser like a naked prisoner weak from starvation and exposure.

"I'm sorry—"

"Shut up."

The cold, calm pressing of the paddle to my skin makes me jump, though she does not strike a blow. It is the mercy touch, to allow me to get ready, and to steady her hand for the surgeon's first cut into my spirit.

And when the paddle is raised up, I hear her voice inside saying *you know the routine,* which suggests that somewhere along the timeline, in her thoughts, in her dreams, she has done this many, many times before…

A loud *whack* burns a flame through the skin of my buttocks, causing me to focus on my own breasts in the mirror for a moment, as if they could anchor me against the impossible wave of heat energy flooding into my bones, my groin and the pit of my stomach…

And a second *whack* tenses me up against an embarrassing yelp held in my throat, holding on the dresser with all the strength in my body…

And then a third and brutal *whack*ing of black fire tinted blue, screaming an acid burning into my backside with force, until I hear my voice press out on its own. The sound is loud enough to ring my own ears, and shocks all who are present—myself, my executioner, and every power and principality therein.

And a fourth blow of heat to my backside reduces the siren to something like an angry scream, colored with an unspoken cry for mercy.

"Save it," she says. 'You're going to need it."

"I've learned my lesson! I swear!"

Her response to this is silence. The paddle quietly touches my bruised bottom again.

"Breathe," she says. Which I do, taking deep, trembly breaths of defeat, unprepared for the fifth blow to my bottom, which causes me to tense and strain while I scream, but this time without anger, and more of melancholy and pleading. This fifth blow reduces me to a weeping, sobbing cry, which I must continue without dignity—even though the sixth blow to my burning skin is yet forthcoming.

"*Liz!* Liz what are you doing to that girl? You stop it right now I *mean it!*"

The pounding on the locked bedroom door only adds to my stress and misery. Mother's anger doubles on her face, and she storms over to the door, paddle in hand, opening it with fury.

"How *dare* you interrupt me when I'm disciplining my daughter!"

"You've already hit her five times Liz. It's enough! You're torturing her!

"Get away from this door, Denise."

"You leave her alone or I swear to God I will call somebody!"

The audacity. The Olympian temerity.

"Oh, you've got balls, bitch. I'll give you that. You get your ass away from this room until I'm done."

'Liz—"

"Shut up! Shut the *fuck* up!"

Fully nude, I turn and catch a glimpse of what I already know, that mother is holding the paddle as a weapon pointed at her own mother's nose.

"And if I so much as *suspect* that you called a fucking cop over this I will beat you to within an inch of your life and I will cut you off like a dead *tree branch!* Now, get away from here!"

It is a screaming anger I hear. A rage echoed into the walls of this palace, severe enough to cause fear in her mother.

"Now, go to your room! And you sit there, and you shut the *fuck* up!"

Grandmother Denise turns away, upon what dignity there is left. Obedience born from a lifetime of servitude, passed from the dead husband to her bitter, angry daughter.

I hear a door close down the hall, and then this one closes again. In a rage purified, blue and black flames phased red, she returns to where I am, and she ties a panty hose around my knees to lock them together, and she proceeds to wail the tar out of me. The blows come fast and hard, continuous and without mercy, until my screaming becomes hoarse and epic.

And when *fifty* of these have passed, she angrily smacks the paddle to the dresser, which seems hard enough to break it.

"Hush up," she says. "Turn around."

What is left of me turns to face her. Face wet with tears. Twisted, red. Sniffing.

"Look at your backside. In that mirror."

I turn back to see the girl in the mirror. To see that the flesh has been seared with a hot iron. To see the raised welts and blackened skin, at least one welt with a spot of blood. Quietly I return to my sobbing, but only loud enough for Mother to hear.

"I said *hush up.*"

While I tuck my lips in, sniffling, feeling the fire burning my skin, she steps away to the dresser where I cannot see, my back still turned. When she comes back, I feel a cold metal against my wrists and hear a click, causing me to plead *'no'* again already.

"Hold still," she says. Clicking the metal handcuff to my other wrist behind my back. "Turn. Back to the mirror."

I am too defeated, too far into this desert to fret. So when she gets behind me, wrapping her arms around me, her eyes high enough over my shoulder to see (as we are the same five feet 10 inches with no heels), I am hardly moved when she raises the wooden ruler in her hand, and touches it quickly to the front of my breasts.

"You have two of the biggest tits in God's Creation. And to tell you the truth... I think they're your biggest problem."

Suddenly, the source of my greatest pleasure is transferred to the greatest pain of my life, as the ruler whacks my nipple without mercy, quick and repeatedly—the ruler spanking the front of my breast to the feel of a hornets sting, causing me to wail as a banshee; a long and lonely sound of lamentation, echoing through the walls and the halls of the Windsor Estate.

Teacher

At the Mt. Mitchell High School, the teachers and students clap a noisy blue streak. Angel Simms steps to the microphone in the Blue Hawk gymnasium. By 'Ms. Angel,' the Teacher of the Year is known.

On smiles of good feeling. Carried along on the current of good will. Angel Simms beams with pride and gratitude, the fifty eight year old mother of two. In the sea of appreciation, Ms. Angel speaks of her thirty five years at the Mt. Mitchell school. The tears of gratitude are many.

In the Sea of Appreciation, her two sons watch their mother speak. Languished, they are, from their own jobs in the far city. The older boy, a lawyer. The younger boy, an English teacher. Like his mother.

When her speech is done, the blonde cheerleader that catches her eye reminds her of the Mountain Girl, and new bruises she put on her buttocks the night before. Jenny May did not cry from the pain.

$\mathcal{T}$he Heat of Summer melts the snows of our unresisting hearts. Through the days of recovery, I have seen three night skies come and go. Denise and Jennifer have both been so discreet, either out of courtesy or fear, not bothering me at all while I hide in my room. Denise has taken to Jennifer like a butterfly to a yellow rose garden, hardly leaving her side, confiding in her things that I know and don't know; inquiring of Jennifer's mother, but never learning the Third Part of the Truth.

And what is the third part of the truth according to Denise Hayes, mother of Elizabeth Hayes—that thin, lithe little white girl of twelve? Why can we go so much deeper with a stranger or a friend than we can with our own so-called beloved family? How is it that Aunt Denise can go so deep into revelation, to drag up truth and secrets from half a generation ago? Of those that concern the thin, beautiful woman who is still her daughter, whose rages must eventually be acknowledged as having a reason, a cause, an origin from somewhere along the way? From where along the timeline, Denise Hayes, where is it that the spirit hath come to your daughter?

I think what's happening between them is my fault, she says. *God forgive me but I'm seeing things, hearing things between them that I used to thank God were out of our lives forever. I was an abused woman,* Denise says, *and I did what I could to hide it from Liz but she knew. 'Bout the only thing she knew about her father was that he despised me and yelled at me all the time. And it wasn't because I was weak or silly or unattractive to him. He never once acted like I wasn't exactly what he wanted. But it was as if something inside him wouldn't let him treat me with respect. If he loved me, to tell you the truth I don't know if I really knew it half the time. But I know he wanted me, and the man was worth hundreds of millions of dollars, so who cares if he really loves me, right? John Hayes wants me, and he wants me to have his children…*

But I still have to ask myself why did he treat me the way he did? What is it about me that inspired it in him? Because whatever it was, Jennifer, it causes my daughter to treat me the same way. And when you mix that in with the things she claims she remembers, the things she never accepts my apology for. Oh God, Jennifer I… I abused her. I did, God forgive me I abused her. I did it in the name of discipline. I did it because I was angry with her. I was angry with her because her father treated her like a little angel and he treated me like a dog. How dare he smile and laugh and play with that little shit like her face is the Sun and her ass is the Moon? That disobedient, disrespectful little mouse. I was worse than Mommie Dearest to that little girl, Jennifer...

After I had the guts to make myself lock her in the closet, the pinches and swats weren't enough anymore. Jennifer, help me understand... why would a mother tie her little girl's wrists behind her back, and take a ruler and paddle her little breasts until they were so red it looked like they could never be white again? Why did I do it, Jennifer?

Jonathan Lovejoy

Book Five

Jonathan Lovejoy

I see the sun, behind a cloud.

I see the rays of the eternal sunshine.

I see the glory of the Throne of Heaven.

I see the sunshine in grieving.

It is the glory of God.

It is the hope of the blessed Son.

I see the glory of the Lord.
The glory of his blessed coming.
The glory of his precious Son.

Behind the clouds of our grieving.
I see the light of his Son.
The shining light of the blessed Son.

Upon a melody of Heaven, I find myself enraptured, but still hidden inside the upper room. When the A Major minuet begins to sway and swing, the piano keys burdened to tell the truth this 29th symphony provides, Mother emerges from her afternoon business at her bedroom desk, drawn to the hymn of Mozart's divine minuet. Having fancied herself an aficionado (because she sat through *La Boheme* once in New York), the Lady Windsor is a slave to beautiful melody when she hears it, which is so far from often as to be closer to never. Not since before her husband was gone, has anyone sat at the piano and played anything even remotely so classical, having the power over her will and desire.

Liz turns the corner from the upper room into the hall, pretending not to notice her mother open her own bedroom door. As the minuet plays from the Steinway baby grand, in piano chords the modern world hath never heard in this arrangement, the Lady Windsor is the savage breast soothed to comfort, walking down the bright railed staircase in awe and million dollar wonder.

Clouds of Judgment are gathering.
As it was when Noah built the great ship.
Clouds of Wrath.
Gathering.

Clouds of Darkness are gathering—
As it was when Noah went in The Ark.
Clouds of Wrath.
Gathering.

Clouds of rain gathering.
There will be no rainbow of promise.
I pray to thee—
Clouds of Judgment are gathering.

See the storm of violence.
See perversion.
When the clouds start to burn.
Clouds of Wrath—start to burn.

Mother's heart burns an end of the world desire unknown, fueled by the strange and beautiful chords flowing from resurrected keys. Softly taking her place from the last step to the uncarpeted floor of the living room, thankful for the echo of sound through the lonely house. This sound has echoed to the second floor, the motherline upper room, from where Denise walks casually to the top of the stairs—descending. Joining her daughter on the huge, cushioned gray sofa. All anger and regret dispersed and sent away, as lies away from the Ray of Truth, as darkness away from a ray of light.

I see the Judgment of the Lord.
I see the Second Coming of the Lord.
The Second Coming of the Lord and Savior

Behold, He cometh on a cloud
And every eye shall see him—
Behold the glory of the Lord.

Behold the glory of his name.
Behold—the wicked are burning.
Unrighteousness dies.

As every knee shall bow to him.
And every tongue shall cry.
Behold, the glory of our Redemption.
Behold the glory of his Second coming—

And now, we all go home
When our Redemption draweth nigh—
The Second coming of our Lord

There is a bright and epic pause in our earthly mansion. The kind when silence is as a white dove, and cannot be rightfully disturbed. But this silence is soon broken proper, when my friend lights the keys on blue and black fire again. I hear the blazing call of the final day, the finale to this self-same 29th sermon, pitched up so skillfully by my friend to perfect beauty and power—*to prevent boredom,* she says. *Classical music is dead,* she says, *because of the stuffy, elitist attitude that everything has to be played at the same low, draggy pitch, even if it sounds worse, even if nobody cares—if I ever play in public,* she says, *my pitches are going to burn—it's the flame that carries the rhythm, the melody and the tempo— the right pitch covers the multitude of sins in classical music—the end of the world is in the right pitch—the truth about the fate of mankind—the voice of God himself,* she once said to me—and this truth, this voice I hear burning the keys of my mother's piano with the fire of God—the flame that burns either the Voice of Life, as to Moses, or the Voice of Everlasting Death as to Satan, and every lost soul under Heaven.

This blazing fast voice I hear, a voice alive, bristling as the Ocean roaming with beautiful and deadly life, churning and boiling as hydrogen fusion, to burn in our sky by day as the Hell hot of the Sun, or the agonizing liquid fire from beneath the Earth itself, seen so briefly in its coolest form, as the liquid light of a Pacific Rim volcano at night. The truth of this fire burns from the keys of the finale; restless strings transcribed down to restless keys and chords of chromatic brilliance pressed down to pure melody—the Voice of Truth and Beauty, which is God.

I emerge from my slumber of self pity, from my sepulcher of brooding, to rejoin the land of the living, to walk among the accursed two—the two who are held captive at the bottom of these stairs by the voice of Orpheus, but risen up from chamber of Hades as the voice of Orpheus in the New World, the sound of the anger of Eschatology screaming Death and Hell from the piano keys, and a world on fire with the Judgment of God.

I walk quickly from my hiding place, seeing the woman who is my mother sit so casually beside the woman who is her mother, both completely dim to the fullness thereof, of this Mozartian prophecy transcribed and displayed for their eyes only, pitched upward just so, pitched upward to Him...

And I am privy to this, this submission that must be; no, I will *not* escape the Judgment of Fire over the unrighteous, and I must sit too, in the line of those who wait. Denise Hayes, Elizabeth Hayes, and the space I now take, the space of Alice Maybelline Windsor. With the two of them, I sit enraptured, at one with the chords of prophecy, played in the Key of Eschatology...

And now we sit spellbound, on the trailing end of this grand finale, but these fireworks being those of lightning, fire and vapor of smoke, the space of every work in the Earth, every work of Old Creation and every work of man dying in a great noise, while every element that created them are burned with fervent heat, so that the world is only ashes and cinder, where the bones of mankind glow as fireplace ember, underneath clouds of soot and devastation. We are spellbound, by the message of prophecy, by the message of the angel's calling, to proclaim the Second Coming of Jesus Christ, and the Judgment of God over the unworthy. We are spellbound by the Great Warning, the final word of warning that says to the laughing hoards, to the sea of skeptics, from where we are plucked out from and forced to listen: *the Earth will be consumed with fire, as we enter the Ark of Safety, as it was in the Days of Noah...*

Enraptured, held captive by the sound of judgment from the keys, I listen to my soul's companion blaze to this finale's end, stepping up to the same two chords upon which this began, the two flames of her passion—

one tinted the color of the ocean, and the other the ocean in the fall of night.

Keys

$\mathcal{I}$ am sick of the outside world. That place of false hopes and shattered dreams. That place of inadequacy and perpetual disappointment. Where I am carried aloft on expectations, and continually dashed against a stone.

"Why can't we just stay here forever," Jennifer says. "This is Paradise. I don't see how you can stand to leave."

"I don't have any choice. Mom wants me to go to graduate school at Harvard or Princeton. That's why she was so mad. I don't even want to be in college at all, and she wants me to go to Princeton someday."

"I didn't know you hated college."

"I hate everything about it. The classes. The books. The stupid subjects. The studying. And that sorority… the thought of those girls. Mary and Judith are a couple of vampires. They can suck the life out of you just by looking at you."

The view from my bedroom balcony is pristine. Breezes rustle the trees of warning.

"About that," she says. "I'm not running from them anymore."

"Look, if you want to be with them, Jennifer—"

"I do, okay? I do."

"But can't you see how cruel and twisted they are? How evil?"

"You see everybody as evil, May. Maybe that's just because of the way people have acted towards you all these years. It can't be easy hauling those boulders around all the time."

"Boulders?"

"Yeah, boulders."

"Well, I didn't hear you complaining about these boulders a couple of weeks ago."

"And you never *will* hear me complaining about 'em either. My mouth's watering as it is."

The comment causes me to giggle just a little, at the thought of what it is I know she would do in a hot second if I compelled her.

"What was that you played for us on the piano? I know it was Mozart but what was it?"

"It was something I've sort of worked on for years in private. I've never played it for my mother, though. She'd beat the Hell out of me if she knew about it. It's really meant to be played by a full orchestra. She would say it was *candy apple music*."

"But what's it *called* though?"

"Oh. It's Mozart's Symphony No. 29. I played the third and fourth movement."

"Do you know the first and second movements?"

"Yes."

"Mozart's symphony…"

"Number 29. In A Major. For me that pitch is dead, though. I have to pitch it up in B flat. You wouldn't know this, but that's why you all enjoyed it so much. Makes the whole thing *so* much prettier. Brings it to life."

"Well, I'll never remember all that, but I've never heard anything like it before. It was like the music was, like you said, *alive* or something. And it felt like I was trapped having to listen to it, you know? It was scary. It was like you were Beethoven or something. How do you even play the piano anyway? It looks impossible. I remember once at the end it felt like I was being stung by bees."

"I guess I kinda did conjure up the Devil, didn't I?'

"I've never seen my mother like that. She was friendly, but it was so real. Like she suddenly cared about you for the first time. I don't know if she was going to your concert before but she is now."

Suddenly, a large, dark shadow moves across the lawn, from a massive cloud devouring every ray of sunlight. The day is instantly cooler, and every tree responds with a new message of brief warning.

"So that's why it's been so hot," she says. "I wonder when the storm's coming?"

"You think so?"

I look upward at the cloud. Brow wrinkled. Mouth half open in dumb girl concentration.

"I'm real sorry about what happened," she says. "With your mother I mean."

I'm unable to answer. I can only look down at the cloud shadow on the big lawn.

"The mother thing isn't working out too good for us, is it?" she says. "We must be the only two people in the world this stuff happens to. But even when I say that, I know better. Does it happen a lot?"

In the Heart of Memory, I see the twelve year old girl with her dress up and underwear down, being held tight over the knee; her mother's legs clamped tight around her, one of the little girl's arms up behind her back, with a maid stripped to her bra and underwear, spanking the little girl with a hair brush to bruising and blood.

"When I was twelve, my mother used to punish me a lot before she sent me to boarding school. I almost got kicked out."

"You?"

"I hated it there. I cursed at the teachers. I even hit one of them. My Mom had to work hard to keep me from being thrown out. She took me home, and she and the maid gave me whippings and spankings for three days. I didn't misbehave anymore but—let's just say that Mom and I don't get along too good anymore. And it's funny—she's always given me everything I've ever wanted. But I still—"

"Hate her?"

"I just don't feel a connection with her. I think we sort of gave up on that when I graduated high school. This was just her way of taking the power back from me. I had the grades to go to Harvard, and she wanted me to go to school in Europe for God's sake. But I wanted to go to school here. And there was nothing she could do about it. So I think this happened out of pure revenge. Something building up inside her for over a year. These grades gave her an excuse to do what she's been dying to do all along."

"Why did you let her?"

"Look around you."

I watch the beautiful Asian girl lower her head. In tragic understanding.

$\mathcal{L}exus$

$\mathcal{T}$he first drops of rain dampen our uneasy resolve. We are committed though, whole heartedly to this journey to the far city. All the way from the mansion here in Watauga County to the Appalachian school down in Asheville, and the summer concert at the Whitaker Memorial Auditorium. But this day has decided to bear no resemblance to the hot summer we've been facing; with thick, dark clouds of overcast pain and weeping, and temperatures dipped somewhere below what modern summers have known. For several days it's been building, this crescendo of cold, until it is now one of the coldest July days in this state's history. And this, remarkably, from record summer heat just two weeks ago. Topsy-turvy is what comes to mind as I get in the car, told by mother to get in the back seat with our star pianist. The four of us take our places in the black luxury car, which is no crimp-backed, ubiquitous design SUV, but a classic, roomy four door sedan, as if any Lexus can truly be what classic status is ascribed to.

But whether or not, our ride from the front of the mansion down the long asphalt driveway is a cruise upon the Wealthen Stream, felt by the four of us inside, as we glide through the massive open gate, and begin this rainful trip to the music hall.

I sit as quiet as the blue-eyed mouse that I am, listening to mother attack my friend with all the standard questions; *"are you nervous Jennifer"* certainly not being the least among them. Part of me wonders whether or not Mother herself would be nervous, if I were to hold my friend's hand. Would it really matter if I did anyway? Does it mean a blessed thing beyond friendship, if two best friends who are women have to hold one another's hand for support? I'm not ready to take that step yet. Does she already know? Does she care?

I'm suddenly held at rapt attention, when she mentions Jennifer's mother. Staring at Jennifer in the daytime gray, to see if the mention of her will cause any anxiety whatsoever. And I wonder if Mother can feel my own nervousness take form, as she tells Jennifer of the lengthy calls and discussions made with her mother, and how Anna May had indeed *"[insisted] that Jennifer stay"* with her until the concert. If there is anything significant about it, Anna May had said, is that Jennifer is the only undergraduate *ever* chosen to solo at this prestigious annual concert, which means that all eyes will be on her this evening. But even with this knowledge, knowing that she is about to be put on serious display, it seems that the closer to the concert we get, the calmer she gets.

It is the calm of knowing, the absolute rationality of true faith, which she has developed into a mountain of confidence, especially where tonight's performance is concerned. Of that which is meant to be, there is no force needed to push it along, as it has its own energy of motion, which some have been accustomed to all of their lives. In this sea of talent, Jennifer Lin May has swam and drifted and set sail, carried forward through the calm and the storm, to be where tonight she can only be by Destiny in its purest form. The piece that her mother had beaten into her for 10 years, the piece she has performed in her sleep, is the piece allowed to be what she performs tonight, the Great A Minor Concerto, that romantic rainfall of regret, this Holy Ghost inspired phrase, portending God's sorrow to an endtime generation, and the few lost souls within who will listen.

Approached by the staff at the "Shitaker" school, Anna May calls it, the semi-prestigious Whitaker School of Music, the only underclassman ever chosen for this summer concert. Even Claire Bullock, whose own lust is as big as her ass is wide, could not push away the demons that tormented her, when she learned that many were calling for a romantic showstopper at the piano this year that was not Beethoven or Rachmaninov, even Claire Bullock could not fight what came to her mind and stayed, because she had known that Jennifer May's signature piece was the best romantic piano concerto every written, and that she *"plays it like she owns it."*

What force of energy did the half-Asian pretty need, to move this preordination along? Prettiness enhanced deeply by a sexiness about the face, passed down from Anna May herself. A face with just enough magic to thrill the local powers that be, to make them fall completely under her spell. *"I think you're a gifted pianist,"* Claire Bullock had said, pretending to not want the girl naked on the floor and straddled, *"so much so that you're going to get an opportunity we've never afforded an underclassman before. The Grieg concerto,"* she says. *"I know how much you love that piece. Do you think you're ready to give it a try? If it was any other piece I don't think I would've bothered you, but you and this piece of music go together like Angel food and white icing, Honey. I know you can pull this off in your sleep,"* words which had made Jennifer lower her head and just nod in agreement.

What force of will hath propelled this energy into being? Yes, whenever something is meant to be, there is no force under Heaven to stop it. These are the powers that be—those unseen forces that do Fate and Destiny's dirty work, the daily busy work that builds every individual life. And these have moved by the Force of Destiny, to poke and prod the right people until needs are met, until action is carried along the timeline, and Jennifer May rides the luxury car through the rain to the Whitaker Auditorium, to play the concerto down through the stage floor to oblivion.

"How can you not be nervous," I say. "I'm not the one going on stage and I'm scared to death."

"Don't be," she says, taking my hand. "It'll be fine."

"You better believe it'll be fine," Mother says. "Nobody can convince me that you're not brilliant."

"The piece I'm playing tonight is a lot more subdued. More subtle. You won't be quite as entertained as you were with my little house concert."

"Honey, I'll be equally entertained no matter what you play. You look so *beautiful* tonight. And I know you'll play as good as you look."

My mother's upper class, frozen libido. And naiveté. It pours from her un-licentious mouth in the innocence of benefactorism and restraint, herself unconcerned with what Anna May has taken upon herself in iniquity. Oh,

Liz Windsor, what would happen to that trusted sensibility, encrusted by years of sublime hypocrisy! What things do you not know, Liz Windsor, that hath now tainted our mother-daughter line—a disease passed to us from this Asian girl you so desperately admire! As you drive on, carefully in the pouring rain, what secrets are you unaware of Mother Dear, that have blazed the heart of every woman somewhere in the flow of time and history? What sins and sorrow, dear Mother, do you think you can fathom, but ultimately, being unable to endure?

"I'm really looking forward to meeting your mother," she says. "If she looks anything like you, I know she's beautiful."

Judgment

The world is going to burn. The Second Coming of Jesus Christ is imminent. Are these the signs of the times—the things we see and hear and feel? On the eschatological calendar, when and where is the so-called Rapture of the Church? Even as I look at the raindrops splashing the windshield, I can hardly stop imagining the splash of sparks and ash, and some sort of fiery rain from the gray clouds all around us. *The world is going to burn,* seems to be the refrain for this part of history, as news floods in from every corner of a condemned world; these whirlwinds from the clouds of mourning, as well as those from the clouds of grieving below, the roiling Sea of Humanity. Mothers who think nothing of drowning or stabbing their children. Husbands who think nothing of choking or shooting their wives. Fathers who think nothing of raping their daughters, and every unbelievable variation of the theme within.

But even my own mother escapes just under the wire, for the things I have endured in the name of discipline. And though she may have thought it, or felt it from time to time, she has never put her tongue in my mouth, nor has she wrapped her thin and beautiful lips around mine. Nor have I felt her teeth at the front of my breasts in anger, as some have endured behind the closed doors of secret. And I wonder how many of the cars I can barely see through this cold summer rain— how many of them carry passengers such as we? How many end-of-the-world examples do I unknowingly see? How many girls and young women, how many daughters—even into middle age—how many of them know what I know, as it was taught to me by a beautiful woman of means, as she enacted this lesson upon her nineteen year old daughter? How many untold messages go undelivered to a scoffing, skeptical generation, who refuses to believe that mankind is evil? And that fifty percent of that evil is woman? For it was Eve who listened to the serpent, and coerced her husband to disobey God, which he then did of his own free will, and cursed mankind for an eternity.

And in these last days, the next comeuppance is overdue—this, the greatest unpaid debt in Creation; the Fall of Man, Paradise Lost, the described condition of every soul ever born east of Eden. And though there were but eight souls taken into the Ark, they were eight souls under the curse of sin, the curse of Adam and Eve passed down through each generation, after the floodwaters were abated. The breath of life, a decision of such Divine Regret, has brought Creation to ruin. Under the Second

Heaven, in the blue prison of the First Heaven, we live in the shadows of God's former Creation—we languish in the echo of the beauty he once made, with flashes of it seen and heard in nature, and even through the beauty of mankind's own creation; as shown by the lights of the great cities at night, or on the art canvas colored by every stretch of the imagination—this beauty seen in the shape, color and sound of every musical instrument, capable of finding and breathing the voice of God in song.

But the beauty of man is fleeting. And these works shall be burned in the fire and the glory of judgment, and payment for the next comeuppance overdue.

aindrops

*O*ur arrival settles on the front edge of a long, cold summer rain, after the sun has disappeared somewhere beyond the horizon—hidden by these clouds of mourning. Amidst the thunder and driving white lights we pass to find a place to park, it seems that the world has already begun to weep for us, to cry for what it is we do not know, and to portend what bleak days there are ahead. Happiness is of least concern to a cold summer storm. Whatever joy there may be for us has been distilled into every raindrop nearby, fallen to Earth upon us and around us, then washed away with every grain of filth and dust of the ground.

In this evening day that glows like the fall of night, the three of us who are left step out into the hardest, the coldest of summer rains we have seen, and begin our walk through the Valley of the Shadow of Death, we three. They are mother, mother and daughter, these three. The generations of black flame sent down—the burning upon the back and backside of Denise Hayes as a child from her mother, even from her husband Jonathan Hayes, a.k.a. John Hayes, down to the exposed breasts of Elizabeth Hayes, to the exposed and gargantuan breasts of Maybelline Windsor, May Windsor, the exposed and gargantuan breasts of mine.

From our parking space in the rain, we are together, these three. Missing the one who is special among us, already inside the Great Music Hall, waiting for the appointed hour. *"Stop here,"* she had said. *"I'll run inside. You guys find a place to park. I'll see you in there. Wish me luck."* Then the door had closed on our pathetic, untalented position, held for a split second in time. Watching the dark figure glide through the rain, to where the A minor key awaits. The melancholy key. The key that glows a cerulean flame.

Through the cold, uncaring downpour we walk. Mother and mother, together under one umbrella. Daughter alone under one.

Rendezvous

The lights of the auditorium are a call to safety. Providing refuge for every hopeless onlooker. In the lobby, some are held captive by the light, milling around like lost souls at a party gathering, only without the glasses of wine, or the glassy eyed looks of epic ennui. This gathering begins to undo the women's raincoats, so that every evening dress is exposed, so many of them black, along with much smooth and freckled skin to show.

"May?"

The voice has a familiar sound, but unfamiliar just the same. I turn to see Anna May appear behind us, as if she had been hiding and waiting. Lurking. We are all in the throes of *fungalooga,* in the warmth of the pride of life. She hugs me as if I were her own daughter, and had been kept away from me for months, though which part of this is actually true? As I hug the lovely Julie Chen looking woman, I am overwhelmed with the heavy feel of her body against mine, the smell of her powder and perfume in my nostrils, and the memory of her lips and tongue at my bosom.

"You *must* be Liz," she says to my mother, pushing through the barrier, through the veil that keeps strangers at bay, and she drops a cheek kiss and hug on my mother like she has not felt since Connie Brown. Laughs and *"I feel like I know you already"* are thrown around unmercifully, while one arm is around my mother's waist and the other brushed surreptitiously against mine.

"Ms. May—"

"Please, Honey. Call me Anna."

"Okay...*Anna.* This is my mother Denise."

"I'm so glad to meet you. Thank you so much for coming."

And Anna May leans in again, for the inappropriate kiss, holding both of Mother Denise's soft, mature hands. Disarming her with in your face closeness, staring and a smile.

"You three," Anna says, scanning the three of us. The looks do run in this family don't they? I see where Maybelline gets it from."

"*Maybelline,*" Mother says, "She makes everybody else call her *May.* So, you must be closer than I thought."

"Are you kidding? I love her. If you don't want her, I'll take her."

More of Enmity's ice breaks and falls away, to reveal Civility's beauty underneath. Their laughs are genuine.

"Anna, your daughter is gifted," Denise says. "We can't wait to hear her play."

"It's so nice to hear that. Thank you. She works very hard at it."

"And I understand that you taught her how to play."

"I don't know if taught is the right word. More like *guided. Coerced. Cajoled. Bribed. Threatened...*"

And the laughter ensues. With mother covering her mouth in pretend shock, while the lovely Asian woman bares every fang in smiling. Denise hardly smiles at all. Watching. Listening. A knowing, unwanted wisdom in her eyes aflame.

Mother! Your black fire is tinted blue! Anna! Your blue fire is tinted black as pitch! From whence cometh these two flames together! Woe unto them—who stand in proximity! To them who might be tormented in this flame!

Oh, God.

But such is life. When the spirits move, to guide two souls into proximity. Two souls of heat and power alone, who burn so hot alone. Coming together in combustion. In explosive energy renewed. Liz. Anna.

Oh, God.

Auditorium

If Anna is supposed to return backstage, we would never know it. She takes my mother by the arm and leads us through this throng of ritzy rabble, all the way down to the front of the auditorium, where the seats have the audacity to be reserved. So smartly, in the stealth of cunning flings us—one by one she does, from the aisle to the seats in waiting—Denise being ushered in first and over the edge and out of her periphery, with me next, feeling too tall and blonde and conspicuous, frankly, feeling the moms and other daughter's eyes on me, and the charge of *'fake'* being made, though my long yellow hair is decidedly genuine, as is the blue in my eyes, and the big in my bosom. But tonight, they feel so heavy and on display, especially when I take my raincoat off to expose them. Though I tried hard, this burgundy dress does nothing to conceal the gigantic nature of them, and I cannot resist the urge to glance around just once, to see who is staring at the "big-tittied blonde" down front.

On the heels of my embarrassment comes the Asian beauty, the talkative, friendly, touchy feely woman who seems in charge of everything, but is really only in charge of us. And bringing up the rear, the tragic end to our lonely quartet is the tall, thin brunette with the operatic face. Anna helps my mother take off her jacket like a lady in waiting, but in remarkable public restraint; as if the eyes of her soul were not already upon what is hidden.

We all sit down in the half empty auditorium, taken in by the tall, royal burgundy curtain in back of the stage, the many seats and music stands for the orchestra, and the grand place of reckoning, where the solemn notes of eighty eight are played. My grandmother sits quietly on the left side of me, exhilarated by the rare evening, I know, grabbing my arm and whispering *"this is so exciting, isn't it,"* drawing a big smile and small giggle from me.

And this spell is suddenly broken by a lovely, snickering laugh to the right of me, the woman who is Liz Windsor.

The two of us are divided anew, and held together by this same force of division. Sitting nestled; settled between us is the beautiful Asian woman, so shapely in the form hugging red gown, worn to distinguish herself in the row from the stage, I know. Comfortable, tranquil between us is the lovely Asian woman, with one hand laid firmly on my thigh, and her other hand on my mother's.

"...Julliard wanted her. I know it, but there was this fat, dumb little bitch who they felt sorry for..."

Mother snickers again, but covers her mouth and begs forgiveness.

"No, no its alright. You should have seen her. Retarded-looking, cross-eyed little Japanese girl. And she was like..." (Anna puffs her cheeks out in hilarious fashion). Mother's lips betray the laughter underneath at last. Loudly. I notice there are some people looking our way.

"I'm sorry," Mother says, covering her mouth. Still laughing a little.

"No, it's alright Honey, look...look Liz... she was as fat as a *pig*..."

Anna's hand is suddenly gone from my thigh, holding now both of my mother's wrists in the strength of her gift. And she makes the puff face again so naturally, that mother descends into a full, pitiful laugh she could not have contained in a hundred years of trying. This laughter, with her arms trapped by Anna's strong hands, unable to cover her bright smile, which Anna takes in upon a deep breath unseen. She has mercy and lets my mother's hand go, so Mother can cover her mouth again.

"I know, it's funny now but I was in Hell when it happened, I was at the audition, and I know that little pig did not play with the feeling and depth that my daughter had. And I know they let her through *only* because they felt sorry for her. Because Jennifer was twice as pretty as that retarded little sow, and they were just being politically correct I know it."

"Well, I did hear your daughter play some Mozart a couple of weeks ago. It sounded like she was on fire to me."

"Mozart always was her—oops I'd better get back there, I need to see her once more before she goes on..."

Anna May stands up boldly, patting my mother's leg, then gathering up our summer raincoats, then disappearing from us somewhere back stage, in the bustling sea of talent and ability. Mother takes a deep breath, and I see her smile—no, I *feel* that she is smiling, with her head slightly turned away, arms crossed, then with one hand over this secret and enigmatic grin.

abin

*I*n the cold, summer mountain rain. In the cabin by the Appalachian Wood. The rain is noisy on the tin roof above the head of the Teacher of the Year. In her bra and underwear, standing beside the bed, Angel Simms massages the naked and mountainous bosom. The mountain girl sits boldly, calmly at the edge of the bed unclothed, but for the small, blue underwear bought by her benefactor. Angel Simms remembers the breasts of both her daughters-in-law, as she watches the lotion disappear upon Jenny May's skin. As to where the feeling hails from that rises, Angel Simms does not know.

With one hand, she massages the breasts of Jennifer Maybelline Breen. Soon, the feeling in Angel Simms' body twitches her once, and then once again. The mother of two lowers her head to the mother of one. Resting her mouth upon the mouth of Appalachian Beauty. The breaths from Angel Simms' nostrils are loud in Jenny May's hearing. When she touches the front of Angel's bra, a third spark twitches Angel's body.

In the summer mountain rain. In the cabin by the Appalachian Wood. The woman climbs upon the bed unclothed, laid upon her back. An immolation in golden hair, an un-waif in full glory climbs atop the teacher woman astraddle. In the gray of stormy twilight, at the rainy edge of mountain night, the fair skinned Maid of Watauga County performs the duty of her calling. With no pushing against a dark destiny; accepting her fate, the Watermelon Girl of Watauga County bounces astraddle. Pounding energy to the body of Angel Simms.

"That's it," she says. *"Right there. Bounce up and down right there Jenny May. Now put your hands behind your back... put 'em behind you... lemme see 'em flop. Flop 'em for me..."*

From whence doth this female breast obsession flow! Angel Simms dare not ask herself. She does not know. As the blonde woman bounces, Angel puts her hand at Jenny May's throat. Squeezing until there are coughs and choking. As Jenny May coughs, she feels trembling start underneath her, and grow to magnificence. The long, loud moan from Angel Simms' throat is shaken by her body's hard trembling. While the woman shakes, Jenny May's breath is nearly taken by the hand at her throat. She feels her eyes begin to strain. Her hands remain behind her back.

When the shaking ends, Angel's hand slips from the Watermelon Girl's throat. In the mountain rain, the choking, coughing noise from the cabin is great. Jenny May did not cry from the pain.

Concerto

*P*ain pushes our minutes along like days, on our rainy concert evening. The school auditorium is filled to capacity with souls, all busy striving to escape damnation, professing a form of godliness, but denying the power thereof. There is a rumbling here tonight—energy bristling through, of the only underclassman ever invited to these hallowed halls to play in this annual summer concert; and all present are anxious to satisfy the lust of the flesh, the lust of the eyes, and the pride of life. All are anxious to see what manner of woman she must be, this "Jennifer May," who has broken such a time honored rule, and set a new precedent for a time honored tradition. *Jennifer May*, I keep hearing in whisper, even as the players in the massive orchestra begin to wander towards their seats. A massive orchestra. A condition owing to Jennifer herself, who told me that one of the problems with these school concerts is that the orchestras are just *"too blamed small to begin with,"* so she and the conductor (female) decided to *"cut the elitist crap"* and put more players on stage, another unprecedented move, with members of the local symphony orchestra called here to pad the cushion, for a substance and depth this annual concerto has not seen in many a year—a full 70 players packed on stage, to support and defend the constitution of this A minor sermon and the young soloist in charge of its delivery.

And as the lights go down to hush all the whispering, and as the applause rises to meet the lady conductor (a Greek beauty named Adina Angelinari, a young teacher whom they say will probably conduct recordings one day), I can remember Jennifer saying something to me about *"pitching this concerto to heaven,"* and as the beautiful Asian girl walks—no, glides out onto the stage in full, snow white gown cut low enough for the back balcony row to see her cleavage, I now remember her using the words *"an A so razor sharp its B flat."* While I clap over what is purely meant to be, over what is as inevitable as a mountain forest tree, I can't help but glance over at her mother—whose humble, awestruck expression doesn't surprise me, but strikes me enough to wonder how it is that there is no animosity in her eyes, and love may be the color of the humility I see in her expression.

Oh, but what love mankind is capable of, this love colored by suspicion! Tainted by every prejudice and preconceived condition ever known! Daughter, I will love thee, but only if I am impressed by thee! Come, my daughter, let us have our part of the rod and the cane—let us have you learn obedience to me, lest we turn this part of your white skin to blood!

In the flood of applause, in the sea of appreciation, we watch young Jennifer May, her own look pitched upward as white as snow. She glides over to the piano, drifting down to rest at the seat of past and future glory. And I watch the quiet smile of hers fade into a somber expression, tinted by sorrow of the ages, the burden of built up energy, and inspiration at the gate.

And when the lady conductor raises her arms, we are all breathless, enraptured, though unknowing of what to expect; so few of us truly understanding what sounds come from a piano concerto at all, let alone this particular one. Then the drums begin to roll in like thunder, growing louder and louder, like a wave of ocean water looming higher and higher, and faster to the smooth and rocky shore—at the far edge of a stormy sea. Then the rolling crashes to a sudden stop, splashed violently away by a bolt of white lightning tinted blue, which makes Anna May jump, twitched in her seat by the reckoning bolt, hearing the opening chord of the Mother Daughter Dynamic, the opening chord of her and her daughter's life displayed—the divine fulfillment of a promise made. Hearing the pain of their lives from the keys, descending down the scales to the bottom, as lightning which crawls slowly like a river of light from the top of the sky to the bottom—as the misery of a public façade shattered, to reveal the core of agony down to the bottom of their souls. Hearing her daughter's hands evoke sounds that flow like water along the scales, that ignite the air moving around her and her piano, to begin the burning of blue and black fire.

And when Jennifer May's opening soliloquy ends, and the orchestra answers in the whining, pleading of the gods, the chorus of instruments that beg a warning to the last generation, I turn to see Anna May's face reduced to pure melancholy, a contemplation of defeat, the uneasy acceptance of total devastation welled up into her eyes, and rolling down her face like rain down the colors of a stained glass window. And we all listen to the orchestra's feeble cry, but heavy in sound and execution, feeble only in its unheard message of weeping and doom to an uncaring generation. We hear the orchestra's song, calling again to the piano as the rolling gray clouds of rumbling, as the churning of a latter day sea, while Anna May grabs my leg as though she might fall into an unseen cavern, and she grips my mother's hand as tight as a haunted house lover.

Then suddenly, slicing through the gray, I hear another calling from the keys; the echo, the reprising of the orchestra's pleading, as another river of lightning brought into being, spread out in flashes across the base of the cloude, high above the Sea of Eschatology. As Jennifer May's hands draw these unique sounds from this concerto, pitched to the Glory of Heaven, written in blue upon the white parchment, Anna May releases both of our hands to cover her face, while her entire body begins to shake in weeping.

Jonathan Lovejoy

Jenny May

Book Six

Grave

*I*n the misty mountain dawn. In the aftermath of pain. The blonde woman stands at the edge of the deep mountain meadow. The lilies of Flowers Canyon glow white in the early mourning light.

The cross at the head of Momma's grave is made of stone. Nearby the tall, green grass over Momma's grave, white roses grow in summer bloom. While overlooking the meadow, Jenny May remembers the choking from Angel Simms.

"You choked me too hard, Ms. Angel. I couldn't breathe."

"*That's why I choked ya. I needed to see you lose your breath and cough.*"

"*Why?*"

"*Cause it feels good when I do it.*"

"*It don't feel good ta me. You ain't never choked me before. It hurt my throat.*"

"*I know it hurt your throat and I'm sorry. But I told you I gotta do it and you gon' git used to it. Ain't ya?*"

"*Yes, Ms. Angel.*"

In the distance, two buzzard hawks soar high over the meadow. A dark premonition pricks her heart. Jenny May did not cry from the pain.

Charlotte

*I*n the heart of Angel Simms, the mountain girl burns like the brightest star. Angel wakes up from her morning dream, of a rope twisted around Jenny May's neck. In her dream, Angel's body had shook with pleasure when Jenny May died.

As the sun climbs to the top of the summer sky, Angel Simms and her husband ride the road south to Charlotte. Images of her two granddaughters cannot take hold in her mind. The teacher's heart burns with resentment for her daughter-in-law. As they ride the North Carolina highway south, Angel closes her eyes to drift. To her fantasy of raping her son's wife.

At the grand, suburban home of her youngest son, Angel watches Julie and Douglass Simms at the swimming pool. Julie Ann Simms. Nary a spark of what she feels inside has shown. This, the heat of resentment towards the smiling young woman, for causing her son to move so far away. For making her have to drive so far to see her granddaughters. Ashley and Amelia Simms.

Requests to Julie Ann for summer visits to Angel's mountain home have been denied. Prayers for leniency go unanswered. From the kitchen patio door, Angel watches the shapely, exotic brunette in her bikini, immersed in conversation with another woman by the pool. A fair skinned, fair haired, fair weather friend. A short haired blonde friend, all too happy to glom on here, at the home of the English professor's wife. A wife with an Egyptian look about the eyes. Hips from the Land of Lopez. Hailed from the Kardashian Kingdom.

Angel watches her son's exotic wife, among the many other voices, faces and splashes in the pool. In the theatre of her mind, she sees the suffering of a mountain girl. The bind of ties that must be. The blood and bruises of a calling. A whipping that will turn a mountain woman's white skin to blood.

In the theatre of her mind, Angel sees a mountain woman scream from the burning of leather to her skin.

Juilliard

*P*ain colors skies of grieving. From the rainy departure of summer cold, along the shores of A minor suffering and grief.

Pain colors Asian eyes of beauty. Those that gaze the reflection of themselves, to see into the soul of ache and grief. Anna May is held enraptured by her own face in the mirror staring back at her, trying to gauge the likelihood of events transpired, and to grasp hold of the power that is meant to be. A last glimpse in the closed door mirror, a last pressing of the reddened lips, then a gliding forth from the lonely suburban house, out into the cooling of summer gray. Along her summer timeline, the rains of the A minor concerto have come and gone, but loom in these gray skies once again.

Comfortable in her favorite tight blue t-shirt and black, tight denim jeans, Anna May puts her travel bags in the back of silver Mercedes luxury, taking one last look at the thick, dark clouds looming above her house. She is held captive by them but a moment, bravely facing the ghosts of warning, whether they be lies or truth. Able to discern the spirits of cause and effect, as they appear in various shades of gray and weeping. These are clouds formed from somewhere along the flow of time and history, dissipated somewhere in a successful past, now coalesced and reformed again, as the portending angel of what is unseen, along the road to ashen gray regret.

Anna May accepts the calling of her life. Slipping into the driver's side of luxury. Coursing the river, the stream of unbelievable events transpired, to bring her where she is today. Driving along the road west from Chapel Hill, to embrace the invitation of a wealthy and beautiful woman at the foot of the Appalachians, whose heart and soul have been touched by Anna May and her daughter.

Thunder rumbles these new summertime clouds, while principalities hold every drop of rain at bay. Along the road to her solemn future, Anna recalls the powers that be—the impossible revelation of prophecies unheard. This revelation, in the wake of heavy applause and cheering, and a standing ovation her daughter was given. Anna remembers how Liz Windsor had tugged and patted her arm so excitedly, reassuring her that her daughter was blessed by God this night, and just as she had told Anna May already, Jennifer May is brilliant on the piano. *She plays with such passion, and where does all that pain come from,* someone had said. *I never really liked that piece until tonight*, someone else had said. And "she should definitely record," and "I've never heard anything like it," and "Is that your daughter up there—where did she learn to play the piano like that..." and on and on, all of them at the end of another hour of well performed, classic orchestral pieces, each of which were soundly dismissed and forgotten. "Jennifer May," was the catch of that rainy night and day; it was as if someone famous had descended and done us all a favor. Yet, this girl is a lonely, depressed nothing. A scholarship baby from nowhere, barely out of the diapers of her freshman year. Even so, her aura on stage was such that could not be denied, Anna remembers—and yes, though the orchestra was too big and Jennifer's concerto was pitched up for pure beauty over melancholy, Jennifer May's piano was still ablaze with blue and black fire.

In the heart of memory, as Anna cruises the Wealthen Stream, she sees the thunderous applause bestowed, when the last notes of Berlioz's *Symphonie Fantastique* is played. The final ovation, the enthusiasm, is likely for the lifting of Berlioz's heavy burden and the end of the concert as it is for the memory of the Asian girl at the piano, delivering the message of eschatology. Anna remembers the congratulatory hugs from Denise and I—and then one hug in particular; one that she still feels in her body, and the sweet perfume of which is still in her nostrils.

"Anna, before we go backstage there's somebody I want you to meet."

Mother leads us all toward the stage, where a middle aged man of intellect is waiting beside his lady companion.

"Jerry Fielding," Mother says, *"This is my mother Denise and my daughter Alice. And this is Jennifer May's mother Anna."*

The John Boy Walton looking man suddenly puts both hands in on the greeting, shaking her hand with both of his at the same time.

"Miss May, when Liz called me and told me to come here, I didn't know what to expect, but I must admit I've hardly seen or heard anything like it."

"Well, thank you, Mr... Fielding. You're very generous. I suppose she was 'adequate' tonight."

The introduction hardly raises an eyebrow from Anna, assuming that he is a local music critic or wealthy friend of Liz's.

"I don't know if Liz told you who I am or not, as if it matters, but I teach piano at Juilliard."

Some words, when spoken...have power. It is an energy beyond hearing, passing into the mind as if by magic, as if a deaf dancer were to read this same word on a piece of paper. The word penetrates to the soul of artistic ambition, where it combusts like a light inside a nebula cloud. Anna May's reaction is as if she learned she were shaking hands with a dead person. Her expression settles to an uneasy calm, and she slides her hand away.

"I'm sorry we approached you like this Anna, but Liz and I decided that it would be better if nobody knew I was here. And based on what I just heard, we were right. Your daughter's expression on the keys was genius. It sounded as if she's been playing that piece all her life. It was technically brilliant but not the least bit stiff or learned. It was like magic. The way she attacked that opening chord, and then the main melody. I swear, I've never heard anyone roll into it like that before. It was unbelievable. She played with such power and finesse. Ms. May, I heard your daughter do things on the keyboard that you can't teach."

In the Heart of Memory, Anna May takes the card from the Julliard man, staring at it as if the blue and black flames were going to burn her hand. Something about the rain and getting back to a hotel are spoken, and as suddenly as this mocking spirit from New York had appeared, it was gone.

As the first drops of rain splash her windshield, Anna remembers the whisper she had breathed into Mother's ear to *come to the bathroom*. Leaving us to fend for our lost and pitiful souls in the nearly empty auditorium, they go to the nearest restroom, to the stall as far away from the door as the far wall allows. In the locked bathroom stall, Anna steps fully against the tall, thin woman who is my mother.

Holding onto her tight, the restroom echo is suddenly around them, of a 40 year old Asian woman, sobbing uncontrollably against my mother's navy dress.

Mansion

The rain falls in a gentle mist, from high into the Appalachian Range, down through the summer forest pine, and into every river and fishing stream.

Still bathed by the pain of her and her daughter's finest hour, Anna rolls onward, embracing the voice of her dyke blood, the memory of Paradise whispered into her soul.

"I want you to come to my house," my Mother had said. *"I want you to unwind and relax from your suffering. Be there when my friend talks to your daughter about Juilliard."* When it happened, the words *I want you to*

come to my house had wrapped themselves around her womb and squeezed before they dissipated. Leaving their imprint and echo in her spirit.

Pulled along by the solemn, sensual promise of these words, by the promise of nipples exposed, pressed and rubbed together until there is a shaking, screaming surrender, she cruises up to the gate of paradise, certain that this is where she *longs* to be, but uncertain that such earthen grandeur is truly where she is *supposed* to be. Yes, this is the address, and yes, as Jennifer told her, *"you're not ready for this house, so just prepare yourself."*

As she rolls her own luxury ride smoothly down the long asphalt drive, past the line of trees and magnificent front lawn, the white building that looms up ahead is surely beyond what is possible without the power of God in a woman's life, and goes so far above what encompasses the word 'house' in her mind that she cannot find the word anymore, as it is blasted to pieces by the word 'mansion.'

A twinge of fear flows through. This, the Fear of Humiliation, which debilitates so many into mediocrity. But born from the old country, this spark of bravery that brought her own mother Min Hai (who became Min Cao)—this spark of bravery that brought her own mother here with nothing; this divine spark attacks her fear, to make Anna understand that yes, she and her daughter most definitely *do* belong here, and they have earned it by blood, and the sweat of hard labour and pain.

But truly, what doth a man or woman receive in this life, except for pain and suffering, that they have earned at all? So many are buried in poverty; buried so far underneath it. Working two jobs six days a week, many laboring like mules under the calling of God himself. And these work themselves to graves of failure, not understanding that this life and the things which are in it are given, and what we deserved has very little to do with what we get. "Give us our daily bread," we pray. Unknowingly, in lack of clarity and understanding, that they are at the bottom of the wealth pyramid by Destiny rather than choice, and that though they eat their bread in the sweat of their own faces, they barely earn enough gold to buy another loaf of it without worry. Blissfully, mercifully unaware of those on the other side of life, who eat bread cooked and cut from the same dough, with not enough days left in forty years to find time to spend the mountains of gold they have earned, though the burden upon their backs is light, and the sweat upon their faces is fleeting.

This Storehouse of Gold, Anna May rolls her luxury car to. In awe of the tall, white pillars and many windows, as she steps out of the silver Mercedes and hurries through the haunted mist of rain.

Reunion

The mansion door opens in that vague fearfulness—the tension that descends over any reunion. But the two of them are aware of what power this is, what blazing heat of circumstances and coincidences these are, from the moment the door swings open, and Mother's eyes see the beautiful Asian face again; and Anna's eyes see the tallish brunette, and a somber, regal beauty even stronger than she remembered.

Anna steps in out of the rain, pulled by a spark of magnetism, able only to hug my Mother in the burden of an oppressive mood.

"Jennifer told me I wouldn't be ready for this. And she was right."

In awe of the grand, open space, she walks arm in arm with the wealthy woman, engaging the spirits of higher class, more profound than those that rule her own house and neighborhood. This is the upper class. The truest definition of earthly success, with none of the fear and desperation of the middle and lower classes around the world; where the reserves of money have taken a life all their own, renewing and replenishing themselves for an eternity. Spaces in time and history given, to exact punishment on the backs of the have nots, that no, life is *not* fair, and you were born to suffer the curse of The Garden of Eden.

Anna glides the dreams of Avarice. The current of wealth and grieving. Up the grand and flowing staircase to the second floor, to the refuge of the Lady Windsor. Past the pictures—the paintings and photographs of Perpetuity. From the corrupted air of Hope down below, to the clean, crisp air of prayers answered. Listening in a haze to Mother go on about her daughter's ability, and how talent always rises, not realizing that so too does oil, fire and smoke. But here, the air Anna breathes is pristine, and free of mankind's greatest curse under Sickness and Death: this, the curse of Poverty.

"Where's Jenny May?"

"Jen—oh, you mean…I honestly don't know. They left here early this morning—"

"Your looks."

"Excuse me?"

"Your looks are stunning, Liz. I just had to say it. You and your daughter are two of the most beautiful women I've ever seen."

"Thank you. And concerning you and Jennifer… the feeling is mutual. Really."

In her characteristic fashion, Anna smiles and turns away without looking at Mother, glancing at the white and crystal décor around the massive bedroom.

"Well, speaking of Jennifer, as I said, I haven't seen them. Which is more than fine for us, I think. We'll get the whole day to ourselves."

Words breathe energy. Substance. Life to a dying world. Underneath the smiles—the coy, polite laughter—is the substance and energy of the ages, on the edge of birth, at the Eve of Armageddon.

Chandelier

Anna May gazes around the unfamiliar space, the chamber of wishes which is Elizabeth Windsor's room. Mother allows the woman a moment to take in the sights and sounds of God's uncompromising favor. Among the white finished dressers and drawers, Victorian style desk and chair, is the focus and center of the room. A bed unlike anything she had ever really seen or imagined, white canopy veils tucked like curtains at each corner.

"This room..." Anna says. "Its magical."

"You like it?"

"No. I *love* it."

"Well then. Its settled. And don't bother saying no."

"What?"

"While you're here, however long that is—this is your room."

"Liz, I—"

Mother takes the opportunity presented. To deliver her solemn hand of dominance, by a firm pressing of two fingers to lipstick reddened lips. Oh, but what tragic fires burn, beneath the crystal chandelier! Already, the crystal glows blue, from the ignition of this flame below. Is my mother prepared, for the quick and fervent grabbing of her hand, held perfectly still by Anna May? What sensations arise, Dear Mother, as the reddened lips glide gently across your fingers! What sensations are these, Mother, that run through your arm to your tiny rose bosom, as the beautiful Asian woman caresses her lips and cheek across your hand for dear life, not caring at all what lines have been crossed? What barriers have been breached, what politeness, civility and restraint have been compromised? And what sensation is it, Mother Dear, that passes as a bolt of lightning to your groin, when Anna wraps your two fingers in a gentle but deep sucking? Oh, thy condemned duet! What spark of flame hath been wrought, that makes the room glow with fire the color of the ocean! Mother! What does it do to you, when you grab this woman's hair, this beautiful Asian woman, and pull her head backward! What does the single grunt from in her throat, the touch of her hand on your stomach just below your breasts, the touch of her other hand on your arm—what do these connecting points, these three—what manner of conduit are they! And what does it do to your body, your soul, Mother Dear, when this beautiful Asian woman must reflect, must return your domination, with the same uncompromising hair pull? Anna hears the lurch of your deep voice leap forth in a hushed, whispery tone. Women of beauty! Mothers of sin! Come together—brave the burning fire within! And what manner of sensations are these, Mother Dear, when the rest of Anna May's pretense vanishes, and she grabs your hair and face, and begins to lick your face with her tongue! The heaviest burden of pre-desire imaginable—the expression of what lives inside, the hunger displayed as she flattens her tongue on your cheeks, tasting and kissing the makeup from your eyes, cooling your face, itching it from her spit, her hands still buried in your pinned up hair with pulling. *Push your tongue all the way out*, she says, which you do without hesitation, feeling the beautiful Asian woman meet your tongue in the licking, then wrapping her reddened lips around it in the deepest sucking, pulling it to the very edge of comfort—then holding it there. Breathing. Exacting more of your inevitable surrender through your tongue. And this slips away into the French Kiss, with both your sophisticated, worldly tongues pushing and sliding against one another! Like two white and beautiful serpents you are, giving yourselves over to the deep perversion— to the flicking of tongues together with mouths open, enduring the desire to drink—the desire to push your lips together. How long, Mother! How long can you suffer the tongue kiss, until you know you must have her soft lips against yours, to taste the flavor of red, the cinnamon burn of your life's inner prophecy revealed? But no—Fate has no mercy for thee—as she pulls away from the tongue kiss, and begins to unbutton your navy blouse with controlled and rapid precision. Underneath, there is the lovely black bra of her desire, and she lowers the navy blouse from your shoulders, then the black straps from this same milky white skin. When she exposes your tiny bosom, she stops and stares at both your nipples, at both your dark and gigantic nipples fully formed, already extended so far outward and beckoning, upon breasts pitched so perfectly in the Melancholy Key, where Mozart's Passion plays his 23rd concerto upon the piano in A. The breasts of cultured civility, the breasts of a noblewoman hidden, but now exposed and overly sensitive, to make the onlooker's mouth water at the possibilities, imagining the feel of such grand and perfect areolas sucked deeply. A breast fetishist's alternative dream, the unique nipples of a goddess, with areolas raised up from the slight breast flesh, and large nipples upon these areolas—nipples poked outward in perpetuity. And what is the energy wave, Mother Dear, that courses through your body, when her tongue slides over every part of your little bosom, focused so heartily upon the meatball nipples of legend, upon *your* nipples, Mother? When she wets the front of your bosom, sliding her tongue across them, with aggression and fever? From whence is the twitch in your body, Mother, when her lips clamp down upon one nipple, and pulls it so expertly into her warm mouth just once, unmercifully, just one slow and singular suck and pull? And now, what is the look in Anna's eyes, mother, as she raises up again, and gazes the queen's bosom—areolas shrunken now by stimulation, nipples wet with spit from her tongue?

As she slowly rolls her own blue T shirt up to expose her bra, what is the look Anna has, Mother, when she raises her own bra, and causes her D Major cadences and chords to drop free? What is the look of awe you have, Dear Mother, for the big, flopping breasts of the forty year old Asian woman? Does the back of your own throat ache, Mother, from the desire to have the phantom milk? The need to drink every drop of her passion, until your soul's belly is full?

Anna steps forward without fear, and lifts both her hanging breasts with her hands. Until her nipples are on par with yours. What does it do to you, Mother Dear, when she touches her nipple to yours? When you see the wrinkled brow, the heavy anguish on her face? Do you like it when she spits down onto both your nipples, and rubs them together with purpose? What is that breathing you do now Mother, that deep, loud breathing? Where does it come from? Why not revulsion, Mother, this is the breast of another woman! Yet, thou art not lesbian, are you? It does not matter! Lust is no respecter of persons, is it? This fire ignited knows no gender, it knows no bounds but lips and tongues, nipple to nipple, the proverbial scent of a woman, and the spark of depravity in your soul! Yes, try Mother. Try to control the deep breathing. Don't you think that she can hear you losing yourself? Don't you think her dyke blood burns with energy drawn from thee! After the friction—after the nipples have burst into flame, she lowers her head to your breast again, sucking only one, deeply and with a hungry purpose—this time having no mercy upon your false chastity, craving the stiffening of your muscles, the feel of your lovely hands in her silken hair, the involuntary twisting of your fingers upon one of her nipples, as you begin to breathe deeper, louder, just loud enough for the whispered breaths to become ghostly voices, the voice of a woman, a feminine voice deepened by body chemistry set ablaze. No, Mother. God will not have mercy upon thy voice; and you know this, when you say *God don't let me scream,* a prayer unanswered, as the sucking suddenly pulls a lightning bolt from your groin, causing you to yelp a deep and helpless woman's noise, amidst the sudden jerking of your body held tight by her as she nurses onward.

And the waves through your body continue, but with lesser and lesser voltage, making you grunt very deep, breathy releases of your body's built up pain and suffering. When this is done, Anna holds you tight. Whispering *yes'* into your ear. Holding you up. Absorbing the rest of your body's trembling into hers. Standing there, the two of you, in the middle of the hardwood floor, below the crystal bedroom chandelier. Mother breathing, head spinning from what happened to her body. From what happened to *your* body, Mother. The two of you. Two mothers, standing there. You in your unbuttoned navy blouse and matching navy pencil skirt below the knee. Anna in her black jeans and blue shirt raised up. Big, naked breasts pressed against yours. Breasts swollen with arousal, Mother.

Anna takes her T shirt off, and her bra. Topless, she leads you to the bed. She helps you remove your blouse and skirt. And bra. (Why is your skirt wet, Mother?) Still topless, Anna slides her pants off. Then her underwear. Bending over nude, her breasts hanging, she slides your underwear off too, Mother. After the hugging, the coming together of spirits uncontained, she tells you to sit on the bed. To slide back just a bit. This, you do, Mother. Exhilarated, your entire white body exposed. Gazing at your beautiful, exotic captor. Knowing that such pleasure is given to but few among us. So few, those of us not Asian, but lucky enough to partake of what exotic offerings there be. Watch her, Mother. Watch the busty, shapely hipped woman climb onto the bed, sitting. Facing you. Sliding up your thighs with her entire self, until you two are as close as possible. Sitting in your lap. Her legs wrapped around your waist. *I need you to tell me something,* she says. *I need you to fuck my daughter.*

Oh, Mother! What dark and cold waters are these! What impending Death is this ocean, which can have no mercy on your feeble breath! *I will,* you answer. To be merciful to her. In such deep and powerful understanding. *Yes,* you say. Absorbing the proud perversion of it. The epic and unholy discomfort of it. *I will fuck your daughter for you.* The sound of the words. The implication of their meaning, true or no, has cranked the engine that is she, has it not? While sitting on you, as though upon your phantom member, Mother, she begins to hop herself up and down, her lower self barely grazing your stomach, but apparently just enough...

And she begins a hot and fast rhythm. A solemn race to capture this feeling she has held back for a fortnight—a woman practiced in her orgasms, a woman held by them as a drug addiction, having kept herself pure for this fortnight away from you, so that her energy is built up to volcanic potential, even to match your own, Dear Mother, when the *years* of repression broke into your body a moment ago...

She hops a fast rhythm, a quick bounce fever without ceasing, her legs still wrapped around your waist in sitting, her mind on fire with you and she raping her daughter into tears and screaming. *Tell me, tell me* she says, eyes closed, faced completely anguished now. *Tell me*, she begs, at the edge of this cliff she has run toward at full speed. *I'm going to fuck her* you say. *I'm going to fuck her...*

And the words light a spark somewhere unbeknownst, somewhere past the breast and the groin, as her legs begin to twitch, and you watch her, Mother, as she grunts and breathes loudly and pitifully, while her entire body shakes as hard and fast as a bowl of Jello on a washing machine.

Jonathan Lovejoy

Haydn

"Restore to my loving arms
The heart of my heart, my soul!
Unreasoning beasts are want to have—
Their fury tamed by love"

Joseph Haydn
Orpheus and Eurydice, circa 1791

The harp echoes the sorrow in every drop of rain. Longing played from the heart of Orpheus, who begs Providence to restore his loving bride Eurydice to his arms. From the new, big bass floor speakers I was coerced into buying, Jennifer and I listen to Haydn's profound interpretation, from his own inexhaustible well of inspiration. The harp twinkles softly above the low, heavy basses plucked gently, until the flowing tenor attempts to fashion the sorrow of the ages through song. We hear the lamentation of Orpheus, breathed so smoothly into the modern era, at the precipice, which is the end of the age we are in.

And when the tenor's velvety tone ends, the harp plinks a single tear for each unresisting heart, supported by the serene and solemn base line below. It is the first such sounds heard inside these hallowed and high class walls, the power of a full orchestra through speakers such as this, so profoundly more robust than any excuse of a sound system we have heard before (since Mother's 4th of July concert, at least). In this sound, I can feel even more glorious potential than even what I heard in the live orchestra several evenings ago in the school auditorium. This, again, courtesy of Jennifer Lin May, whose own credit card is still burning emerald green with envy.

And when the Song of Orpheus is past, I hear a whining, desperate cry of violin strings, joined by mysterious harmonies in full orchestral song, weeping for the evil intent of mankind, and the inevitability of his burning destruction by fire…

Then suddenly, after this brief repose, I hear the end of all mankind echo across the countryside, born from the Trump of God, the voice of Truth and Beauty itself. In Andante's gentle breeze, in this twilight of falling rain, Haydn calls the angels of Jubilee again, to warn the world of its impending destruction. *What's this called*, I am compelled to ask, as the orchestra weaves in and out, over and under, through and around the

Judgment Song for a Trumpet. *Its Haydn again,* she says, turning the volume down a little. *Trumpet Concerto in E flat, second movement.*

"I like the trumpet," I say. Dimly. Touched somewhere near but so far away, to increase what is already deeply uncertain inside. And when the main melody returns unsurreptitiously, I hear *Hail to the Lord of Heaven and Earth. We bow to thee O Lord our savior, we bow to thee, O Savior. Hail to the Lord of Heaven and Earth—we glorify thy name, Lord Jesus. Set us free…*

And from my soul's fear of the Ruins of Eschatology, I am reminded of the Rule of Eros, here in the latter day, these signs of the times; the abandonment of the woman's natural use of the man, as the entire earth is suddenly burning with black fire tinted blue.

"They're on a honeymoon in there, you know."

From my comfortable cushion chair, I gaze across the room at the lovely pianist. With her stereo remote, Jennifer lowers the Voice of Divinity.

"I know you can sense it," she says. "They've hardly left that room in three days."

"I know. But Mom says they have a lot to talk about. She said your mother is such a sad and beautiful person."

"Give me a break," she says. "Please…"

Jennifer wrinkles her mouth, rolling her eyes. Sighing, turning her face away.

"Well, she is."

"Is *what,*" she says.

"A very sad and beautiful person. Right?"

"You see? That's the power she has. She freakin' *raped* you, May. And you're acting like she's as sweet as a baby deer. Sad and beautiful. Sad and beautiful my yellow ass. You know what—the only thing sad and beautiful about my mother is the face she makes when she's cumming, okay?"

"I'm sorry. I didn't mean to cause problems."

"You didn't cause problems," she says, lashing a snappish tone. She gets up abruptly and leaves the room, leaving me to suffocate in the vacuum. In the wake of her departure, I am drawn from the room into the hall, adrift as unknowingly as a leaf on a trickling stream. While these mountain rains continue to fall, I flow the waters of this part of the timeline, to find Jennifer already downstairs, walking past the piano without so much as a glance, then out the front door to the grand entranceway. In full golden yellow braids, I bounce bosoms too heavy and healthy, skipping down the staircase quickly, across the massive livingroom and out the front door behind her.

The evening day is covered in clouds of melancholy gray. Clouds still burdened by a cool summer's weeping. In the gray twilight, we stand under the roof of the grand entranceway, sheltered by luxury unimaginable. White painted. Gold fixtured. By the echo of Paradise on earth.

"Every time I come out here," she says, " I can hardly look at this place without wanting to cry. Truth is, I wish I could stay here forever."

"I never did before. But for some reason, this summer's different. I guess it's because you're here. And your Mom."

The comment bristles her into motion. She turns and strolls a few steps away, leaning against one of the two main columns. In the distance, the trees rest on the edge of gray and silhouette, drowning in the darkened rain.

"Are you mad at me?"

She turns to look at big, blue eyes. Blue eyes of fear and desperation.

"I don't think I'll ever get used to it."

"What?"

"Oh… you. Maybelline Windsor."

"Jennifer, what did I do? Please tell me. Don't punish me and not tell me what's wrong. Please."

"You didn't do anything, okay? And maybe that's the problem. What are you, an angel or something? Have you looked in the mirror? If Cindy Margolis had a prettier sister it'd be you. Your hair is so golden yellow it doesn't even look real. You've got long, supermodel legs and a big, Kim Kardashian butt. And your tits… your tits are probably bigger than Oprah's. You could have gotten into any college in the world, but you went to an unheard of place like Appalachian. God, even when you stink, you smell like old cookies."

"I do not."

"Yes. You do."

"Well, that's no reason to get mad at me. Because of how I look."

"My God," she laughs, "you didn't really just say that did you? *Don't hate me because I'm beautiful?*"

The comment serves its poisoned purpose, and I can only wince in sorrow, and gaze out into the rain.

"Honey, it's not you," she says. "Come here."

She moves her face close to mine.

"Look at me. You know I'd rather gouge my own eyes out than make you feel bad."

"I know."

"I'm so sorry. You're too beautiful for words. You know that. And you're as sweet as pie. But… you do smell like old cookies when you need a shower."

The comment pushes a small laugh out of both of us. And my own laughter goes up, when she lowers her face into my bosom and shakes her head quickly back and forth. Making the famous boobly noise with her lips. Motors and boats. Boats and motors. Tickling me.

"No," she says, calming to a plaintiff stare. "It's not you."

"Then what's the matter?"

Afar off, a great distance away, there lies a truth that only she can see.

"Anna May."

"So that *is* what's wrong. Your mother. Her being here makes you uncomfortable."

"Well how about you? Aren't you the least bit weirded out by her? Or have you forgotten so quickly?"

"Trust me. I'll never forget."

"My mother should be in jail for what she did to me," Jennifer says. "For what she did to you. And now… she's at it again."

"She hasn't bothered me at all. Did she do something to you?"

"Maybelline… don't you know?"

I close my mouth and stare. Unable to imagine the unimaginable.

"I thought you and your mother had a breakthrough at the concert? If you want me to I'll—"

"My mother is fucking your mother, Maybelline."

The words '*how do you know*' need not be asked, as my mind is grabbed away from dumbness and denial, and thrust into the Heart of Revelation; which rises me up from where I am out into the rain, then down into a window at the far end of the front of the mansion, wherein are two women who have immersed themselves, who have done naught but trade orgasms for all of three days—the door of this room locked from the inside. Here, I am forced to gaze upon the sight of my mother's nude body, thin, shapely and strong, as the spirit within has come to full measure; with the nude Asian woman imprisoned underneath her, the Asian woman gagged with a cloth in her mouth and a stocking tied tightly around, while the brunette woman's teeth bare down another bite mark onto the Asian woman's naked breasts in grieving.

Lovers

"How do you explain it?" Mother says. "This thing with us?"

"You don't explain it. You just go with it. It's too impossible to explain."

In the nighttime of deep, early morning, Anna is awakened by the thunder outside. She lies to the side of Liz Windsor, her leg and arm over top of her.

"Maybe this is an easy thing for you," Mother says. "But I still can't believe it's happening."

"How many more times will you have to cum before you accept the truth about yourself? You're a closet dyke, Honey. You always have been. You just ran into the right woman at the right time."

"Are you a lesbian?"

"I'd be lying if I said I were. I'm not attracted to the typical lesbian type. I'm not interested in the lifestyle, and I've always been very attracted to men. I just don't feel like I'm a gay woman. I'm very comfortable being feminine, I love being a woman... I always have. But still, since I was a little girl, I always had fantasies about sleeping with other women. I never wanted to do anything about it, though. I never dated a girl, and I never considered it. Never thought I'd ever do anything about these feelings. I just accepted that they were part of my fantasy life."

"So you're saying its possible for a straight woman to crave lesbian sex, and still be straight."

"Yep."

Lying still, in the haze of half sleep, Anna rubs her hand across the eternally raised nipples of the brunette woman. Mother takes a deep, exhausted breath, and enjoys the echo of deep pleasure passing through. In the heart of memory, she can still she Anna's face in deep, anguished concentration, feverishly rubbing her own nipple against hers; from the nipple stimulation alone, Anna's body had shook with a powerful orgasm.

"So, you've never been with another woman?" Mother asks.

"You're my first one," Anna says, with a Phariseean honesty. "But like I said, the fantasies have been burning me up for 30 years. I don't have to ask you, I know you hardly even thought about it. Let alone did it."

"That's... not exactly true. I did think about it sometimes. But I always blocked it out. I've hugged women before that I've had a deep attraction to. And there was one that I think I might have if it ever came up. But she got married and moved to Washington D.C."

"Really?"

"Just some hugs, we shared. She was my best friend. She was there when my husband left me. But sometimes the attraction was deep, and I couldn't really understand where it came from."

"Women naturally lust after one another," Anna says. "But you'd have to go through the Gates of Hell first to get one of them to admit it."

"Now *that,* I understand. Because I'm telling you right now, we can't tell another living soul about this."

"Don't worry. I get it. I guess I wouldn't want to broadcast it either. But…"

"But what?"

"I think my daughter knows."

The types of fear are many. And uniquely distinguished.

"How would she know? Did you tell her?"

"No. No, I swear. But I can sense it."

Amidst the rumbling thunder, Mother takes a breath of trembling, epic defeat.

"But you don't know for sure if she knows."

"Relax, Honey. I was just teasing. All my daughter knows is that piano."

The breath my mother releases is as deep and sensual sounding as they come, this side of Climax Mountain.

"Don't scare me like that. *Please.*"

"Scared you're gonna get caught?" Anna says. "You don't think they haven't heard one of us cry out at least once? Remember the scream you let out when I stuck my dick up your ass—"

"*Don't…*don't remind me."

"I had to cover your mouth with my hand—"

"I *know* that. *God,* I feel guilty enough as it is. I won't be able to look anybody in the eye for a week."

"Just admit it. At that moment, the pleasure was so big, you didn't care who heard you. And I know it because you shot off like a rocket from just *butt sex* alone. You're as hyper-orgasmic as I am, Liz, more even. Admit you loved it so much, you didn't care who heard you."

Lips apart. An answer lost somewhere in my mother's spirit. A deep, defeated sigh.

"You're all the same," Anna says. "Riding your husband's cocks, closing your eyes, imagining that cock is attached to another woman."

"I never did that."

"No? Well, I did. A hundred times. But in my heart, when I was alone… a thousand."

Book Seven

Chopin

The hours roll swiftly along, emerging our mothers from their stupor, wherin they partook to excess of Perversion's wine. They have milled around among us with the utmost care, as though the last three days had never happened. As to the tension between the four of us, who can tell? Mother-daughter tension is as perpetual as the Moon around the Earth, or the Earth around the Sun. Beatings and paddlings and secret sex among us—they are the same as music, school and money. It is the Curse of Eve—passed through the motherlines—that mother-daughter tension is palpable and ever present.

Three generations of us glory in the emotions that ebb and flow, taking part in a rare dinner cooked and eaten rather than ordered at some restaurant. This late summer afternoon, this daylight evening finds us still lost in the rain of summer, enjoying a home cooked southern meal. Every batch of home fried chicken ever cooked is unique to the day, and ours has chosen to be uniquely good. Grandmother, Mother and Me, Anna and Jennifer, we had all eaten heartily and happily through our Mother-Daughter tension, until it was lifted and carried away by the talk of Jennifer on the after dinner piano.

We sit here now, in no mood for television or shopping, carried away by the angelic sylph maidens, *Les Sylphides,* and their ballet gathered together by Fate itself: Chopin's Prelude No. 7 in the key of A Major drifts to us from an Opus 28, to remind us that inspired melody is King, and in art, instinct is more important than intellect. Jennifer May, solemn and determined on our early evening piano, waltzes us through effortlessly; a spirited dance without effort upon the keys, which seems to establish at last her authority as a pianist of merit, even if it is only for the four of us who listen. And when the Grand Waltze Brillante begins, the lilting beauty of her playing, full and smooth, almost orchestral, causes her mother to reach for my mother's hand…

But after only a few seconds, Mother slides her hand away as casually as she can, trying not to appear as if she'd just been stung by a bee.

I clearly see Jennifer look up from the keys, glancing in their direction, at the bodies and lovely hands in motion. And there again rises this perpetual tension, as the revolution of the Earth and the Moon. And then I must endure another tragic glance, the one directly into my eyes from the piano player, as if to drive home the point that *yes, I told you they were fucking, didn't I?*

I listen to the girl channel every fear and frustration into her playing, which seems magical on this fifth and final number, as it had on the four which came before it, these five played as heavy and robust as a single piano can allow, always with great emphasis on the bass keys for the fullest effect, and not played with the delicate, careless tinkling that even the established masters always seem to resort to. Jennifer May interprets Frederic Chopin for us as follows: The Prelude No. 7 in A Major, Op. 28, followed by the Waltz in G flat Major, Op. 70, then a reprise of the Prelude No. 7, to set up the Waltz in C sharp minor, Op. 64, and finally the Waltz in E Flat Major, Op. 18, the aptly named *Grand Waltz Brillante,* which when channeled through Jennifer May's heavy playing is surely as Beethovenian as ever. She attacks music with controlled abandon, displaying the truth in passion, with no regard for purist criticism, unafraid to flow stiff, staccato passages legato, and to pitch whole pieces from their original keys up to where they are perfectly beautiful to the ear and the soul. Jennifer May's piano playing is fearful, sounding as though the piano itself is come to life, with a message from somewhere forward along the timeline, of our rapid approach to the end of this age, and the coming storm of fire and judgment.

And while she blazes the fiery blue and black sounds into our world, the professor of the Juilliard School of music is held prisoner outside our rainy door, afraid to knock or touch the doorbell, lest he interrupt the voice of Eschatology.

Jerry

*J*ennifer's latter day sermon ends on the echo of our enthusiasm, what little smattering of applause we can find, after a quarter of an hour has passed. While we clap for her—the Mother, the Mother, the Grandmother and Me—I cannot hold my admiration inside, cheering the best cheerleader whooping and wooing voice I've got, bringing forth even a bravo from my mother, so unafraid to perform it for us, which is clearly what she's doing whether she realizes it or not. Jennifer stands up from the piano and walks towards us, clearly embarrassed, and we all let out one last cheerful exclaim for her, and her ability to make us hear the end of the world in her piano.

Our little gathering is suddenly interrupted by the loud metallic call from the front door. There is always so much to fear, from a fateful knocking at the door. Mother glides away from our Jennifer-worship to the tall, white double doors, opening one side, to see what ghost of hopeless humanity has drifted in out of the rain.

The Lady Windsor braves a shockwave through her heart, prompting her to step outside under the entranceway, where the columns support the shelter above their rainy repose.

"I heard it again," he says. "Dark magic. She is a sorceress on that piano."

"Oh...how long... I mean... were you listening? How much did you hear?"

"Enough to know that I've never heard Chopin played like that before. She's so confident in what she does, she plays *Chopin* in higher keys, and the result is pure beauty. Her technique is so smooth and polished, its flawless. And her passion and power... I hear laughter *and* pain. She brings pieces to *life*, Liz. With her, it's not just somebody playing music. She can make you hear a piece you've been listening to your whole life sound like you're hearing it for the first time. It's professional ability. Recording talent."

"Well," she sighs. "What's the bad news?"

As if conjured by the question, the big door opens again, and the Asian mother steps out, in favorite tight gray skirt and white summer blouse. Her lovely smile is genuine.

"I'm sorry to barge out here like this, but I *thought* I heard you, Mr. Fielding. I didn't know you were coming. Is everything alright?"

The John Boy Walton-looking man smiles and takes a deep breath, not hiding the echo of disappointment in his expression, as if he is reporting to a mother that has not yet seen her daughter's house after a twister.

"I was going to call, but I knew I had to drive down here again. It's good news and bad news, sort of."

The two women gaze determinedly at one another. Searching.

"The problem is that she missed the audition dates, and the transfer deadlines. Besides all this, our sophomore class is filled to the brim. Normally, none of this would have mattered, because I didn't think she was gonna be anywhere near as good as you said she was, Liz. But my problem is—she *is* that good. And that puts pressure on me I thought I wouldn't have to worry about in the first place. I looked at her freshman audition tape and frankly, I wasn't prepared for her to be special at the concert. And now, I'm stuck trying to figure out what to do."

Anna turns away in silence, trying not to appear as broken as she feels inside.

"But, the good news is that she can apply for junior transfer this fall, while she's still a sophomore at Whitaker. And she will have to audition again."

"Jerry," Mother says, shaking her head. "That's unacceptable. I'm sorry, but I can *not* accept that."

"Look, Liz I heard her play, too. You think I don't know what a travesty, what a tragedy it is that she's stuck at Whitaker, and not in New York with us?"

"Jerry, you know how things like this work. Applications, deadlines, procedures… they don't mean a *damned* thing. People do exactly what they want to do They let in who they want to let in, they help who they want to help. And I've been around long enough, and I've helped enough people to know when it really is, like you say, a travesty or a tragedy, and I'm telling you, Jennifer May not being given special consideration, a helping hand into the best music school in the country is an artistic tragedy of the worst kind."

Crossing his arms, the piano teacher breathes a sigh, turning towards the sheets of twilight rain for comfort.

"And you know what I'm talking about when I say how things get done. Because as much as we try not to face it Jerry, it always has been, and always will be *who you know*. Because I could make you an offer you couldn't refuse and you know it. And I would make that offer as a friend, Jerry. A friend whose desperate for a special, life changing favor. But I believe so strongly in that girl's talent, and in your integrity as a judge of music and character, that all I need to offer you is the opportunity to help this young girl. To help her climb as high in this profession as she can. But she's going to need you, Jerry. Your school would be her golden ticket. And I know she deserves it."

Suddenly, at that moment, as another spirit is called forth, a Waltz in C sharp minor plays from an Opus 64, a truer raindrop melody than any other, so called; played at such upward pitch, swung so powerfully in waltz time, slow enough to call Poseidon from deep sea slumber to listen—notes strung together like Christmas lights climbing to the top of a Frazier Fir on Christmas Eve, slowing down upon the last light, then skipping forward to alight as the Star of Bethlehem, at the top of the Appalachian forest tree.

The three of them are held captive for a moment, watching the waltzing spirits of mountain rainfall begin to fade away. And then the truest melody ever conceived for the keyboard proceeds, sung from Opus 28, this brief and crying melody; this Prelude no. 7 in the melancholy key. As the melody slices through the cloud of untruth and resistance, the Lady Windsor stares at Jerry Fielding in pure, righteous judgment, allowing him no room for mercy. Still gazing at his old acquaintance Elizabeth Windsor, then glancing at the hopeless expression of Anna May, who gazes into the glow of darkened rainfall, he opens his little phone and dials whatever beeping can fly him to the home phone of his colleague in upstate New York. Somewhere in the self-assured mumbling, Anna hears the words "*I say we push for the fall*" come forth.

After less than a minute, he hangs up the little phone snapped shut, and slid un-surreptitiously back in his front pocket.

"My grandmother had a saying about getting the job done. '*Money talks, and bullshit walks.*' And Miss May, your daughter is *money.*"

"What are you saying, Jerry," Mother says, touching his arm. Unreservedly.

"I'm saying that I've heard enough, Liz. Miss May… I think it's time I met your daughter."

ossini

also will laugh at your calamity;
I will mock when your fear cometh.

Proverbs 1:26

The Barber of Seville plays the theater of our minds, in the aftermath of joy and happiness grown. Early this morning, I was awakened by one of the most beautiful melodies of all time, transcribed to Jennifer's piano, echoed through the house. I can remember laying there, barely awake, unable to remember the composer's name, and often unable to remember whether I was really awake or dreaming.

Curious, how it is that some dreams can seem more real than life itself, as I am still questioning the vision I saw before the music woke me, with Jennifer standing fully nude, while her nude mother paddled the palm of her daughter's hand with a wooden ruler, hard and fast enough to make Jennifer tense up and scream one loud scream. This, I realize was only a dream. But what of those other sounds and images? Yes, the man from Juilliard was here last night, and yes, he did say that he will send Jennifer an application by email for her to print out, fill out and mail out to his office to bypass the online confusion. And yes, he did say that barring some unfortunate, unforeseen event, Jennifer May will attend the Juilliard School of Music this fall.

Jennifer stands outside in the summer morning breeze, while the clouds take a break from weeping. The sky is thick and overcast across the Windsor estate, down to every horizon. Jennifer sits in easy repose, at the table on the back patio; gazing beyond the pool to the grand and open back lawn. Wondering where it is that she has come from, how she has drifted here, and to where along the flow of time and history she will arrive. What is this echo of Heaven and Earth, and who is that tall, blonde angel that picked her up from the Valley of the Shadow of Death, and carried her to a place of Hope and Light?

A noise, a commotion at the patio door. The sound of door sliding technology—smooth. To signal the end of tranquility.

"I heard you playing Rossini this morning."

Jennifer does not look at her mother. She only listens to the clip-clop of black heels, the movement of casual, burgundy dress cloth in her periphery.

"What did I tell you about playing Rossini?"

"I woke up early this morning—it was on my mind."

"Sounds like you've been rehearsing it. Playing it behind my back."

"I think… I think I've earned the right to play whatever I want."

Facing away, gazing across the lawn, Anna May feels a rush from her heart to her womb, or rather her groin. She suppresses a smile, and lowers her head.

"I don't know why everybody's so afraid of Rossini's music," Jennifer says. "Inspiration scares the Hell out of people. I don't love Rossini either but that overture is as close to the truth as anything I've ever played. It is pure, undiluted genius."

"Yes, you're right. That level of musical stupidity *is* pure genius."

"You don't know you're talking about."

"I don't know what *I'm* talking about?"

The sudden memories of the scars on Jennifer's back, and the offer from Jerry Fielding last night justify Anna's bewilderment.

"Those who can't do, *teach*," Anna says. "I couldn't have a career as a concert pianist. But I promised you when you were twelve years old that you would play the world stage before you were thirty. How old are you. I said how old—"

"Nineteen."

"Watch your tone," Anna says, turning her head slightly towards her daughter. Finding her in the periphery.

"Rossini's music is the end of the world," Jennifer says. "It's the voice of God laughing at the wicked. Laughing at hypocrisy. Rossini's music is Divine Insanity. Its God going crazy from his grief at having made us. Having to listen to our lies. Having to watch us hurt each other. Rossini is God's madness. Laughing over his own agony. Laughing at me. Laughing at you."

From an energy, she knows not where, on an involuntary turn and step, Anna May whirls around and walks toward her daughter with calm determination, watching Jennifer look up at her boldly. Then, on the beat of her last step, Anna raises her hand and brings it down like an axe against the trunk of a tree, her open hand smashing against the side of her daughter's face, causing Jennifer to yell a small shriek from the shock.

"Is God laughing at me now? Put your hand down to your lap. Is God laughing at me now?"

With as much boldness as is left, Jennifer stares through the steady tickle of tears that roll down her face.

"Is God laughing at me?"

The daughter looks up at the mother. Insolent. Bold. Prideful without speaking a word. Defiant with only the sniffing of tears. Braving the fire of a mother's wrath kindled.

Anna's angry expression suddenly goes calm. She stands up straight, glancing at the patio door with profound interest, perhaps to see if they are alone. Then with a tragic, steady calm, she straddles Jennifer in the cushioned patio chair and takes both her daughter's ears in her hands. The howling noise from her daughter's throat is the music of domination, brought on by the solemn twisting of her daughter's ears backward as though she were a disobedient German Shepherd in training.

"Is God laughing at me?"

Not waiting for the answer, she twists Jennifer's ears again, to hear the word *'no'* howled in a pathetic, begging siren of defeat.

"God's not laughing at me now, is he?"

"Please…"

The audacity, the steel-heartedness, the stubborn temerity of this little dyke bitch, who owes her very existence to her, the nerve of her to not answer the question directly prompts another twisting of her ear, another howling *'no,'* and a whimpering *'I'm sorry,'* and *'please forgive me,'* and *'God's not laughing,'* and *'I swear I won't play it anymore.'*

The two of them rest in their scene. The dynamic of their lives displayed. The Asian mother in the burgundy dress and black heels, straddling her nineteen year old daughter, her hands still pressed calmly to the sides of her daughter's head.

The weeks pass into oblivion, with the rise and fall of every new sun, and the fervent heat of summer days. These are days of Heaven, our last days in the warm light of hope.

Money is the greatest anti-depressant known to man. It allows the four of us (and Denise) to leap from luxury to luxury, like angels leaping from cloud to cloud, not having to suffer the corruption of the ground below. We know nothing of Poverty, nor the sorrow of his dirty, unhallowed walls, and broken hearts of unrequited want and need. Carried aloft, the five of us, many miles east over the ocean, to settle on the white sand beaches of the Ivory Coast, along the shores of Barbados in the Caribbean Sea.

For two weeks we languish here, far North of Christ Church, west of Bathsheba, able to rest from the pain of poisoned ambition and relationships uncertain, whereby the modern mother-daughter dynamic is defined. The grandmother stays to herself, pretty much, always able to find a book to read or a television program to watch, staying in the palatial hotel as much as possible, while the four of us waste no time, flaunting our half naked butts on the beach. And here, along these shores of Ivory sand tinted blue, I am unashamed of my body, understanding full its dimensions, and the power of its disproportionate proportions in the top of my bikini.

"There's something I want you to do for me," Anna May says to Mother, watching Jennifer and me go from the beach ball to the Frisbee near the sky blue waves that roll ashore.

"What's that, Honey?"

"Look at my daughter."

Liz opens her eyes from the shaded, jaded rest, seeing the slim but heavy hipped Asian girl in the black French cut string bikini playing Frisbee with a giant breasted blonde.

"When you and I first got together," she says, "can you remember what I said about Jennifer. What I told you to say?"

"I'll never forget it," Liz says. "It's the most perverted thing I've ever heard."

"How do you feel about things like that. Perverted things?"

"You mean dirty talk? I guess I love it."

"Remember what you told me about your daughter, when she brought home those bad freshman grades? You were strapped on when you told me."

"I know."

"Remember how hard you started pounding into me while you told me how you punished her? I was underneath you. Watching you. Studying your face. I saw your eyes roll back. I saw you lose your mind. I felt your body jerk. I heard you crying to God for mercy. And before I screamed to both God *and* Christ, I remember thinking how lucky I was, watching a woman as beautiful as you lose herself in the strongest orgasm she will ever have in her life. One that most women will never have. Because they don't understand. But you do. Don't you?"

"Yes."

A strong, sudden ocean breeze blows Anna's hair, while it carries their daughters' Frisbee to a greater height. Blowing a breath of renewal through our mothers' jaded, shaded rest.

"Because of the Juilliard thing, my daughter thinks she can disrespect me. A couple of weeks back, she said that when she plays Rossini, it is *'God laughing at me.'*"

Liz turns away from the Asian woman in the blue bikini, to gaze at the Asian girl in the black one.

"What are you going to do?" Mother says.

"Do you understand the agony? The power you feel inside? The aching in your groin? The life or death feeling in your spirit? True murderer's rage, when your daughter is insolent? Or when she defies you or embarrasses you? Can you understand that lust, that craving to inflict pain? To exact punishment?"

Liz gazes at the busty young blonde in the yellow bikini. Watching the way her breasts bounce when she runs.

"Yes," she says. "I understand."

"Then you'll understand when I tell you I want you to punish my daughter for me. I want you to punish her the way you know she needs to be punished."

Mother sits up taller in the reclining beach chair, her long, white leg sliding slowly, smoothly against her other leg. Knowingly.

"So you say she's been an insolent, ungrateful little *cunt*."

The word spoken, the somber expression on my mother's face takes away Anna's ability to speak, nearby a phantom shortness of breath.

Hotel

In ignorance too epic to know, Mother's afternoon suggestion has me dimly dragging my grandmother happily around the island, looking for everything, finding nothing. *"I want you to take your grandmother shopping,"* Mother had said. *"Buy us all two dresses apiece, hats, swimsuits, sunglasses, whatever. And don't shy away from those little open markets, they've probably got the most interesting stuff anyway. I'm keeping Jennifer and Anna with me, I want to talk to them about Juilliard..."* And like a dumb, dull, lumbering lump, I got dressed in the hotel, sliding my dress on over the bikini that never touched the ocean today. It is just too comfortable to take off, I realize, sliding my sky blue T-shirt and matching faded jeans on, still unafraid to display the curves I've been given while I'm here. Grandmother Denise and I, Aunt Denise—are soon out of the elegant hotel room and on our way to look for everything. And to find nothing.

And what is it that the grandmother and me don't know, at the edge of the pendulum swing? When the energy flows from happiness to unhappiness, for the one who makes our piano sing? What is it that grandmother and I don't know, when the paddle emerges on the pendulum swing?

"Mom, I said I'm sorry. Please. Miss Windsor please don't do this!"

Can I imagine what pain there is, when Mother's paddle burns the black bikini hips in time! The paddling fire comes out of her mouth in a loud, guttural scream, her head held tight in Anna's hands, her wrists bound together in front by stockings. *"Rest your hands between your legs you little bitch—don't you look back at her! You look at me—look at yourself in this mirror! Watch the insolence* (whack!), *the disrespect* (whack!), *the ungrateful little bitch* (whack!) *come out of your fucking mouth* (whack!). *Liz, do it!* (whack!) *Do it!* (whack!) *Beat the fuck out of her!* (whack!) All of this, while holding her daughter by the head and throat with both hands, watching her scream and cry to oblivion.

In the hotel room in Barbados, Mother's victim pressed against the dresser, in the aftermath of having watched Anna go topless and belt whip the girl to a frenzy, after having then spanked the girl's breasts to red and bruising, my mother wails the tar from her lover's insolent daughter, driven forward by the need to see blood on the girl's white skin. Concentrating the paddle to one spot on her buttocks, Mother pounds the paddle into the screaming girl; full, hard swings of the paddling wood, drawing her arm far backward and fast forward, while the daughter is held still by her mother.

After a long while, after one hundred hard swings with the paddle, after having cut the daughter's white skin to blood, Mother backs off, face somber and stern, watching Anna drag her daughter violently to the bed by her throat. Anna throws the crying girl to the bed and slams herself hard on top of her, still wearing her blue bikini bottoms only, Mother in the black one piece that shows her long legs and small, shapely waist and bottom. Mother's anger, her paddling strength comes from the long, strong arms and powerful leg muscles naturally built, and a tight, athletic waist and chest unburdened by the long and heavy, swinging breasts of her topless lover. She puts the paddle on the big King sized bed with its opulent, gothic carved darkwood headboard, so much darker than the blood stained paddling wood. Liz walks around the bed, watching the mother lay her topless, blue bikini bottomed body full atop her daughter, then sliding this blue bikini bottom down from her hips, while her daughter cries and sobs without ceasing. *"Liz, come here."* The words ring true through every nerve in Liz's body. And she climbs serpentine onto the bed, then onto the body of the girl, where both women are now laying side by side on top of her, pinning her motionless to the bed. *"I want you to stop crying,"* Anna says. But to no avail. *"Your mother told you to be quiet,"* comes the heavier, deeper voice. *"Kiss her, Liz,"* Anna says. Her own voice trembling. Without hesitation, my mother leans down to the tear stained face, and kisses Jennifer May full on the mouth. *Oh God,* flows freely from Anna's voice, as she begins to squeeze herself tighter against her daughter, suddenly convulsing once mightly, her body twitching the lurching forward of itself, while she watches the promise of her life, the unspoken desire of her heart manifest itself to her. In the aftermath of this heavy, involuntary spasm, she pushes her lips to my mother's cheek, until my mother raises up and joins her in the kiss, moaning at the feel of the Asian woman's tongue, unable to prevent her own body from its sublime and fervent tremble.

Still pinned helplessly underneath, her skin on fire from the paddling wood, Jennifer May gazes a sight that surely none other have seen; of her own mother on top of her, kissing her best friend to an orgasm.

*B*arbados

*T*ragedy soars high above the clouds, in the wake of our so-called vacation, our respite from the spirits of ashen gray regret. This plush, cushioned gray seat calls the body to relaxation against its will, to force one to ponder the finer things in leisure. The five of us are alone in this part of the cabin, safely protected from the stench of failure and mediocrity, and the teeming masses that go in thereat. Oh, what sins and secrets do we try to escape—what demons do we attempt to flee from, when we hide ourselves in luxury! Hardly a word passes between us on this flight—Denise being engrossed in another one of her thick literary books, something about a hundred years and solitude, and not about a wizard girl named Hermione, as it probably should have been.

Spirits of boredom are held at bay for me by thoughts of what I see in Jennifer's eyes whenever I look at her. It is a mournful, defeated expression, as if joy and hope have been stolen in a blast of trauma, and carried into the bowels of the earth and held prisoner. Across the aisle from me, in her cozy, comfy cushioned chair, Jennifer gazes catatonic out the window, watching the angels take cloud form and rest motionless in the sky below. The heart and soul of these clouds is a stormy revelation seen only by an accursed few; those unlucky enough to have had the flames of violence and perversion heaped upon them—passed down through the branches of the proverbial family tree, the tainting of a spirit with poison— the burning of blue and black fire.

Jennifer gazes at the fluffy white clouds, at the silver linings that glow with Heaven's glory, and can find nothing to grab hold of, as though the bottom of our plane has just fallen way, and she tumbles towards the clouds, hoping to bounce on a mountain cushion of cotton softness, only to find herself falling faster, her vision obscured in the crystalline, icy cold.

I want to call across the aisle to her, her chair so close yet still so unblissfully far away. I want to speak out, but just behind us both are the invisible chords of domination; these invisible ties that bind, those born from ancestral farmlands somewhere deep in the Asian countryside, and those from the shores of Old Great Britain. Spirits of what was, born into the women of our far and distant past, sent down through the motherline; resting heavily upon these two—the hearts and souls of the uncovered, these two, breasts still sore from the pain of perverted youth, these two— who sit quietly behind us, their attentions vacillating from magazines to laptops to phones, and to an Ipod filled with classical music. Holding us captive, these two, so that I cannot say a word, even though Anna and Liz do chatter every so often. Holding me captive, these two, so I am not able to call my best friend's name, and tell her that yes, I remember when it was that your hopeful expression died, and I know from whence the sharp and evil blade cometh.

"Don't cry, Jennifer," Mother says, still pressed heavy on top of her, kissing the tears from Jennifer's eyes. "Your mother still loves you. But she wanted, she needed you to remember this. For the rest of your life, you'll remember this. And you'll remember to never disrespect your mother again..."

In the Heart of Memory, Jennifer feels, she smells the perfume and oppressive weight of both grown women pressed down on her, both struggling to hide spirits now spent from trembling. *Now go take a shower,* her mother says. *When she kissed you... I pissed myself...*

Will you ever disrespect your mother again?

No.

No, what? Anna says sharply, pushing harder against her daughter.

No Maam, Jennifer says. Defeatedly.

In the Heart of Memory, Jennifer feels the weight of the women lifted, the weight of Death and Hell. She raises up without their help, slowly, stiffened by soreness, from the raised lump on her left buttock, and the bloody welts from the paddling board. What is it that I imagine you see, Dear Jennifer Lin, when you look in the bathroom mirror? Is it the face of God's curse? Is it the face of humanity burdened with suffering? From which pain comes the tears you cry, Jenny Lin? Is it the pain from your spirit, cracked by your mother's epic betrayal, then shattered by the Lady Windsor's epic depravity? Are your tears born from physical agony, the sores burned onto the skin of your backside, which is hard and sensitive to the touch, a third degree burn from fires invisible, the fires of Violence and Perversion in which we burn? Are the tears from a broken heart, when you hear your mother speak the word: *Barbados* out loud in her thickest Asian accent, causing the Lady Windsor to snicker then guffaw into a full laugh. What is the end-of-the-world sound you hear, Dear Jennifer, when Anna's bikini is taken off, and she is on all fours on the bed when you turn the shower on? What is it you see, Jennifer Lin, when you make sounds as though you are in the shower, then slowly creep the bathroom door open just enough? Is it the sight of my mother standing on the floor at the corner of the bed, the top of her one piece down to her waist, with your mother nude and on all fours on the bed—the Lady Windsor slamming herself into the back of your mother with the assurance of a white horse in heat? What is the slapping of flesh together, Jenny Lin? What depravities doth it entail? Where does my mother receive this natural skill you see, as she slams a dog's portion into the back of your mother—starting, stopping, slow, fast, then one final, fast burst, that bends my mother over your mother's back in siren from the core of her spirit. Mother! Where doth this phantom member hail from? From whence doth this secret dyke blood begin! In the Heart of Memory, Jennifer hears the noisy hotel shower, and she watches my mother in the aftermath of her own trembling, standing behind Anna May, one hand between Anna's legs rubbing feverishly, the other hand rubbing both of Anna's breasts without mercy. Jennifer watches this end of the world sight in shock and disbelief, as her mother soon raises up straight, leaning back against the Lady Windsor's body, and begins to shake violently from the waves of pleasure passing through.

Airplane

The pilot's voice plays the Theatre of My Mind. Drifting me awake, in time to see a flash of light illuminate the dark, booming thunderheads in the distance. All around us, far to every horizon is a thick carpet of dark gray clouds tinted darker, as if we have flown into another place in time. And I hear the noise of the plane drowned by the crackling, screaming thunder, as if the sky were being ripped apart with every flash of light in the clouds…

And suddenly, the stormy, cloudy world outside our window vanishes in a blinding flash of light, and a blast of sound surely never heard from the ground, with nothing but this single plane to impede the mountainous wave of noise energy, rolling past our stalwart journey forward, but not without a profound shaking and rattling of the plane, and every nerve within—this, followed by the cacophony of screams, both man and woman, berating their own stupidity for being here, and their inability to escape judgment and damnation…

The pilot's voice coalesces into cogency, into coherent speech in my mind, and I hear something said about *"fireballs coming again,"* and not being able to *"land the plane in this storm."* When I look back, I see my grandmother bent over with her head tightly covered by her hands and arms, as if she could wish this cataclysm away. The motion this plane rocks is unnatural to say the least, as if it were grabbed by the unseen hand and shaken to its limits. From what I am able to gather, my mother sits bolt upright, her hands clutched on the armrests, her eyes closed, face in tight and determined meditation to a God she only thought she knew, a God she sought through good works and piety…

And across the aisle from her, one seat back is her lovely Asian counterpart, whose eyes are blared open, who jumps at every flash of lightning in the evening day. And across the aisle from me, I see Jennifer held still by the flashes of lightning in the clouds, which we both bear witness to, now accompanied by trails of fire and smoke from the clear evening sky above the carpet of clouds, a sky still illuminated by the sun already set, beyond the stormy clouds of agony below our plane. From nowhere above us, like falling stars they come down burning in orange fire and trailing pillar of smoke, falling though the black clouds beneath us unhindered, lighting them up as they pass through to the unseen ground below.

As I gaze out my window, I see a sudden bright and thick bolt of lightning arc from a high place, towering miles up into the sky to nowhere in particular, appearing as a lightning tower, flashing the bright center of its origin, among an infinity of smaller bolts which crackle from the cloud it comes from. This tower of lightning flares up again, and suddenly the wing by my seat is blown in fiery pieces by a passing fireball, and Anna May's deep maniacal screams dominate the chorus of them that I hear, as the plane makes a sudden, downward slide towards the fiery clouds below...

Though I am unable to utter a sound, I am privy to a symphony of weeping and gnashing of teeth, hearing the name of God screamed deeply from a woman's voice, as we pass through the blackened clouds of thunder. Every dream and wish of the imagination of man about a plane falling from the sky is manifest to us; the noise, the screams, the feeling in the gut of falling from the top of the world to the bottom, where only the pain and burning agony of death awaits...

And suddenly, our plane blasts through the bottom of the stormy clouds, where the reason the plane couldn't land blazes apparent—the ground below us, every building, every tree, every part of the open ground is on blazing, burning fire of Hell, where the elements it seems will melt with a fervent heat, and everything we have ever known or loved is burning up as far as the eye can see...

Then suddenly, a monstrous blast of noise, cold wind and flames bursts into the cabin where we are, and I look back in time to see Anna May and my mother burning like trees in a forest fire, writhing and screaming in torment...

And at last, in the icy cold and burning with fire and brimstone, the place where Jennifer sits with her eyes closed tight is blasted away, leaving a gaping hole where she used to be, while our mothers still sit behind me burning alive, as I gaze the clear view of the burning city below us, and the rain of fire down from Heaven…

And I hear my name screamed in these flames by Anna May, whose own face is beginning to corrupt, and turn to ashes in this flame.

"May. May, wake up!"

I am shocked awake in the safely landed plane, looking around me frantically, staring at everyone as though they were made out of glass.

"I didn't mean to scare you, Honey," Anna says. "It's time to go."

Audition

Desperation permeates the halls of the Juilliard School, along with the spirits of high ambition and fear. The elitist tension is palpable here, phasing through every wall like magic, flowing through the cracks under every door, down the halls and around the corners, and into the mouths and lungs like so much smoke, causing the untalented to have to take at least one deep breath in defeat. Those that belong here are chosen, though not as many would surmise; these two spirits of God, the one called Fate and the other called Destiny, administrate the ebb and flow of this current with as much tangibility as the world will ever see from them, these people all possessing Divine gifts in some degree or measure. The sights and sounds of entertainment in the forms which we take for granted, which we so cavalierly judge on a whim; singing, dancing, acting, composing, and yes, even the lowly musician—these cannot be *honestly* taught to the general population. To the average man and woman at large, such efforts to learn these to any degree of beauty or flair of original expression, such efforts would (and do) prove ultimately futile. And even among the elite, among those gifted with these arts, there is the prevailing, inner knowledge that talent without inspiration is mediocrity. No struggle, no sacrifice, no learning curve can conjure artistic inspiration, which is as fleeting as a bolt of lightning, or a blast of thunder from the clouds. And this ever present fear flows just beneath the surface, the fear of being outed as a poster child for Mediocrity. And so, this fear must be controlled and eventually conquered; held at bay by Delusion, and her twin sister titan Denial. But for a select few, for those chosen from the beginning of Time, there resides in them no fear of who they are, nor of their ability for artistic expression. Among performers, in the sea of talented pretenders on the piano at this school, there is one who knows. One who flows with Time and History. One whose piano glows. One whose expression rises from the East. Burning blue and black fire.

We sit still in the far back of the music hall, in the shadows of grief and recognition. I sit alone with my grandmother Denise, at my mother's request, while Mother and Anna sit together several seats away. "They certainly have become friendly, haven't they," Grandmother Denise says. "They spend all their time together. It's like that whenever your mother gets a new friend. But I haven't seen her this close to anybody in a long time..." *Trust me Granny. You ain't seen shit!* The vulgar, disrespectful words blast into the space of my mind, causing me to smile at my grandmother and to touch her hand in full, fungalooga repose.

One of the details of my mother's tragedy in Barbados, one of the reasons given for sending Denise and I away that fateful day, is so that they could discuss Jennifer's audition, created and dominated by her mother, of course, with pieces by Schubert, Liszt, Prokofiev and somebody named Schumann, pieces I imagine as having collected the dust over the years, brought to life every so often in the academic halls, heard only by the academic musical elite, those who have the tolerance to listen. Even a sonata by Beethoven, which as surely as the sunset, will shine no moonlight in this audition hall today. Sitting a good distance from us, the two women whisper constantly when the faculty comes in, which must surely be more than what normally watches an audition, all of them aware that this girl has already failed once, and is here again because she is supposed to be somebody special, somebody who played the Norwegian's *Great A Minor Concerto* supposedly as well as Beethoven himself would have.

These lies and exaggerations fill the cloud of rumor here, ad nauseam, until the process of watching another so-called prodigy's bubble pop is now something of a growing tradition. The spirits of Here We Go Again have joined the small, talkative crowd of piano students and teachers from all over the music division; including people who have taught Grammy nominated musicians in the past. A jaded, heaping handful of them now sit and wait for her to come out on stage, a stage so reluctantly approved for this failed retread, who seems to have captured Jerry Fielding's mind and body.

Jennifer Lin May walks out onto the stage in her black blouse, charcoal gray skirt and low black heels, walking straight to the piano without fear, but in undeniable, relaxed confidence, with an air of definite humility. I feel the hush fall over the audition hall, and every breath half taken, as the somber mood falls over her expression.

She raises her hand and brings them down in a chord from Rome 1816, by way of New York 1825, when it became the first Italian opera performed in this country's history. The sounds send lightning to the heart of everyone in the seats, who in watching a generation of students in this school, have never heard this level of audacity from the audition stage. As the overture from the Crown Prince of Melody plays, my mother looks over at Anna May, and studies the mixture of humiliation and anger in her expression.

*I*nsanity

*O*h, what solemn promises are made, unbeknownst to those far below, and their giddy bewilderment at what they see on stage! No, Anna. This is not Rachmaninov or Bach, as you had so specifically required! Sit there and listen to God's happy, mocking laughter at your failure! Hear the brief call of hilarity from the Throne—the echo of divine laughter at the wicked! Yes, Anna May—what you hear in this closing crescendo is Divine laughter and pain! And your daughter's insanity, her madness continues through the Bagatelle in A minor. Yes, Anna, Beethoven's lowly and exalted bagatelle! How did she do this, you ask, when did she do it? How did she get Jerry to help her ruin her life and yours with such epic and blatant disregard? You were not there, Anna, when Jennifer walked into

Jerry Fielding's office and handed him a piece of paper, and yes, his reactions at that time echoed your own at the present! Sinking his head, telling her *there's no way Jennifer, you've got to be kidding.* But Jennifer's look is stone cold in the office, telling Jerry that she is not going to play those pieces her mother chose. Jerry had looked over the list again and again, trying to justify it, trying to justify his decision to get involved in this madness in the first place. Unbeknownst to you Anna May, Jerry Fielding had taken the deepest breath of his natural life, and conceded to watch her fall to Earth like a shooting star.

Listen, Anna, to the question of her virtuosity answered, by Mozart's Sonata in B Major, K. 281, by the whirlwind 1st movement *alone*, and its flashes of lightning in the rain! And now, the calming breeze, the hush over every inquisitive mind; yes, Anna, it is the dreadful Opus 28, the Prelude No. 7 from Chopin, the purest glimpse into Christ's composition ever born! *She'll be laughed off the stage* is the voice that plagues your mind now, Anna, while you wait for them to get up and start walking out one by one. But who can stop gazing at a car wreck—at the bloody bodies lying in the street with blankets over their faces? Who can stop watching the oncoming twister, as it lifts a house nearby, turning it into a floating mass of bricks? Is this why they do not walk out on the Waltz No. 7 in C sharp minor, from Opus 64? Is it the beauty of the Waltz No. 11 in G flat from Opus 70 that holds them captive? No. It is the end-of-the-world audacity, the end of the age boldness they see displayed, as Jennifer May plays these simple, beautiful pieces with such authority, such ease of command as they have never witnessed in person, and can hardly remember from the old records, the cassette tapes, the compact discs or the computer! Is this a joke? High School Recital, redux? But maybe, it is a joke less funny, when Book Nine of Rossini's *Sins of Old Age* opens up, and the phantasmal *La Savoie aimante* drifts out like a ghost from 1868, presuming to aspire to Beethoven and Chopin in depth of feeling, and to Mozart in pure musical expression! Listen to the A Major Sonata K. 331, which begins at the second movement in slow, impossible minuet time! It proclaims the coming of the *Rondo Alla Turca* which, unbelievably, actually comes out of Jennifer's piano, but played as though the piano were a living thing with a voice. Just as a bird sits in a tree and chirps a message unknown, so too does the Turkish Rondo, this third movement from the same sonata in A, as though Jennifer's hands and technique were guided by a Schubertian spirit. Drawing harmonies from the keys that lend color and voice to this monumentally overplayed piece, so the affect is as if hearing it for the first time, not just with the mind, but the spirit as well. These are the Spirits of Jubilee. Of the origins of music itself—from the first notes composed and plucked on a string, to those on a string orchestra on the eve of the Second Coming. Surely enough, Anna knows it is the end of the world, when she hears another *Péchés de vieillesse* bang to life, the essence of Rossini from the *Sins of Old Age*, drifting across the hall in operatic authority to the Anna May mind. On this, your devastation is complete, my Dear Anna, when you hear the tragic conclusion to what you believe is the worst audition in music history, the most blatant and disrespectful, blasphemous and defiant display of your daughter's whole miserable life, all come together like a string of bullets and night tracers flashing from a stationary machine gun at you, killing you with Rossini's Trifle No. 12 from Book Twelve, the *Siberian Dance,* amidst the intermittent flashes of lightning here in the clouds of rumor, and the words in your mind—*nobody can blaze a finale on the piano like Jennifer May.*

Anna closes her eyes to the enthusiastic applause scattered below, hearing, *feeling* the bravo voice of Jerry Fielding pierce her heart like a sword.

Letter

Dear Jennifer,

 "We are pleased to inform you that despite the unusual circumstances of your application, we gladly welcome you to [this year's] sophomore class at the Juilliard School of Music. Everyone here agrees that you gave one of the most unique and special auditions we've ever witnessed. Your natural ability is nothing short of extraordinary. We look forward to adding your unique talents to our student body this fall. Enjoy the rest of your summer and we will hopefully see you soon."

     Sincerely,
     Jerry Fielding

Beethoven

*M*oonlight drifts though the early morning house in sound, from somewhere far below, through the walls of her upper room. Anna May arises from the most troubled sleep of her life, glancing in the summer morning darkness at her Lady Lover, so sound and fast asleep at her side. Does anyone know that she has slept in this room every night in the month she has been here? Of this, Anna does not know. She only knows of the sounds her daughter makes upon the intrepid keys of life, the keys of who they have been, and of who they will forever be. For what purpose, what reason does she play the ghostly music now, except to drive home the point that she is her own woman now, and that the years of struggle and sacrifice, the years of training, the years of nails scratched across the back of Anna's own soul mean nothing to her. As Anna drapes the silken robe over her naked curves, she listens to the solemn chords of defiance, drifting as the sound of moonlight from below.

On this journey through the night, Anna is unaware of the forces that guide her each fateful step, those that guide her down the detour of her chosen path. This was the path of reconciliation, to admit a gracious defeat to her daughter, to tell her gladly that her job is done, to welcome her with open arms—away from a dark and dreary past, to a future of hope and light. To listen to her daughter's inspired Moonlight Sonata, a playing born of the Spirit, so that it is uniquely good, conjuring every mournful and depressive mood without effort, until it seems as though one may lift from the floor, and drift though the walls into the night.

Anna is pulled from this path of reconciliation, this path of redemption and renewal, to walk the road less traveled, the road to rage and revenge. With resignation, in the calm of uneasy acceptance, Anna goes to the bottom drawer of her lover's mirror dresser, and slides open the place where these Grapes of Wrath are stored. From underneath the silken fabrics, she pulls a pair of small, tight black underwear, sliding them on underneath her robe, but wearing no bra over a bosom in D Major. Still pulled along this detour, this alternate path, she pulls the razor sharpened kitchen knife hidden away under the silken fabrics, then stands slowly upright, sliding the cold blade into the side of the black underwear like a hungry Amazon Warrior.

Anna glides through the pre-dawn darkness, as if drawn unawares, as though these steps are taken of their own accord, in powerlessness to deny their intent. She stands at the top of the stairs, watching her daughter play, feeling the unique sounds drift into the world, knowing that perhaps she is the private witness, the lone observer to this phenomenon, one of the greatest performances of this sonata ever played, as though an angel were dispatched to this piano, to draw sounds from it in grieving to hear. On the chords of this *adagio sostenuto,* on this sustained grief and melancholy, she takes each step in slow defeat, knowing that she must eventually be seen, but that this movement cannot be disturbed.

On the closing chords of her daughter's grieving, Anna steps into the space of the *allegretto,* the Call of False Hope, the Hope of Redemption, to a generation beyond repentance. Jennifer does not look away from the piano, except to close her eyes once, refusing to look at the woman who drifts to her as a spirit, as the woman who gave her life, and took it from her so abundantly. Eyes still closed, on the keys of false hope, she feels her mother behind her, but does not see her robe slip to the floor, nor does she see her topless, in black underwear, her blade sheathed in the cloth like a jungle warrior princess.

She does not see the glorious shape of her mother's figure, the small waist curved outward to the extraordinarily widened hips, reminiscent of the Nova Curve, which flares excitement and desire in the hearts of women and men. Jennifer is only aware of the firm left hand gripped on her forehead, as she is so accustomed, reminding her to play with power and precision. When the second movement ends, Jennifer hears *take off your clothes,* causing her to look back at the woman, but only in the periphery. Obediently, she removes her white tee shirt and white sweats, leaving her white underwear in place. *There is no finale to this performance,* the mother says. *Play the first and second movement again.* And Jennifer does this, with greater feeling than before, as though perfection were infused with pain. This, channeled by the hand she feels on her forehead again, and the naked breasts pressed against her back.

She closes her eyes, resigned, pledged not to witness a single key not pressed, but only to feel the energy flow from her mother's hand through her mind, from her mother's breasts through her heart, through her arms down into the piano, to glow this piano with blue and black fire once again. This sustained melancholy ends, and her fingers find the Hope of Redemption on their own, and suddenly she feels a sharp, cold pain flash from one side of her neck to the other! She opens her eyes, in time to see a flood of red pour down from the screaming pain at her neck down to her breasts. Jennifer's hands lift from the keys of false hope on their own. And she grabs at the blood soaked wound at her neck, trying to speak, but being unable. *Play!* her mother says, grabbing both of Jennifer's bloody hands and slamming them to the keys, pressing her weight forward onto her daughter, feeling her struggle, hearing the hopeless gurgling amidst the smell of blood and fear, set to a clamor of cacophonous chords from the piano, as her daughter paints the keys with her own blood in desperation. Not playing them, but grabbing at them, pushing at them, trying to grab hold of the drowning water, to keep from sinking to a watery grave. But in this ocean, in this Sea of Lost Hope, there is a pulling at her bare feet; the hand of Misery itself, which seeks to grab hold of every soul in its vicinity, and whirl it down into nothingness, where there is only outer darkness and despair. This despair lays atop her daughter's back, keeping her hands at the keys, feeling the life drain from her daughter's body in blood, their scene illuminated by the glow of soft lighting in the room. Anna leans heavily onto her daughter's body, her hands clamped hard to her daughter's wrists, her daughter's head down on the keys.

The blood has ceased to pour, now only spilling slowly from the neck wound, spreading over at least a fourth of the white keys on its journey to the bottom of the piano, then dripping into a puddle on the hardwood floor. The mother lays there. Aware of what must happen to her body, wondering if she will exclaim to God. But she breathes and tenses, readying herself as the feeling travels from her breasts to the center of her body, and she holds on to her daughter's wrists right as the wave jerks her entire body once, hazing her vision, then jerking her body three times more. Through a powerful effort, she holds her voice to mere grunting; a deep, animal grunt done but twice, the rest of the scream energy pushed outward in breathing. She lays there, on top of her daughter's dying life, absorbing the Sorrow of the Ages. Feeling the Pain of Death. Already, the cold, lifelessness raises her up, and she removes the warrior cloth from herself, until there is only her flesh exposed, her buttocks in the open for every judging and condemning spirit to see. From the pocket of her blue silken robe crumpled to the floor, she lifts the vial of poison, yes, that intrepid poison, kept with her as a loving companion for over a year now, as the key to open the Northern Gate, when she must journey into the second heaven. And what of God and Christ she knows, she asks their forgiveness for her life, and she swallows the liquid in a thirst unknown, as a desert maiden lost in the heat, kneeling at the oasis fountain in her last delusion. She closes the vial, dropping it nearby where the bloody knife fell loudly to the hardwood floor. Then she walks back to where her daughter lies cold upon the keys, and takes hold of her daughter's wrists again. Positioning herself over her daughter's back with her arms stretched out, holding her daughter's wrists, her legs drawn tightly together.

Anna May lays there. Over her daughter's back. Aware that her daughter's spirit is forever gone. Lamenting the rise of evil in her life, and the look of terror in her daughter's eyes as she died, wondering where it is that her beloved mother could have gone.

Jonathan Lovejoy

Book Eight

Jonathan Lovejoy

schatology

I saw a mother and daughter dipped in blood
On the eve of Eschatology
Two hearts and souls dragged through the mud—
Enslaved by their piano key

The fires of rage and sorrow combine
Both mother and daughter just the same
Lavender souls on the Winds of Time—
Tormented in this purple flame

Jenny May

As it was in days before the Flood
Upon the modern piano key
I saw a mother and daughter dipped in blood—
On the eve of Eschatology

*G*hosts

*I*n the Heart of Memory, I can still hear the way my grandmother's voice came out of her, when she called my mother's name. In the wake of this tragedy, in the rising wind and rain of their departure, we stand helpless at their graves, hardly able to process that the beautiful bodies in these coffins will soon be below ground, and will lie corrupted, returning to the dust from whence they came. While Mother and I stand stubbornly at the gravesite, drawing strength reluctantly from one another in this storm, it is the sound of Grandmother's voice that still permeates my spirit, from the day we were touched by the end of the age.

I can see Denise rising up from the night's slumber, determined to quench this thirst with apple juice, a drink she has hardly given a second thought to, but knowing it is the Juilliard girl's favorite drink; what a privilege it will be to have at least this small part of the Jennifer May dynamic as a part of her! The Juilliard School of Music, Denise says in her mind, walking past my mother's locked room, wondering if Anna May is inside. *When are they going to stop trying to hide it*, she thinks, dying of a sudden thirst for apple juice like what she has never had before. But when she gets to the top of the stairs, in the fading daytime dark of morning, she sees something at the piano that surely was not meant for her eyes, with a naked and full hipped Anna leaning over her naked daughter's back at the piano. Oh, but Grandmother Denise, why can you not turn and walk away! Is it because they are so lifeless and still? Is it because you have caught a glimpse of the unnaturalness of their position? Or is it because you can clearly see on the floor by the piano seat, on the floor by Anna's feet, a puddle of black liquid spilled from somewhere?

You clear your throat once, then once again louder, wondering what perverted Mother-Daughter meditation this is you have stumbled onto. Hoping that is what it is. *Jennifer?* you say. *Anna?* Knowing that this unique sight in world history will now become a part of you, and must be burned inside you forever. You take the stairs in your morning thirst, wrapped in your morning robe, still craving apple juice from you know not where, as you descend the stairs in fear and bewilderment. You approach the back of the piano slowly, away from the keys, as if you still refuse to believe what you see. But the truth of the matter is this, Grandmother— reality cannot be denied. And the reality of what you see on the floor is *blood*, and what you see on the blood stained piano keys is death.

Denise walks around to the other side, where she can see clearly what will haunt her dreams forever. Jennifer is bent over and laying her head on the piano keys, her head turned to the side, the front of her naked body covered in blood, her arms stretched out wide towards both ends of the keyboard. Laid on top of her, over her back is Anna May, naked, her hands gripped tightly around Jennifer's wrists, as if holding the girl's hands to the piano keys. Their eyes are open. And it is this revelation—that these open eyes do not see, that they are as lifeless as doll's eyes that stare—this revelation pulls my mother's name from your lips in a voice that is low, almost whispery, causing you to run away from the piano back to the stairs, stumbling upward on them as if the two women have suddenly come to life. They are part of the Zombie Apocalypse you've heart tell about as you run, feeling icy fingers clawing at your neck and ankles. Somehow, you make it to the upstairs hall of this fine, grand palace mansion, running clumsily, heavy stepped down the uncarpeted hall to the door of your daughter's room, trying to open the locked door, but being unable. And then you knock, Grandmother, calling your daughter's name once, which is surely inadequate, you hear; so you allow your mind to see their dead eyes again, and you feel their cold fingers' icy touch at your throat, and you hear their husky voices in your ear. Then you slam on the door like a madwoman, and you call the name *Elizabeth* to Heaven and Earth, so that every wall and windowpane reverberates with the fear and the sound of it.

On my own now, the only straggler left at the rainy prestige funeral, I'm glad for my mother's intolerance and impatience with these proceedings, her *'get in and get out'* mentality displayed. Their coffins are closed now, but I can remember the beautiful white Asian silk they wore, giving them both such an angelic appearance as they laid asleep in their coffins. This tranquil funeral scene, with every requisite eulogy and grief testimony, bore such stark contrast to what I saw of them in the mansion. In the heavy, windblown rainfall, under skies that crackle with harsh lightning, I stand under the tent shelter at the burial site, alone with the sight of their coffins, still imprisoned by the Heart of Memory. It is where I still hear my grandmother screaming my mother's name as if she were on fire. Mother opens her bedroom door, a second after I open mine, scowling pure puzzlement and caustic confusion at Denise, even grabbing her and saying *Denise what's the matter*, shaking her on the word 'matter.'

The pian... is all that mother hears her say.

What?

The piano! wails out of Denise now, as I see mother walk frustratedly past her down the hall towards the big living room. I see Mother stop at the top of the stairs, turning to look at Denise, who can only shake her head without a word. Mother hurries down the stairs, but must walk slowly through the haze of shock and disbelief, as she sees her naked lover sprawled dead on top of her daughter at the piano, with the keys underneath them stained red and black with blood.

From the staircase, so monumentally busty in my gray sports bra, I watch the priss, prim and proper take a beating, where dignity must step back and flee—and my mother says "*God please no*" so loudly. Then "Oh no," covering her mouth as she walks behind the scene, until she sees their faces. Their dead eyes look at her, gazing into her soul, to strike a spark of icy fear, and mother let out a siren that starts low and finishes high, unsuppressed by the effort, sprung forth from inside her as if by magic. It is the scream we all feel, so representative of the scene, as she is held prisoner by their dead eyes, with a look of horror on her expression. In the Heart of Memory, I see Mother stumble away from the piano back towards the stairs, climbing them past me, holding her hand over her mouth, the horror still in her eyes. Denise follows, taking my hand saying *Alice please don't look. I beg you, please come back.* But how does one coax the Moon away from its next phase! How does one coax a hungry dog away from a meal? How does one coax a prisoner away from dreams of freedom! Except with God, these things are impossible. As it is with my grandmother's feeble attempt to pull me away from this scene. *I can't look anymore,* she says in defeat, going up the stairs to hide in her room—to hide from the truth, as if that could make it go away. *This is not going away,* I hear my mind say, as I take the first step downward, unable to take my eyes off the naked woman at the piano.

We are all travelers along the River of Time. Powerless as we drift from place to place, either in hope or fear, watching each fateful scene drift towards us, with no power to turn either this way or that, but having to go where the current of predestination arrives; then to disembark by Divine decree—into a scene of joy and prosperity, or to a scene of fear and devastation. The scene drifts towards me, as I am pulled on the current of fear. But as in a dream, I take these slow motion steps to where the mother and daughter lay sprawled at the piano, but sprawled with purpose, as if placed and positioned by an unseen hand. This hand hath disrobed them to nudity, to expose their secret shame for the world to see, and I know that it is not for me to touch them. I take my fateful steps, in the curse bestowed upon me at birth, moving slowly past the back of the mother, who is leaned almost straight legged over the back of her daughter. The mother's arms are out as far as they can go, giving her the classic silhouette of a cross. And I continue my drifting walk, disembarked from the River of Time, moving slowly around their scene of bloody Redemption, amazed at the browning blood painted on the keys. And I am moved around to where their faces are displayed in tranquility, expressions peaceful in reconciliation, in their special and unique resolution, as they prepare to proclaim the modern mother-daughter dynamic, and what churns beneath cultured civility.

I am unable to move, unable to look away, unable to run from what I am charged to see, as the Spirit of Fear leaps into my body and cause me to tremble, while I study the tranquility in their lifeless eyes, and the redemption on their peaceful expressions. And I am struck again in my soul, as if a part of my spirit is cut away and vanished, feeling it leave my body and drift away, on its journey toward the second heaven. Past the Moon and the stars, faster until every galaxy flies by at a speed unknown, and sights that no man can know; the fullness of what declares the glory of God, whose echo we strain to see in the fall of summer's night. As their spirits have departed from me, leaving me spent and alone, I am turned away from their bloody, tranquil scene, around the back of this baby grand piano, away from the Ghosts of May, apart from the demons who will roam the world in their guise. Moving slowly again, I am called away from the Valley of the Shadow of Death, away from the Valley of Fear, to find my way back to the River. Upon the River of Time, I am again a weary traveler, drawn away from this fearful scene by the current of Fate, to another place along the timeline, to another private time in history.

A swirling wind pulls me from the Heart of Memory, where I can see the two coffins bedecked in flowers, and the black and white photos, one each of the beautiful Asian mother and daughter. Turning away from their peaceful scene, I drift through the hard wind and cold summer rain, toward the black luxury car parked on the asphalt cemetery road, where the grandmother and the mother wait patiently inside.

Death

We disembark our rainy, windy chariot, the three of us, making the short, hurried walk through the downpour to the sheltered entrance, then into our fine and fancy home. One of the disadvantages built into this seven figure home is the conspicuous absence of a front garage, which would make things so much easier. (Where is the garage, for God's sake?) I must admit that even in the rain, I couldn't care less.

The hardwood floors echo our discontent as we walk to the stairs, climbing them apprehensively, as though we have not done so a thousand times before. But rounding the corner to the upper room, I am suddenly struck by the need to enter the serpent's lair, and confront it for being what it is, even while the green, serpentine eyes will glow at me from the dark.

"Aunt Denise, can you give us a few minutes? Mother and I need to talk."

"Sure, Honey," she says, hugging us both, kissing us both on the jaw and walking down the uncarpeted hall toward her room. We stand here in the hall, my mother and me, not avoiding the quiet stare-down, set to the music of matriarchal footsteps echoing down the corridor. The opening of the Denise door, the closing of it, ends this concerto's smooth and melancholy opening, whereby now the cello and the violin must play. Statuesque, fully dressed in black, mother opens the door to her bedroom and drifts through, while I follow her boldly inside, closing the door again behind me. I walk slowly through the beautiful room, gazing at the exquisite décor, from the lamps to the chandelier to the bedposts and canopy.

"The world never got a chance to hear," I say.

"What?"

"Her brilliance. The laughter and pain she played that piano with."

Mother turns away silently, walking over to the mirror, taking the pins out of her pinned up black hair. Her hair shines like a raven's feathers in the sun when it falls over her shoulders, grown to halfway down the length of her back.

"Her audition was on fire, wasn't it?"

"I suppose," Mother says, brushing her hair. "I thought it was beautiful, but the truth is, her mother hated it."

"She did?"

"She called it a circus audition. It wasn't the program they had worked out."

"Circus audition," I say. "Well, Juilliard thought different."

"No. *Jerry Fielding* thought different."

"Well, it wouldn't have happened at all, if it hadn't been for you."

"You know me," Mother says, still brushing her long, black, shiny hair. "No matter what you know, it's still *who* you know that counts."

"Did you notice Jennifer's father? He seemed more inconvenienced by the whole thing more than anything else. Where the heck was his grief— your wife and daughter just died, for God's sake."

"We all grieve in our own way," Mother says. "I understand that you and Jennifer were close. It's going to hurt for a long time."

"Sometimes, I think they died because of us. Because we triggered something that was already inside them."

"The only thing that was inside them was *insanity*," Mother says. "You saw the way they died. Is there anything normal in that?"

"Was there anything normal in Barbados?"

Fleck shards of phantom glass appear. Shattered and whirled dangerously around us. Mother stops brushing her hair, placing the classic wooden brush onto the ivory colored dresser.

"So you know about that. About her mother's harsh discipline."

"I know about her mother's perversion."

"What you call perversion, Anna called punishment, precision and perfection."

"Oh yeah? What do you call paddling a bloody bruise onto somebody else's daughter's body?"

"I call it *discipline,*" Mother says, undoing the buttons at the top of her black dress. Staring at me the whole time she slips it down, stepping out of it. Walking to her room sized closet. "What I did, I did willingly and without remorse. I saw how insolent and disrespectful Jennifer was, I just never said anything. Anna said she wanted, no, she *needed* for Jennifer to remember her punishment so she would never disrespect her again. I'm sorry if you think that had something to do with them dying but frankly, I don't."

"Jennifer told me everything."

There is an icy stare between the two of us. One replete with loneliness. Echoes of pain and suffering. And death.

"So, she told you I helped her mother discipline her. Why are you making such a big deal out of it?" In the closet, I watch Mother pull out her favorite navy dress, then walk past me back to the room, over to the mirror.

"I wonder... sometimes I wonder if we didn't somehow contribute to what they did. Maybe we triggered something that was already there. Don't you think?"

"I told you, they were *insane.*"

"Maybe. And then we pushed them over the edge."

"How, exactly?"

"Like this..."

From somewhere deep within, motion rises up to step me forward, to the beautiful woman in her slip I call my mother. Then I lean forward, kissing her full and sensuously on the mouth. She pulls back as if my lips were burning hot and slaps me with a force I had not thought was possible, a look of genuine shock and disgust on her face.

"What the *Hell* are you doing?'

"Jennifer and I... were lovers."

The disgust drains from Mother's face, replaced by painful realization, to join with the shock that remains.

"Do you know why Jennifer was so good at playing the piano? Because her mother used to beat her when she practiced. Since she was a little girl. And when she was sixteen... her mother raped her."

"Jennifer May was a goddamned *liar!*"

"Oh, you don't want to know how I know."

"Why, because she licked you into believing it? You're right, I *don't* want to know."

Mother turns in her slip, back towards the mirror. Quickly, she slides into her navy dress, to conceal the slip over her tiny rose bosom. In the mirror, a tall blonde in a black dress drifts up behind her.

"When I first met Jennifer's mother, she pressed me up against the kitchen counter and pushed her breasts against mine. A few days later, when Jennifer was at the mall, her mother raped me to."

"I will *not* stand here and listen to these lies."

"I swear I'm not lying. I swear to *God.*"

My voice chokes on the power of *"God,"* and a stream of tears pours free when I blink.

"What do you mean, she *raped* you? How can a woman rape another woman, Alice?"

"She was wearing a strap-on under her dress."

The words continue in choking, until both my eyes are red and tearing. Mother is unable to hide her new shock, covering her mouth and looking at me through frustrated eyes of defeat.

"If you're telling me the truth, then why didn't you just push her away? You're stronger than she is. Why didn't you just put a stop to it?"

"I *tried…*"

"Then you should have tried *harder!*"

"I *couldn't!* She had so much power and control over me I felt *paralyzed!* I had to do what she said! Mom, her daughter was my best friend. They were millionaires. She was married to an investment broker. Jennifer told me that her mom was a TV reporter. She had complete and total control over me. You met her, Mom, you *know* what I'm talking about!"

Mother looks down and away from me, gazing into the Heart of Memory, to the first time Anna May put her lovely mouth to her nipple.

"And I tell you something else she did too…"

"Stop. I can't listen."

"She had Jennifer and me both in her room. She made both of us take our clothes off—"

"*No!*"

She screams it with deep conviction, a rage born from within. But what is there left for me to fear? A beating?

"What happened in Barbados? Why'd you do it?"

"Shut your mouth."

"Why did you do it?"

"I said *shut up!*"

Suddenly, it's as if I'm seeing her for the first time. As if the woman who raised me is a stranger.

"Those people you love to impress with your money and your good works. Dinner parties and fireworks. Oh, *God* if they only knew."

Suddenly, my breath is taken by a strong hand to my throat, and another wrapped tightly into my blonde locks of hair. The look in her eyes is the same vacant, merciless stare I have seen before.

"Say one more word," she says. Her hand is so tight over my throat that the word "*Barbados*" can barely come out. But it does.

And I am resigned to the beating I receive. Slapping me over and over again, forward and backhanded, even knocking me off my feet to her bed, where she climbs on top of me with a strength unbelievable, holding me down by the neck and literally *punching* me in the face. I have never been in a fight in my life, and there is a part of me that is exhilarated, but held in check by an underlying fear and respect for this woman. I cannot bring myself to fight back, though I am tempted, imagining my own hands around her throat as well. Perhaps we are grief and rage. The two of us. Burning in the same lavender flame as the ones who went before us. I am plunged into the Sorrow of the Ages, because one whom I loved, and who loved me as well, was taken from me so violently—so permanently. And perhaps the rage my mother feels, as she drags me to my feet—perhaps it is the humiliation, a great wave of shame, caused by the sudden and tragic death of her partner in crime, her sexual soul mate—the woman she had imagined and lusted for 20 years, finally having phased in from the spirit world, to tease her with an unfulfilled promise of perpetual perversion, then phasing back into the gray world from whence she came. Maybe that is the rage that causes her to drag me upright from the bedroom by the neck, my eye cut and bleeding, my nose too bleeding but not broken, escorting me down the hall where I reluctantly walk, having no choice but to go with her or fight. To fight physically, this, I cannot do. Somewhere in the haze of it all, I hear my grandmother's voice of pleading, pulling my mother's hand away from my throat, so that Mother turns her rage at her own mother, grabbing her by the hair and slamming her head against the wall, making her mother fall to the floor in unwilling and lightheaded repose, unaware of her bleeding forehead while she lays nearly unconscious. *"Mom, please"* has the audacity to escape my swollen lip, and she hits me in the face with her closed fist and knocks me stumbling to stay on my feet. The tall, strong brunette grabs my neck and my blonde hair and ushers me harshly to the top of the stairs, where I imagine I will soon go tumbling from. *Walk these stairs,* she says. *Walk these stairs with me or I swear to God and Jesus I'll throw you down.* And because I cannot fight, I must submit to the humiliation, and I take the stairs with her in a clumsy hurry, until at last we are at the bottom. Will I be taken to the kitchen and burned? Will I be stabbed? These are what the Ghosts of May wait in lonely anticipation for, watching me be walked by my throat across the hardwood floor, where I am soon spun around toward the Death's Head Piano, it shall be named, as she slams my face onto the keyboard with all her might, causing me to see a purple flash of light, then I feel myself falling towards the keys again at an alarming rate, slammed into them again by Rage itself. It does not matter to me, if I slip and fall from life. Perhaps that is why I antagonized this lady grizzly in the first place, hoping I might possibly be beaten to death. Whether or not life slips away, I do not care, as I fall to the floor beside the Death's Head Piano, hearing the demonic chords still echoing in my ears, as I imagine that now I can leave this horrible woman behind, and fly to where it is that my beloved could have gone.

Shakespeare

"A local tragedy leaves a community in Watauga County stunned this evening. Brenda Johnson from NBC news reports:

> [Reporter:] *"Shock and disbelief might best describe what the residents of this small town community feel this afternoon, after a local teacher was shot and killed in her classroom today by her husband, who then turned the gun on himself."*

"She was the best teacher in the school," [a student says]. "She was everybody's favorite. She knew how to make it fun so we wanted to learn."

"I actually liked her English class, [another student says]. *She had a unique way of teaching us Shakespeare—she let us read modern translations and helped us understand everything about the plot and characters even before we read the play. And then she would let us act out some of the scenes in class. So it made the experience of reading the play so much better, because we actually knew what Shakespeare was talking about. She was Teacher of the Year for a reason last year—I mean, she really cared whether we learned the stuff she taught us. And they say the average test score in all her classes was the highest in the whole school, which was really cool, I guess. So, I just can't believe this happened here. I'm just glad nobody else was hurt."*

[Reporter:] *"Students say that it was during their 10'oclock English class this morning when suddenly the door opened and in walked a man in his fifties, wearing a brown leather jacket and carrying what was described as a 'large present.' But when he opened the white box adorned with a red ribbon, what was inside turned out to be a most deadly gift:"*

"All I can think about was the scene in Terminator 2," [a third student says], *"when the terminator took the sawed off shotgun out of the flower box. That's kind of what it looked like. The box had beautiful red and pink roses inside, and he pulled the gun from underneath. I mean, we thought at first it was a surprise like a hunting gift or something, then he aimed the gun and yelled "Jenny May!" and he shot her in the head."*

[Reporter:] *"The prevailing question is 'Why,' says the Watauga Senior High School principal. 'How could such a loving and dedicated teacher and member of our community meet with such a horrible tragedy?*

"For the rest of my life I'll wonder [the principal says], *how it is that such tragedies can happen, and how anybody could want to*

do harm to such a kind and sweet woman as Angel Simms."

[Reporter] *"But the story doesn't quite end here. True, the prevailing question is 'why?' But the answer could lie in the pages of a journal found on the passenger's seat of the husband's car, indicating that the teacher had been having an affair."*

[Police officer] *"All of the students concur that the gunman yelled 'Jenny May' before he shot the teacher. The journal chronicles the end of what we've learned was a twenty year relationship the teacher was having with a younger woman, whose name we simply cannot release to the public at this time. The teacher, Ms. Simms, was fifty seven years old, and this woman is 39 years old, which means that the alleged affair began when the woman was nineteen. The journal chronicles 20 years of an ongoing, physically and sexually abusive relationship between Angel Simms and the young woman, who for now we'll just call 'Jenny May.'"*

[Reporter:] *"Although the Sheriff's department did refuse to release the name, our conversation with the murdered teacher's family revealed that the young woman in her journal is named Jennifer Maybelline Breen, who lives in this isolated cabin, high in the Appalachian Mountains of Western North Carolina. The cabin is located miles down this dirt road, deep inside the Appalachian Forest. A place that was hidden until today, lost somewhere in time, but is now suddenly, and tragically, revealed to the modern world. Brenda Johnson, reporting for NBC news, in Watauga County, North Carolina."*

Maybelline

This is one of the out of the way places. Lonely. Bleak. Desolate. Lost on the fringes of the modern world. Hidden in the shadows of the end time. Divided from civilization by a curtain of darkness, a shadow cast by a canopy of pine needles, evergreen and ever changing forest leaves, thick enough to block out the sun, or to hide the face of the rising Moon. A place where access is a single dirt road to nowhere, that stretches from the Appalachian highway to another world. A place lost deep in the annals of time, on the dusty pages of unwritten history.

This is the woman who lives in the house. Beautiful. Naïve. Kind hearted. A woman of great faith in God and little faith in mankind, whose only concern up 'til now has been how to survive, and how to cope with days and nights of neverending loneliness. Now, her concern is paradise lost. A tragic interruption to idyllic days of peace and seclusion. Newspaper men and women. Magazine reporters. The occasional television reporter with lights and camera. All quietly refused or kindly turned away. Weeks of soft, inoffensive refusals of questions and company, until the modern rush has come and gone. Until the mountain ghosts return to haunt her cabin in the twilight, in the clearing by the Appalachian Mountain Wood.

In the mansion below the Appalachian Wood, overlooking the Great Lawn, Denise Hayes thinks of the news report. Jennifer Maybelline Breen, her granddaughter, and words that have to be spoken. Words long, and far away overdue. She braves the burden in her spirit, in the cold rains of November, under the hidden face of the Forest Moon. Underneath daytime clouds of grieving, the second local murder suicide of the last few months cannot be denied, as Denise is suddenly a prisoner of what she knows, by the cabin in the Appalachian Wood.

In the Theater of her mind, she rides the highway with Calbert Simms, the husband of Angel Simms, as he drives the road in the evening day, hiding in a rental truck, a truck unfamiliar, following his wife, to see where it is she goes so often in the Watauga County twilight. Denise is pulled along this road, unwillingly, feeling desperation drive onward, to search for unwanted answers forthcoming, unwanted truth uncovered, unwanted revelations revealed. She sees the teacher's husband drive onward, following pale, metallic blue consumption in Hyundai Sonata form. The Sonata turns onto the inconspicuous dirt road, at least a half mile away, a half mile up the road less traveled. The teacher's husband is not relieved, believing that many years have passed since she has seen Jennifer Maybelline Breen, after the mother, Alice Jean Breen had died. *Why didn't she tell me she was still coming here? How many years? How long?*

He glides a smooth and disquieted turn onto the twilight road, lights unlit as they should be, wondering how it is that houses were ever built anywhere near this chasm of nothing, this world of pure twilight silhouette. Denise Hayes bounces and rocks the old mountain road with the husband of Angel Simms, unable to dismiss the rising of bewilderment, and the rule of apprehension. Riding slow, the spirit of Calbert Simms, drawn by the red Sonata lights so far ahead, as they flash bright in the evening day, in the darkness of a twilight mountain wood. And miles down the dirt road, he sees the shining red Sonata lights turn towards a ghostly silhouette in the early evening dark, the headlights flashing onto the century old wood of a mountain cabin, of a kind heard so much about, but so rarely seen in the modern day. He moves the truck to an off road place, where the trees forever hide him from his wife. Parking. Killing the black truck engine. Sitting still in the world after sunset, not caring at all if she peers down the road in daytime darkness, wondering where the truck is she thought she saw.

In the Theater of Her Mind, by the power of her soul's grieving, Denise Hayes sees the passing of the half hour, until the Calbert Simms sky says color me black, and the pinpoint of every star is visible. In the terrifying dark, in the country mountain blackness, Cal Simms abandons the truck for the dirt road, to wander this road with a destination in mind, this being the destination of Truth, shining from the front window of the cabin in the dark. And what is the sound you hear, Denise Hayes, coming at Cal Simms in the dark? Is it the sound of a woman being tortured, sound of a woman screaming to high heaven in the dark? Are these the sounds that draw Cal Simms from his truck in the first place, born from the end of the half hour come and gone? These are the screams of pain. The screams of defiance laced with despair, lasting but for a moment, before vanishing somewhere into the night. And you see him hesitate, Denise, on the road to revelation, wondering what manner of silence this is, and how long it can possibly be. But Cal waits, at least a quarter mile from the cabin, breathlessly waiting, until he hears the beginnings of another manner of crying out, the unfamiliar voice of a woman in travail, in the torment of the deepest physical pleasures known. This sound, the unmistakable *ooh, ooh, ooh*-ing of a woman's reddest heart unleashed, drawing him closer and closer to the cabin, slowly to the glowing window pain in the dark. And as one of these crescendos rises again, now joined by the grunting sound that is his wife's voice, he peers cautiously, with pinpoint care into the cabin, where the shock of his life is immediately shown—that of two naked woman in motion, one on her back in screaming pleasure, held down by the other on top of her in slow, hard pumping rhythm.

She is the most beautiful woman he has ever seen. The woman on her back, this pigtail braided blonde screaming—no, *yelling* loud enough for all the stars to hear, as she suffers the super heightened feeling, the lightning flashes of one forced orgasm after another. His hand over his mouth, unable to believe his eyes, he watches his wife raise up and begin another session of hard, tireless pumping by missionary while she looks down upon the two largest breasts he has ever seen or imagined, rocking back and forth like bags of water, flopping to the beautiful woman's chin and down to her flat stomach and back again. Cal Simms sees his wife's lustful daze, a gaze burning through a haze of spirit lust, each rocking of the younger woman's breasts bringing her closer to her own truth and devastation. And to his horror, the source of the woman's earlier screams is near and apparent, by the glint of a large safety pin in her right breast, and what must surely be a great trickle of blood. He sees his wife bend her head down to the breast unencumbered with blood, pulling the nipple into her mouth in one mountainous sucking, releasing the breast to its tremendous wobble again. Then, as if on the edge of her endurance, the wife lowers herself again to the younger woman, whose high pitched moaning cannot subside, the wife pinning the younger woman's arms tightly, their breasts mashed greatly together. The wife then continues her rhythm; a slow, hard pumping, her buttocks rising and falling mightily, each pump slamming the beautiful young prisoner closer to a cry for mercy never before gleaned by man. He watches them. Every tragic part of his mind and body made aware, having now eaten of the Tree of the Knowledge of Good and Evil. Of this forbidden fruit, he partakes, watching the young woman writhe and stretch her beautiful face back toward him, seeming to have looked him directly in the eye, causing him to duck down and raise up again, amazed at the loudness of the woman's pleasure screaming in the mountain dark. This final orgasmic scream, truly her third or fourth in the quarter of an hour, activates the rest of the wife mistress mind, causing her to see the cliff she must fall from, going over the edge into the space of her first and greatest orgasm of tonight, and Cal Simms is forced to watch his wife's eyes roll back, and listen to her voice rise a siren to a mountain height, the other side of which is the convulsing of her body and animal grunting, to join the shaking leg and the loud whimpering of the Mountain Girl, the mountain woman underneath her.

In the mansion below the Mountain Wood. In the cold November Rain, Denise is held prisoner. Enraptured to tears by the Theater of Her Mind. Imagining the stumbling, retching Cal Simms, scrambling away from the glow inside the mountain cabin to the dirt road in the dark. Feeling the ground rise up to his face. Stumbling a rumbling, clumsy fall. Lying there in the road on his knees, hearing no screams from inside the ghostly cabin. Standing up, toughing out the spinning of the stars above him. Pledging to not fall again. Walking fast, hurrying. Jogging in the dark, to whatever dark tree he parked the rental truck beside. Catching the glint of wheel metal in the dark. The words 'Jenny May' burning his heart and mind like hellfire as he cranks the truck. Lights blaring now. Rolling away like a living energy in the mountain dark.

Denise is transported now. Forced to speed along the timeline forward. A fortnight passed from the discovery of the mountain girl. Two weeks boiling in lust, burning the acid of betrayal, suffering the memory of his wife's marital chastity, her belief in the corruption of the marital bed, that the best way to stay close to God is through long periods of marital celibacy; having kept him at her beckon call, waiting sometimes three, sometimes six months for her to receive a 'word from the Lord' about the undefilement of their marital bed. Keeping him bathed in lust for the thick buttocks, the feel of himself deep in her rectum, the way his vision hazes as he shakes, brought on by the way she lowers her head and cries out when her anal canal is breached. Living for the passing of the weeks, until he can subjugate her again, in the manner of Sodom and Gomorrah. Two weeks from the revelation of endtime adultery, where all of her sex is pent up and poured out upon another woman in secret; this, for two decades unbeknownst. A score of years in cuckold. In the fool's naiveté. Beaten and ground to nothing by hypocrisy—chewed by it, spit out upon the ground and left for dead. For two weeks, even after the discovery of the journal, and the further revelation of depravity. The revelation of an impending choking, and a burial deep in the Appalachian Woods. The revelation of Death.

In the Heart of Revelation, Denise moves forward along the timeline. To the morning at the Watauga County School. When the English class for the teacher of the year is in session. When the perils of Romeo and Juliet are made known.

"O Brawling love
O loving hate…
O happy dagger!
This is thy sheath.
There rust, and let me die."

Cal Sims steps out of the car in loving stillness, in the easy drawl of motion slowed to a Divine crawl. In the ease of slow motion command, he steps toward the school, walking to the rhythm of a heartbeat poisoned by love, by the betrayal of Love and Devotion, by the drumbeat of a dark destiny, and the marching strings of cruel Fate. And Cal Simms opens the door of the Watauga County High School, believing in the power of Fate over chance, understanding that those who believe in chance do so out of fear, afraid of God's autonomy, of his complete and utter control over the choices of women and men. O dark and cruel mistress Fate, have mercy on a dying life! Do not take the bodies of my living wife and I, to kill us, and bury us in the poverty field!

In the wake of this begging spirit inside, Calbert David Simms walks alone, his feet echoing in the school hallway, already allowed to walk past in the trusting and friendly atmosphere, not yet crossed over into post-Columbine, post Nine Eleven, and post Virginia Tech paranoia. Cal Simms walks the halls of insanity, at the Watauga County High School. Knowing which door holds the key to victory. The knob turns upon this unlocking key. Sliding the door open to young faces. Hopeful faces. Melancholy and happy faces. The faces of youth, still held captive by a sunny outlook, and the possibilities of a bright and sunny future. Like a dark cloud passing overhead, a cloud blocking every last jot and tittle of sunlight, Cal David

Simms glides into the room as a cloud of bewilderment, as a thunderhead conundrum, as the rumbling thunder of wide eyed skepticism and wonder. And as the woman turns from the white chalkboard towards him, he lays the box onto the bookshelf and takes the elongated wood and metal from under the green paper beneath the red flowers fallen to the floor. In the din of silence, interrupted by only a single scream, he turns to the March of Love and Hate, pointing the Winchester at the head of his wife, who is holding the blue marker in her hand, having decorated the white board among the letters written in black. In the wake of a single scream let loose, he yells sharply, in brilliant authority the words *"Jenny May!"* pulling the trigger to his wife's stunned expression, cracking the air as a bolt of lightning from this cloud, causing a splatter of red brains and bone in blood to splatter from the back of his wife's head to the white chalkboard in front of the class. And the white lightning sound is followed by the booming thunder of screaming voices and chairs being pushed and pulled around, every hopeful expression replaced by hopelessness and fear. And in the midst of chaos born and bred, where screams whirl with gunsmoke and blood, the man turns the rifle to himself under the chin, cracking the air in the room again with gunfire, and a splattering of red blood paint on the wall and the ceiling.

In the mansion below the Appalachian Wood. In the Theater of Her Mind. Denise Hayes sees and hears the thunderous screams and endtime chaos in the classroom. Watching the older children succumb to fear. Watching the teacher's blood run down the white board in a group of slow, steady streams.

Jonathan Lovejoy

Book Nine

These are the last days, before the Second Coming. In the Appalachian school, under the drowning November rainfall, I am resigned to this. Hauling my books around again from class to class, drowning in talent without inspiration. Mediocrity, droning from the front of every class, from the hearts and minds of frustration.

Three months already into my sophomore curriculum, I walk the rainy campus of dreams, book bag and umbrella in tow, still grieving the loss of my other half, in mourning along with the Whitaker School of Music. So many of the students that care seem to know I was her friend. I've had many smiles and condolences this semester, all trying to be as genuine as they can, but being totally unable. Word gets around, as only one talkative bird need go chirping in the trees, before his message is spread throughout the entire forest. I think that maybe, the entire school knows what happened at my house. And these many months have been spent dodging the phantom looks and the perceived whispering. But as Luck and Fate would have it, I am only about a month away from finishing this first semester of my sophomore year, and thanks to my mother's ruler and paddle, among the collection of 'B's' is at least one 'A' waiting to be recorded. But there are times that I wonder whether or not I even belong here. And this concern is made more vivid whenever I am unlucky enough to meet Death and Hell in blonde and brunette locks, wearing their Psi Alpha Omega pins. The cruelty they show me—both subtle and blatant—is unfathomable. And they are not ashamed of wearing this cloak; doing things to me that most have only heard of, but never imagined they could ever see.

The memory of them falls as a gentle rain, as I walk to my Abnormal Psychology class today. One of two classes where I have to endure Mary Adonna and Judith Spencer's snickering and evil looks, and sometimes just outright laughter. The first day, when they walked into the small classroom, Mary said *Oh, my God* out loud, then put her hand to her mouth briefly. The vision forms in the rainy mist, where I see Mary and Judith walk into the classroom together and laugh loud enough to embarrass themselves, were they truly capable of doing so. But where I am concerned, they cannot go too far, they believe, and I am a victim of their wrath and hatred for me.

It is the dream of every Lifetime TV viewer. Every sorority B-movie lover. But it seems that every member of Psi Alpha Omega has decided that I am a target, having already lit up at least one chalkboard with the words *"Maybelline Windsor sucks dick!"* and *"Maybelline Windsor licks clit!"* Still walking this cold, rainy path to nowhere, my mind is drawn backwards past the chalkboard, to the first day of the Abnormal Psychology class. When class ends this first day, they wait for me and escort me outside in what was then the heat of August, telling me how sorry they are about my friend and how *"this would have been her year if she were here, because we were going to ask her to join us again. We're sorry if it looks like we were laughing at you, Babe, but we were just so glad to see you back. Especially after what happened to your friend,"* Mary says. *"I'd really gotten to know her,"* Judith says, *"and she seemed really sweet, a lot sweeter than the bitches we're friends with, you can believe it..."*

I walk in the air of their social ingenuity. Trapped by chocolate chip mint smell of fungalooga, which speaks to a lonely soul starved for company. Mary and Judith are suddenly so much less threatening, so much less evil, seeming as though they were sent here to pick me up out of the mud, and walk with me arm in arm to the end of this trek in a desert. I despise school, but maybe now I'll be able to survive my mother's decree, that if I bring home a 'C' on my report card she's going to tie me up and beat me like a dog. So I languish in fear and misery every day, which is where Mary and Judith have found me. *"What time is your last class?"* they say. And I stupidly, gleefully tell them. To set myself up for an invite to the sorority house in the afternoon.

I remember sitting in my last class that day, cursing my stupidity for having gone at all, having to sit there for an hour to listen to the academic whore coo and smile at me about literature I am only going to read because I don't want a beating from my mother at Christmas time. Every minute ticks by like an hour, while I imagine that Mary Adonna and Judith aren't as bad as I thought, and maybe the shock of Jennifer's murder has softened their hearts. This thick necked, misshapen English professor bent over from heels way too high is making me sorrier by the minute that I just didn't skip this four o'clock nonsense and go on over to the Omega sorority house early. So, I pick my pencil up and begin to focus on how many different kinds of flowers I can draw in the margins of my notebook. My eyes have glassed over with *ennui.* I'm already half dead from the swirl of literary names on the syllabus, seeming to remember the name Yeats only because the name is impossible not to contemplate. Did Yeats and Keats meet to eat beets? Probably not, since they died a hundred years apart. Did their ghosts meet, then? I'm sure I'll never know. But I do know there is a chamber in Hell called English Literature 201, and were this not a required class I would run like a scalded dog to get out of here.

But time must eventually move on, and all suffering on this side of the grave must end. This mercy of God descends at the end of the longest 50 minutes of my life, and I hurry past the young phantoms and shadows roaming, taking every step toward the exit door as if in a dream, where the faster it is I walk, the further away it is the exit door moves away. But after this slip backward in time, I am launched forward again to the door, and step out into a future of Hope and Light. On this brief and steady stream of false hope I glide, giddy with optimism, thinking of how pleased my mother will be when she learns of my newfound dedication, my newfound focus and social determination. How do you like me now, Mother? I'm going to finally become an Omega, the most beautiful sorority on campus, I'm told.

On every campus, there is one sorority that seems to cast for what is only skin deep, houses full of mothers and daughters off the printed page, women to love and hate and desire; women whose beauty is in some way or another uniquely compelling—those flocked and gathered together like white doves, to baffle any onlooker as to how it is possible. And yes, as I approach the campus' only brick sorority house; a two story mini mansion complete with black window shutters and immaculately landscaped lawn, I suddenly feel a breath of wind through my spirit, which is the wind of privilege, a sudden complacency about who I am, and what I see when I look in the mirror. Maybelline Windsor, I am. And I may as well begin to own it, with my shoulders a little further back, and my head up a little higher, and my gigantic breasts pushed out a little farther.

I open the door to the sorority house and walk inside. Confident. Smiling. Suddenly unashamed of my blonde braids and big bosom. I notice that the inside is kept as beautifully as the outside, with the expensive vases and sofas and end tables and coffee table, so smartly done in golden oak finish, and not weighted down in dark wood antiquity.

$\mathcal{S}$odom

$\mathcal{A}$s soon as I walk inside, I'm struck by two things. One, the sheer number of pictures on the lovely dark gray walls, which I see everywhere, as though these spirits were inclined to the notion of white walls being too unsophisticated to let in here. Pictures of everybody's mother and sister and sorority sister it seems; women with modern hair going all the way back to the mid 1980's, to when this new sorority was founded. Women whose eyes are bright with ambition, whose teeth are white with lust for life, and whose faces are aggressively committed to appearing happy on the outside, hiding their true emotions underneath public perfection, working to conceal the lust of their flesh, the lust of their eyes, and the all consuming pride of their life. And among the sea of pictures on the wall, walks the occasional source of my second fascination, which is the level of natural beauty I see on the faces on the girls around me.

I'm struck by just how much one of them looks like Jordin Sparks (I think her name is Kerry), sitting on the sofa with a study book in her hand, smiling the biggest pretty smile I think I've ever seen, waving big, pretty fingers at me with boldness and personality. *I think she might be taller than me*, is the message in my head involuntarily, putting her at nearly six feet, as I look away from the big, strong, light skinned beauty, to the face of determined, frustrated lesser beauty at the top of the stairs in exquisitely silken blonde hair, done up long and shiny in a manner worthy of the name Mary Adonna. *Maybelline*, she says with a smile, beckoning with her finger for me to climb the stairs to where she is, which I do unashamed, despite the ridiculous bounce of mine underneath my pink button down shirt.

She waits up there. Watching me burdened under the heavy back pack, too lazy and stupid to take it off, even though the busty effect of the straps on my shoulders is tragicomic at best. A big eyed, bit teethed, big tittied dumb bitch is what am gladly now. Ready to be rescued from loneliness by one who had likely marked me as an enemy, but who has turned the leaf over, and now sees me as a friend.

She smiles and greets me, telling me to take that 'mule pack' off my back. She helps me loosen the strap and slide it off my shoulders, dropping it near the dark gray wall here in the upstairs hall. "*It's so beautiful in here...I just love all these pictures... all the girls here are so pretty... everything feels so perfect in here, I don't know if I can handle it...*"

I so happily turn the corner into her room, the room she has earned by privilege, being a junior now at the Appalachian school. I move dimly into this upper room. A room she has waited for all of her young life. I move forward, my time crossing over into her time, a meeting she has envisioned from days long gone, a meeting she has touched herself to quiet nighttime trembling to; a meeting that must take place, from the moment I saw her outside the registration hall a year ago, to this moment inside the room of the sorority hall, inside the beautiful cage in pretty girl prison.

I step lively in, with confidence, comfortable in my own skin, relishing the weight of what pokes the top of my pink button down shirt so far outward and rounded. And as I begin to ask her of the carefully coifed cougar in the picture on her fine oakwood dresser, I feel the departure of the presence I felt before; the departure of *fungalooga*, the spirit of forced happiness and joy. I turn around in time to see the arrival of sensual wickedness in her face, accompanied by her brunette friend coming through the door behind her. *"Is anything the matter,"* I say, so pathetically, with such heartbreaking hope and naïve helplessness. *"I don't know if you've realized it or not, but... you're in trouble."* And when she says this, the door opens on its own, and in walks the light skinned warrior girl named Kerry, and then another behind her, the least pretty among them, but with the greatest look of sadistic satisfaction in her eyes. A girl so ironically Asian, but with an iciness about her dark, slightly unfocused eyes, and a hidden toughness about her lovely expression.

"That's a pretty pink shirt," Mary says. A calm voice of Truth and Reason. *"Why don't you take it off?"*

The types of fear are many, and uniquely distinguished. Among these— is the Fear of Rape. It is the fear I have not known before, though what Anna Lin May did to me could likely be called rape; it was of a kind that comes with the unwilling consent every woman recognizes, but knows she dare not speak of it, lest she be made a fool of. And when this violence is done by another woman, the act is under lock and key—a self imposed exile that is deeply permanent, as if no crime hath been committed, and no violation of human rights was done. What Anna May did to me was rape, yes, but what weak *"no's"* and *"please's"* there were could hardly stand up as genuine refusals, as I was psychologically powerless when she slid the strap on member up inside me. And that selfsame spirit of dominance, that same spirit of violation I feel now, multiplied by four, behind the locked doors of this sorority house upper room.

"I'm just gonna go," I say, trying so pitifully to walk past them, but quickly realizing that I am unable, and that even the rage that lives deep inside me is not powerful enough to save me.

"Take your shirt *off*," Mary says, "or we'll gladly do it for you."

"Please let me go," I say, my fear coming out through my brow wrinkled expression. "Please."

This last please enrages the twenty year old girl, who comes at my shirt with both hands, tearing at it with a vengeance, the other three watching in shock tingled with gleeful enjoyment, Judith covering her own mouth with both hands, watching her expose my gigantic white bra in the ripping of the top two buttons, and the slight tearing of the pink fabric from my shoulder. I try to push her away, which is impossible without fighting, which I am sorely afraid to do. She stops trying to tear the rest of the shirt off me, and they all stand around and stare in amazement at what they see, and what they have been privileged enough to see. "Take it off," she says, breathlessly. And as I undo the last button or two, I can already feel the rising reservoir of sorrow at my eyes, making me afraid to blink, lest the tears betray the pain and fear in my heart and soul.

When the shirt is off my shoulders, brunette Judith attacks by pure instinct, and pulls the shirt down my arms and flings it away, staring at me with her big, Egyptian eyes as though I had killed someone she loved.

"Put your arms down," Mary says, which I find it impossible to do. *"Put your fucking arms down to your sides!"* she says, spitting the hitting words, on the rhythm of hard blows to my arms. Smacking them with the palm of her hand as hard as she can, until I have little choice but to submit, having already blinked unbeknownst—causing the tears to run down my face in tragedy. The pain of betrayal is epic. It is as vast as the ocean on the edge of a hurricane, as terrifying as the crashing waves of a stormy sea, as the roaring of the thrashing, sounding sea. Suddenly, from nowhere, the tall, lightskinned girl grabs me by the neck from behind, as if she were an experienced, arresting police woman, then the Asian doll (named Melinda) and the brunette Judith attack me with punches that I can't block, my arms flailing to handle the choking from behind, the pain in my stomach from the punches coursing through my bowels to my back, one punch causing me to make a sickening grunt from the impact. By fear and instinct I begin to try to fight, finally, but the strong girl drops to my legs, wrapping her arms around them, while the other two girls tackle me easily, making me crash in a heap to the carpet, big cleavage pushed up over the white bra, while I am pounded in the arms and face and stomach, while the big girl holds my legs and feet immobile.

The two girls try hard to move my hands from my face, but cannot. Until the big girl moves up and helps grab one of my arms. My face is exposed, and I endure at least four hard punches to my exposed face before I am able to block them again. But what power of God's mercy holds my arm to my face now, so that the skin of it is not cut like a boxer in the ring? *"Hold the bitch down,"* Mary says, which they do gladly, seeming to me as heavy as marble statues come to life, and I suddenly cannot move a muscle while they pin me on my back. And when I see the scissors in Mary's hand, I take that last true deep breath of strength I have, and I scream *"Help me!"* at the top of my ample breasted lungs, before Mary covers my mouth. With one hand, my mouth is covered, while with the other hand, she cuts my bra in half at the front, causing one of my breasts to fall wobbly and free. The four of them are mesmerized, I suppose, holding my arms and legs down, Judith holding one arm to the floor with her whole body, while the lightskinned Amazon and the Asian tough girl hold me flat on my back, laid heavily on top of me so that I cannot move. My other arm is pinned to my side. I am as helpless as a mummy in a tomb, wrapped every bit as tightly by living flesh and hatred.

Then I see the Lady Adonna. I see Mary brandish a gigantic safety pin, which renews my attempt to struggle and scream, with one of them (which one, I cannot tell) holding her hand so tightly over my mouth I cannot breathe. *"Let her mouth go,"* Mary says, opening the pin, *"I wanna hear her scream and I don't care who the hell else hears it."* They release the suction grip, and even the spirits who watch are taken aback by the wailing, defeated tone of my voice, which is overwrought with long, breathless sobs and pleading. And then, I am made aware of God's curse upon mankind, when I feel the sting of a thousand wasps concentrated into one, pushing through the skin of my breast at the front nearby the nipple, a pinpoint of pain, of a fire worm burrowing through the meat of my breasts, a pain that continues through my body, my lungs and out through my voice in a loud, long wail of woman's woe and defeat, a sound passed down from

Eve through every generation, reminiscent of the sorrow of the ages, and the pain of all mankind.

"*Nobody,*" she says, holding me by the throat, "comes to *my* school, and acts like they are better than me… *I* am the most beautiful woman on this campus, not some fat breasted bug eyed backwoods *hillbilly* Ellie May Clampett looking *bitch! I* am the Queen of this school! *I* am the Alpha and the Omega! *I* am the beginning and the end of your whole *fucking universe!*"

Her stares are so Satanic, so serpentine in the eyes, that I should know the greely eyes, the eyes of Hatred itself. Then she spits a massive glom completely onto my face, below my nose and mouth so that I can smell the stench, and grow nauseous from the thought of it down the back of my throat. "Turn this bitch over," she says, standing up. "Take her pants off," she says, while I am sprawled flat on my face to the dusty smelling, worn down carpet of years, feeling the burning agony in my left breast, and my tight jeans being slid quickly off without mercy. And I brave this cold indignity, the cool, air conditioned breeze on my legs, riding up to between my legs, as my underwear is pulled unceremoniously off and tossed away.

I lay sobbing. Trying to gather enough breath to cry louder, but there is only the quick and breathless whimpering, unable to imagine the pain of this last mile. Before long, I catch a glimpse of the naked 20 year old woman, wearing that which pertaineth to a man, hung down pale and realistic from herself, to represent the fullness thereof, and the magnitude of endtime perversion. "*Please don't let her,*" the wailing voice returns, my face laid against the dusty smelling carpet, "*please don't let her do it to me—*"

"*Shut the fuck up!*" the light skinned Amazon blurts out, a voice of frustrated malice of forethought, and hellish unbridled torment restrained. And then I feel a liquid dripped to my bottom, which makes me plead again, and the Amazon barks *"I told you to shut up!"* but which I cannot obey, when the finger penetrates my backside, feeling like a piece of wood stretching my skin to rear pain. And then, after an eternity in Hell, I feel the tip of my rectum spread out from a pushing within, a pushing that slides up rapidly, seeming to tear my insides from the outside in, as if a blade were being introduced to my bowels deep within. With the lubrication aid and desire, I hear Mary Adonna exclaim *Oh, God* in a gruff voice, and she pushes all of an inch times eight deep into my backside. Laying there. Listening to my whimpering die down, pushing, squeezing her hips in a motion, hardly moving the member outward, hardly able to break her concentration enough to see my face twisted in a silent cry of ugliness, the famed ugly cry, where there is no dignity, nor remorse from breaking under pain and suffering. The girls watch in a lust they have never known, listening to me make the famed coughing sound of the ugly cry, where the sobbing is long past, and all that is left is the pain that caused it. Soon, I feel an unmistakable rhythm, not faster but decidedly harder and more determined, and soon I hear her voice become a wailing itself, and then the calling to God and Christ for mercy.

*B*lood

*I*n the drowning rainfall. In the tears of November cold and grieving. I brave this long and lonely walk to class, resurrected from the Heart of Memory, and the painful images in the Theater of My Mind. I have been pulled forward through the months since the day of my pledge, my invitation into the truth. Pulled forward, past the brave and merciless bumping into me on the campus grounds and in the halls every so often. Even past the day this very month, when I was stopped by them outside and condescended to unbelievably, with smirks and sarcasms, until I was distracted enough for one of them to get behind my legs on her knees while the other one pushed me flailing to the ground over her back. The oldest tripping trick known to every post pre-school graduate and primary school alum, had me falling down, downward with the scraggly Autumn trees rising up, up, upward into the pale November sky.

I cannot imagine what those who saw us thought as they walked past us, seeing the sophisticated, beautiful sorority types (named Kerry and Melinda) act so ugly and unsophisticated for the whole world to see. Yes, even beyond that day, I am transported to the present, the present of rain blown in from Melancholy Bay, and the mourning for a world that spins us toward the Evening Day.

My walk into the classroom is greeted by a loud snicker, causing me to turn and look over to where Mary Adonna sits with her hand over her nose and mouth, her eyes bright with laughter. The two of them watch me walk in my black sweater over a white collar shirt, black jeans, black tennis shoes and matching umbrella—they watch me take the walk of shame to the other side of the Abnormal Psychology classroom. I try not to notice Mary looking at me, and Judith shaking her head as if I were the most pathetic two legged dog she had ever seen, hopping around on its hind legs as if it were as normal as noon day. Like the two legged dog, I hop around in front of them stupidly, committed to believing that I have hope for the future, and that I have a right to be out and about, the right to see and be seen.

Soon the professor comes in, the youngish black man with a moustache and impeccable taste in shirts and slacks, always wearing a dark, pure color like burgundy or dark green with matching tie and black or charcoal gray pants. The friendly professor named John Parker guides us into the text, where we hear the lecture on the impact of violence in early childhood. Truly,

I have to admit that I don't hate this class, the way that a white swan doesn't exactly hate the passing of a raincloud overhead, blocking out the hot sunlight.

The end of this enlightenment sees me rising quickly, obliging the glancing professor with the smile I know he craves every single time. Could I guarantee myself an 'A' in this class? Likely. But my concern now is with escape. Escape back out into the rain, and another long walk back to my room, to sit and contemplate the perils of parental depression, and the spirits of black fire that burn the Windsor family tree.

"Hey Windsor," I hear yelled up the stairs at me. "How's your tit?"

And there is the most vulgar eruption of female laughter I've ever heard, screaming up at me from below. The spirit of fear erupts again, like a flash throughout my entire body, inspiring me to tucked lips and disbelief that I actually have to go downstairs and into the lobby where I know they are waiting to humiliate me again. An irresistible urge to see me broken. On this truth I glide slowly down the stairs, resisting my own urge to turn and run back to an empty classroom and hide there for two hours until my next class. By then, surely they'll be gone. But no. I've come this far. I may as well go all the way.

The four of them don't say a word while I take the last few steps down into the lobby of the building. My foot touching the lobby floor activates a mysterious trigger, and Mary whispers something to the tall lightskinned girl—the Amazon—and the tough Asian girl slightly less pretty. These two leave the empty lobby void of the bygone crowd, save for myself (who is a tall, sad looking blonde with Jenny braids), a silken haired blonde with a pretty face, and her raven haired, beautiful brunette companion.

I swim through these shark infested waters with pretend bravery, putting my hand on the bar handle that runs across the door. But a white, lovely hand grabs the door handle with me, before I can swim free, back into the Rain of Days.

"Where are you rushing off too, Windsor?" she says. "We know you don't have class for another two hours."

I glance over at Judith, whose lips are tucked in, to prevent the giggle that tickles her spirit.

"We just wanted to ask you about a little T and A, that's all," Mary says. "Tits and ass and such."

Her brunette friend actually turns her head and closes her eyes, working harder to prevent the tickle from coming out in a snittling snicker.

"I'm getting a woody just thinking about it," she says. "It worked out better than I thought, because you had more tit flesh for me to grab than the other girl would have. Oh, but she had a nice ass didn't she? I'll bet you wiggled it like a plate o' Jello didn't you? You nasty bitch."

Outside, the rains fall with greater assurance, picked up by a strong November wind. The Amazon and the Asian step back in from the rainy shelter.

"Back outside," Mary says.

"But it's raining…"

"Back outside!"

The two girls reluctantly go back, leaving us alone in the lobby void again.

"Oh yes," Mary says. "They remember too. The tears. The blood. The best I ever got off in my life."

"You better watch your back, bitch," Judith says.

"Oh, yeah," Mary agrees. "Cause to tell you the truth, we're wondering whether or not we finished the job. Because what we did to you, was just the beginning for what we had planned for your friend."

I turn away from the fearful rain spirits, staring Mary in the eyes.

"That's right. When we were done with her, we were going to take her up into the mountains, tie her to a tree in the woods, and leave that piano playing bitch to *die.*"

The sudden flash of my friend in the dark, Appalachian woods, bound to a tree by her neck, naked and helpless, calling to God to give me a dream of where she is, this flash powers a strength in my body, that flows to where fear and shame reside. I feel the cold terror subside, as if an infusion of heat has happened, flowing from my spirit into every part of my body.

"So, next time you make it to the cemetery, say hi to your dead friend for me."

The Book of Abnormal Psychology suddenly becomes a weapon in my hand, when who I was begins to fade, and I feel the anointed sword of battle, when my body whirls around and smashes the book hard into her face, knocking her backwards in a sickening, shrieking yelp from her, covering her face suddenly with both hands as though she were blinded. Then I turn from my right to my left, Abnormal Psychology in my hand, and wham the book hard enough to make the brunette's head turn to the side, seeming to fly white spit (or is it a chipped tooth?) from her mouth as she falls backward to the floor like a pedestal holding a glass sculpture in a museum. Book tossed aside, black book bag slid down to the floor, I am a figure dressed in black, lifting the wobbly brunette up by her hair and neck, escorting her fast and head first into the glass display, shattering the thick glass down on top of her and noisily to the hard tile floor. Judith falls limp to the floor amongst the glass fallen in pieces like diamond crystals by the wall cabinet, our scene watched over by plaques and portraits in gray, faces of antiquity, and ghostly eyes from Perpetuity.

When the Amazon and the Asian come back inside, eyes wide, mouths open, I stand there as though I have the wings of an angel on my back, and the flaming sword of the Lord in my hand. I move over from the broken glass to the stairs, watching them go to Mary and Judith, hearing *"are you alright"* and *"get that bitch!"* When she lowers her hands, I see the bottom of her face covered in blood. As the strong Amazon comes fast towards me, I run fast up the flight of stairs, to escape the strength of a jungle she-demon rising. But when the big, high yellow skinned girl is apt to take the last step or two, I return quickly to the top of the stairs in front of her, and kick her in the gut like a battering ram into a door, sending her off her feet and tumbling backwards to the concrete stairs and rolling down in classic fashion to the hard tile floor, where she lays there like a half dead deer at the bottom of a jungle pit. Standing over her is the tough Asian, helpless, knowing that I am bigger and stronger than she, and that if she doesn't know Karate or Kung Fu, then her Asian ass is grass and I am a blonde lawnmower.

I run down the stairs toward her, where she hesitates out of fear, fear of Mary and fear of my tall, blonde self coming at her. But she breaks away as if I were wearing a badge, bursting through the door out into the rainy weather, followed too closely behind by me, and I push her as she runs, causing her to fall down the brick steps to the brick landing below, where I am on top of her immediately in the downpour, my braids getting wet, holding her to the wet bricks by her neck and ignoring the bloody scar on her forehead. It is suddenly my greatest pleasure in this rain, to find her non-existing little breasts in her white shirt. And I bend down quickly, making sure she cannot move, and bite down as hard as I can through her white shirt fabric, tasting the soap and the cloth, feeling the lace bra fabric imprint in my mouth, listening to her scream in Hell's agony while I bite her breasts through her white shirt. Hard and long is how I like it (that's what she said), until I am almost positive that the soapy taste in my mouth is mixed with blood. And yes, when I raise up, I see most definitely that it is, betrayed by the spot of blood on her soaking wet t-shirt, above where her pathetic little nipple hider dares try to masquerade as a bra.

I stand up in the rain, watching the cars go by slowly, challenging any one of them with a stare, then looking back down at my tough little victim, watching her face twisted into an ugly little ironic grimace of what my beloved's face had been. I hurry back up the brick stairs, thankful that no one has seen us yet, opening the door and going immediately to the big one, dragging her weakened lump of a body over to the door and pulling her arm halfway out, then I slam the door once with all my might, then once again just as hard, hearing the girl scream with all her jungle power, finally able to gather enough strength in her half dead body to pull away. Whether the sound I heard is the snapping of her radius, whether it is the cracking of her ulna, I'm sure I will never know. Roll over, bitch. Hold your arm close. Hold it in. Futilely.

"This isn't over bitch!" Mary says. "Do you fucking hear me! You are *dead!*"

With the brunette still on the floor immobile, I am suddenly a fire rekindled, going over to the bloody faced sorority girl where she sits, eyes blackened already from what has happened to her nose, and I raise her up from the floor with both hands clamped around her throat, then I slam the back of her head against the wall until she is weakened, then I am on top of her on the floor, raising her t-shirt up, followed by her bra. With her naked breast exposed, I clamp my teeth full force into her breast above the nipple, hearing her choked scream, waiting for the Lady Vampire's nourishment to touch me inside. Then I raise up in full and final control, satisfied by the bloody teeth marks I see above her pale areola, and I begin to choke her to death. I choke her for every welt on my back I ever received, for every bruise, for every spot of blood and broken skin, for every insult, for every drop of my own blood spilled, for the agony of needles and pins, and the raping with blue and black fire. For the life and death of my beloved whom they tormented, I press my thumbs to her windpipe, and pledge to bring justice to the Ghosts of May, and lay vengeance as an offering at the head and foot of their graves. As her eyes begin to bulge, as her tongue begins to darken, as her face begins to puff and swell, I feel the Spirit of Battle coursing through, and a need to feel her go limp, and watch her spirit leave her body forever.

Suddenly, I can no longer hold myself down on top of her, as I feel myself lifted by arms many times stronger than mine, and I smell a scent I am familiar with all round me as I try to escape and return to battle. But the black professor's grip is just too strong, a natural strength to overcome even my own rage unleashed. He holds me there, my psychology professor, pressing my head against the wall away from the scene I caused, staring me in the eyes, holding me still by the side of my head, saying over and over, *"Maybelline, please come back."*

Death

"It's the mercy of God," Mother says. "None of the four girls are pressing charges."

In the mansion, three days after my private battle was fought, I now listen to Mother's intended lesson on choices made, and the consequences for those who make them.

"Can you tell me why you did it?"

Silence.

"Two of the girls had bite marks on their breasts. One had a broken arm. You nearly choked another one to death."

Our new silence is broken only by the sound of her defeat, breathed in the deepest sigh of her life.

"You've been expelled. They say that you can't go back for at least another year. I got them to agree not to fail you in your classes. You'll get an incomplete for every class. But you won't be able to go back until next fall."

In my mother's room, beneath the crystal chandelier, I sit in her uncomfortable Victorian style chair, resigned to my status as a prisoner, accepting that for the rest of my life, this woman is the beginning and the end of my world. And I'm not sure where my motivations lie; whether it is the money, the mansion, or Mother herself, that has me gripped now in a tomb of melancholy surrender. Whatever it is that she desires for me, it is what I must endeavor to persevere.

But when she goes to her closet, and emerges with a leather belt, then tells me to stand up and strip down, something in me rises up, to power my legs to run towards the door of her bedroom, and I unlock the door and run out into the hall. Clutching, clawing for the memory of where to go. Turning towards the room down the other end of the upstairs hallway, my soul whip-lashed by every call from her voice to *"come back here or I'm sending you to a private girl's school, I swear it! It's what I should have done in the first place! Alice Maybelline Windsor you come back here!"*

At the end of this long flight to freedom, in the wake of traumas most have never known, I make it to Grandmother's room, banging and screaming on her locked door in fear, to be rescued from the wraith flowing at me down the hall; long headed, pale, long armed, holding a black leather belt in its outstretched arm. Fate has mercy, causing Grandmother to open the door quickly, to let me come running pitifully inside, my eyes blared wide open in fear, closing and locking the door behind me. Then suddenly, I hear a *slam* against the door, causing me to jump like I was hit with a hot spark from a falling sky. My voice is pitched up to a frighteningly mousy tone, saying *"don't let her in Grandma please don't let her in."* The mousiness gives way to a pathetic wailing, born from the spirit of fear, and a renewed terror of being in any way punished again.

"Denise! Denise you open this door or I swear to *God!"*

"You've beaten this girl enough Liz, I won't let you touch her anymore—now you get away from this door or I swear I'm going to call the police on you."

"Don't you *dare!* You wouldn't dare embarrass me like that."

"I wouldn't want to Liz, but I'll have to, for Alice's sake I'll have to. Just go away and we'll all talk about it tomorrow. Please!"

After no response, there is another shaking of the doorknob, and then one violent screaming and banging *"open this door you bitch!"* Then, like the lion locked away from prey she has stalked and lost, civilized, cultured, footsteps turn and walk away. Grandmother hugs me tight, kissing me on the forehead and cheek, escorting me to her own comfort cushioned chair.

"We won't here from her anymore tonight," she says. "She knows I'm on the edge of calling the police on her and she doesn't want to be embarrassed. You just rest here honey. Later, I'll get your night clothes and you can even sleep in here."

"What about Mom?"

"Don't you worry about her. I'll talk to her tomorrow morning. It's time that we had a talk about things anyway."

I am more than glad for the calming effect Denise has, as we settle in for the evening, the images blaring from her television serving to bathe us in modern day tranquility. As I sit in Denise's comfortable chair at her insistence, while she rests in her wooden desk chair nearby, I am struck by a sudden unfamiliarity, and a realization that I hardly know my grandmother, and I've hardly spoken to her or been in this room my entire life. As my mind begins to swirl, settling me down to near sleep, I'm struck by another revelation, smiling at me from *Big Brother*, and Anna May's striking resemblance to Julie Chen. I blink my eyes in half sleep, noticing Chen look away from her interview, seeming to lock eyes with me from the other side of the television, enough to cause a spark of sudden fear…

As Anna May stares at me from beyond the grave, I am shocked fully awake by a loud *thump* at the door, followed by another and still another. Why is mother back, banging on the door like a fool? This question is answered, unsurreptitiously, when a splinter of wood cracks outward from one of the thumps on the door, then turning into a larger splinter, joined by several other splinters of wood. And we stand in fervent disbelief, Grandmother and I, as the splintering in the door grows violent, until the wood near the doorknob is destroyed by the tip of a hatchet blade chopping thru. "Oh, God," Denise prays. "Oh God please help us… I'm calling the police Elizabeth!"A threat fallen on deaf ears, I suppose, as the chopping continues, in full Kubrikian rhythm and song, until we see the flash of the entire hatchet blade flash through. A scream erupts from Denise, calling on the Spirit of Fear. Through the jagged hole in the door, a lithe, white hand appears, reaching inside, unlocking the deadbolt, and the lock on the bedroom doorknob. Then, she enters. A beautiful, angry women carrying a small axe.

"Put that phone down," she says to Denise, "or I'll take it from you." With tears in her eyes, defeated, Denise lays the phone down on her desk, then moves over to where I stand dumbfounded. Denise places herself in front of me. Between me and the Spirit of Death. "Come here to me," the Lady Windsor says, tossing the hatchet onto the bed. "Come here to me," she says, "and take your beating like a woman."

"When is enough going to be *enough!*" Denise says. "Do you think you're the only one whose suffered! We've all suffered! All of us are in pain! Do you know how many beatings and rapings I took from your father over the years? So what! I still loved him and life goes on! So, I locked you in the damned closet when you were little. So I took a wooden spoon and tried to burn the skin off your little breasts, so I tied your ankles together and whipped the blood from your backside when you were sixteen, how many years are you going to make us all pay for it! Get over it!"

We have backed into the wall by the rainy window, both watching her walk toward us slowly, her black leather belt folded conspicuously in her hand.

"You're a lazy good for nothing," she says. "The more I give you, the more you take. No more. The sass. The disrespect. The laziness. I'm gon' strip you. Then I'm gon' beat it of ya."

She stands close to us now, where I can smell her sweet, subtle perfume. "Go to my room," she says, "and take your clothes off."

"No!" Denise says. "I won't let you touch her ever again. If you do I swear I'll—"

"Call the police?" Mother says, her mouth displaying the somber, sickened frown, the complete disgust she feels for her own mother. Her belt lashes across Denise's face hard, then across her hands as she tries to cover up, cowering to the floor, while Mother unfolds the belt by instinct, whipping her Mother across her head, shoulders and back like a plow ox on a mountain dirt farm. And suddenly, I cannot stand idly by and watch her give this pain, and I grab her belt hand, then I grab her by the face and shove her heavily away. But she ignores me, returning to the task of beating her mother, drawing out a pitiful shriek from Denise on the floor. I catch the belt again, enraging her to sling me around, then begin to whip me across the face, head and shoulders as well.

But independent of my will, on its own accord, my hand grabs the belt from her, attempting to wrench it from her hand, even among the barrage of blows from her other hand to my head, which seem to be knocking my brain around in my skull. So what choice do I have, but to bite her knuckles as if they were that of a pig on a plate; holding her arm, grabbing the belt while I try to bite the blood from her knuckled hand. Without so much as a whimper, she lets go the belt and pulls her hand away.

She stands quiet. Panting. Brave but cautious. Knowing that to attack me without a plan, to walk into whatever rage there is around me would be like attacking a small grizzly bear. So, if this animal must surely be dealt with, one must have the greatest chance of survival first, no? And for Mother, for the angry, beautiful brunette woman, her greatest chance of survival lies not in the belt on the floor, but in what she picks up from the bed. "You're going to take your beating," she says, eyes beginning to water with rage and frustration, brandishing the extension of herself confidently in her hand. "You will obey me, or I swear to God I will bury you in the *fucking woods!*"

There is the ring of Truth. The horn signal of revelation that can no longer be denied. I inhale slowly, then exhale the last cold breath of fear from inside me.

"Fuck you, bitch."

It may as well have been an open gate at Churchill Downs, and she a mare with lightning in her belly. She glides at me with the hatchet blade raised to sink into my skull. But all she manages is a frustrated chop to the desk chair raised, *burying the hatchet* in the malice it was intended, allowing me to push her backward. Oh, but what athleticism there is, in a woman bent upon revenge! Indeed, Hell hath no fury. She grabs the chair and pushes me backward until I am against the wall by the rainy window, raising the hatchet to bring it down on the chair again, her eyes focused on what damage she is prepared to do. But when she raises her arm, her mother grabs the hatchet arm, and screams for me to run. Mother turns and shoves Denise to the floor, then raises the hatchet blade in startling determination, bringing it down full into her mother's thigh. The sound Denise makes is purely inhuman. Like the shriek of a she-wolf dog stabbed through.

I throw the chair to the side and grab Mother by the hatchet arm, but she pulls away, running into the hall where I foolishly follow her, yanking my head back by pure instinct before crossing the doorway—yanking it back in time to see the hatchet chop fully into the door frame by my face. The spirit in the woman's eyes is blood lust, harnessed into battle mode, a gift inherited from her corporate shark of a father. But whatever these spirits of combat may be, wherever it is they arise in my blood, I am too burdened by this self same lust to dominate this woman, to make her sorry that God formed her flesh these forty some odd years ago, and breathed life into her accursed body. While I take hold of the hatchet with her, she is only an empty shell to me now, the enemy risen in battle, whose life I am commissioned to take, and whose blood I am commissioned to spill.

I take hold of her throat with my hands, my lovely hands, through which all unknown masculine strength now flows, and I begin to squeeze her throat hard enough to make her see stars. Pushing her, slamming her against the walls of our fine upper hallway, finally able to get her off balance by yanking her downward by the hair until she falls on top of me, both of us holding tight the hatchet handle for dear life, for dearest life, for unhappiness lived, for pain and agony unsubsided. I am able to quickly push her lighter frame from on top of me, and I straddle her in the hall, one hand on her throat, the other gripping the hatchet, pulling it slowly away from her grip. With an effort from I know not where, which is no effort to me at all, I raise the secured hatchet up without a thought, releasing her throat, and I plunge the hatchet blade deep through the white blouse fabric into her chest, causing her to make the sound of a she beast in wolf form stabbed through, in the place through her chest, at her tiny rose bosom. A quick, howling yelp it was, a cry to God for mercy too late, the departure of a soul condemned, by her own hatchet through her tiny rose bosom.

I sit here. Alarmed by the wave of pleasure through my groin, as if I could be nowhere else in the world but here, my hand on the hatchet handle buried in my mother's chest, watching the life slowly fade from the eyes of Hatred. Then her struggle ceases, her eyes roll back and slip closed, and I hear the famed last breath come forth like a ghostly apparition.

Tombstones

The tombstones of the women I knew and loved. In the graveyards of Appalachia. One, of the woman who never bore me, who never gave birth to me, who never brought me screaming into a condemned and dying world. A woman of straw, of deep and abiding lust, a woman unforgiven for the life she chose; the life underneath the charity and good works, underneath the smiles and cultured civility. A woman who pulled me bloody from the womb of another, and carried me helpless, and screaming down from the mountain, to thrust me cold in a crib of luxury, to raise me in the brutality of neglect, and the agony of love unrequited, killed by the heat of jealously over thoughts of my real mother whom she never saw, but felt through the image of my blonde hair and blue eyes, and the bounce of a heavy bosom. The wealthy Lady of Windsor rests, having no earthen ties to have been cut, only that of hatred for her own mother, and of the daughter whose lonely heart she never knew. Whose hatred inspired her life to irony, to kill her daughter with the blade of unkindness, having received by that same blade her reward and comeuppance overdue.

And I see her ghostly counterpart, her partner in crime, the woman who materialized into her life as a sexual soul mate, a kindred spirit in deviance, the rarest pairing in the history of the Mother Daughter Dynamic. Mrs. Anna Lin May, a woman of straw, a woman too, the bearer of scars; scars passed down to her from her motherland, from the farms of centuries past, from the Asian countryside, and brutal, blood-soaked depravities unmentionable, to burn within her a lust greater than the Lady Windsor, a lust she often wore about her hips, hidden underneath her garment, exposed in secret eschatology, shown to her daughter in the Evening Day, revealed to even the Lady Windsor in stroking, moving upon it as though it were a natural part of her, until her own body was laid waste in the cataclysm of energy known to but few women ever born, yet understood by an untold multitude in denial. A woman unafraid to display the end of this age behind closed doors, and the apocalyptic violence and perversion therein. Whose private life spilled over onto her daughter at the piano, to manifest the tombstone of Jennifer May. The Dove of Music, the heart of love that was sent to me. Whose heart of beauty, whose grace and gift for melody upon the keys was transcendent, as an angel whose wings are lifted from the canvas of grieving, to be borne into this ethereal space, to bring love and beauty into the end of this age, through the burning of blue and black fire.

At this gravesite, by this Tombstone of Appalachia, my weeping can know no ends, as I am carried aloft by grief itself; to where longing is condemned to go unfulfilled, and where mourning will not be comforted. It is the pain of loss unresolved, of scars that cannot heal, the loss of a loved one unassuaged, whose memory can inspire only grief, and the sorrow of the ages to come. With all of my heart, I loved Jennifer May, in matrimony of the soul, and of this, I pray that even in Paradise, where there is no more pain and suffering, she can know that somewhere in time, I loved her, as she walks in the River Valley, along the shores of Cerulean Sand.

Of this grief, O Lord, I pray that this cup will pass from me! That I may not endure the pain of her memory, nor the loss of her essence from my immortal soul! Bear me up, O Lord, to endure the burning of her memory in me, and the icy cold of this lonely walk, when her soul is far from me! And now, I must leave her grave far behind, so that I may return to life, and not bear a blade into my flesh, and rest forever at this grave again!

To the tombstone of an angel, I drift, the tombstone of Angel Simms. A woman of straw, my unwitting guide along this path, down this River of Fate, into the Sea of Destiny. A woman with two sons she loved, who she raised in loving kindness, a woman whose heart bore charity for the youth, and compassion for their thirst for knowledge, whose calling it was to guide the course of learning and the enlightenment of young minds, but whose secret way was an end of the world lust for young girls and younger women, whose course was an apocalyptic hypocrisy, of a kind so unfathomable, that the world may never process what she has done, nor the manifestation of her tombstone.

From the incredible sight, the pre-Armageddon silhouette of the Angel Simms grave, I now return to what life it is I have left, to find the strength to carry on, and to find she who bore me from along the timeline, and left me in a condemned and dying world to suffer. On the memory of grandmother Denise's words, on the strength of what I know, I leave the pain of the Appalachian school behind forever, and the tombstones of the women I knew, to ride the highways of Appalachia, to find out once and forever—where it is that my lost and beloved mother could have gone.

$\mathcal{H}$ome

$\mathcal{I}$n the misty mountain dawn. Along the roads of the Appalachian Mountains. I drive a car of midnight luxury. Looking for the road less traveled. Looking for a dirt road to travel on. In the Appalachian Woods, I turn smooth luxury onto a long, dirt road. Riding slowly amongst the many trees. Gliding the unfamiliar landscape. Waiting to see what it is I have only heard about. What mine eyes have never before seen. On either side of this long dirt road, the winter pines loom ominous in the early morning light.

In the glowing light of dawn, the thick forest trees disappear from the right side of the road. To the right of this road, there is a vast clearing, where I see a small house and a small, empty crop field. Atop the roof of the log cabin, smoke billows from the chimney.

In the early morning cold. By the light of Winter's Dawn, I step out of the car, an image of fair skin, blue eyes and long, blonde hair in the mountain morning. The call of lonely birdsong is plentiful.

At the door of the cabin, I knock with timid authority. In the humility of the Lamb of God.

I knock again. Waiting patiently for the footsteps' arrival at the door. The door of the cabin swings open. There is a woman inside. Her pioneer skirt is long and quaint. A woman of beauty such as to defy description. Her big, blue eyes are sad and beautiful. Her braids are golden as the sun.

When I speak the words of truth to her, Jennifer Maybelline Breen steps out of the cabin. Her somber expression is awe and joy. The color of her beauty is humility.

In the misty mountain dawn, the lovely woman hugs her daughter. Jenny May did cry from the pain.

The End

ABOUT THE AUTHOR

Jonathan Lovejoy is a graduate of the University of North Carolina at Greensboro, with a B.A. in Religious Studies, and a graduate of Liberty University with an M.A. in Theological Studies. He currently lives in Winston Salem, North Carolina.

For more info on the author's life and career, visit jonathanlovejoy.com.